Praise for the Edie Spence series

"I was swept away in the force with which it built and the raging rush to the finish. I'm more attached to Edie than ever. This is urban fantasy of the highest order."
—Angie-ville

"An innovative read that offers a whole new look at paranormal creatures and the humans who happen to live in their world. Readers are sure to enjoy this book and will be eager to see what awaits Edie next."
—*Romantic Times*

"I enjoyed every bit of this book. The Edie Spence series is for sure one of the best UF books around."
—*Under the Covers*

"Immense fun with incredible world building. Alexander adds wonderful new facets to old myths and legends and a completely new spin on everything."

"Steamy and entertaining . . .
and the cliffhanger ending

"Full of action, fantastic characters, and situations that will make you want to kick some bad guys where it counts."
—*Urban Fantasy Investigations*

"The story is richly detailed, the plot is complex, and Edie Spence is absolutely delightful. A winning blend that's not to be missed."
—*Rabid Reads*

MORE . . .

Also by
Cassie Alexander

Nightshifted

Moonshifted

Shapeshifted

DEADSHIFTED

CASSIE ALEXANDER

St. Martin's Paperbacks

This is a work of fiction. All of the characters, organizations, and events portrayed in this novel are either products of the author's imagination or are used fictitiously.

DEADSHIFTED

Copyright © 2014 by Erin Cashier.
Excerpt from *Bloodshifted* copyright © 2014 by Erin Cashier.

For information address St. Martin's Press, 175 Fifth Avenue, New York, NY 10010.

ISBN: 978-1-250-03794-7

Printed in the United States of America

St. Martin's Paperbacks edition / January 2014

St. Martin's Paperbacks are published by St. Martin's Press, 175 Fifth Avenue, New York, NY 10010.

10 9 8 7 6 5 4 3 2 1

ACKNOWLEDGMENTS

I'd like to thank all the usual suspects that make writing these books possible—my husband Paul, my alpha reader Daniel Starr, my agent Michelle Brower, and my editor Rose Hilliard. There is no possible way I could do this (and on this schedule!) without their support.

I also got some special help on *Deadshifted* from Ian Tregillis, Ben Hanelt, Deirdre Saoirse Moen, and Stephen Blount. Ian and Ben (especially Ben) put up with endless what-if questions from me, and Deirdre and Stephen were fantastic resources on cruise ship logistics, operation, and engineering. Their help was invaluable, although as always any errors are all mine.

I can't wait for you all to see what's in store for Edie next—I hope you enjoy it, and thank you for continuing to read!

*A woman knows the face of the man she loves
as a sailor knows the open sea.*
                              —Honore de Balzac

CHAPTER ONE

I wake up with a start, gasping for air. I have to tell Asher something.

Everything's bright and orange, and I can only see through one eye. The other eye's swollen shut; it burns when I try to open it. Water slaps rubber, over and over, in endless slow applause. I remember the sound from childhood, floating down a lazy river in an inner tube, drunk from beer my older brother had snuck me when I was sixteen.

"Edie? Are you okay?" Asher's leaning over me. His voice is hoarse.

I have to tell him something.

But I can't. There's rope in my mouth. And I can't pull the rope away because my hands are tied. My feet too. I'm hog-tied, and when I move, my shoulder starts to throb.

"Is it still you?" Asher asks me. I don't know why he's asking. I don't know what he means.

I have to tell you something, I try to say around the rope, even though I can't remember what it is.

"I'm so sorry, Edie. I'm so, so sorry. It is you, right?" he asks, and his voice cracks.

I want to comfort him. To tell him that I'm okay, even

though it's clear that I am not. He looks so afraid right now. I've never seen him this afraid before.

"We're going to be all right. We're going to get away from here. I'm going to save you," he says, more to himself than me. He scuttles backward and brings up what I realize is a paddle, then leans over the side of the orange thing we're riding on, paddling for all his might.

Inside my mind, things slide into place. My ties, our lifeboat. What I want to say to him.

He's paddling so hard to nowhere that salt water is spraying my face.

And I remember.

Everything.

I had a death grip on the balcony railing and was looking down at the ocean with trepidation. Our room on the *Maraschino* was six floors up, maybe four down to the waterline. I couldn't help but wonder just how deep the sea was after that.

"Edie, it's not like I booked us on the *Titanic*," Asher called from the doorway of our room.

I turned around to give him a nervous grin. "I know," I said, then returned my gaze to the sea. He'd planned this trip for us. A chance for us to get away from the weather in Port Cavell, to go on our first official vacation together. It was just what we'd needed, especially when winter rolled in with a white-out blizzard that'd lasted two weeks, making it impossible for us to get to the clinic where we both worked, me as a nurse and him as a doctor. We met before I knew he was a doctor, I swear.

Our cruise had sounded fabulous up until my last-minute packing extravaganza this morning. That was when I realized my period was a week late. My luggage had felt like I'd been carrying an anchor with me ever since—and it was why I was staring out at the ocean like it was a

Magic 8 Ball now. I was hoping for a sign, a yes or a no, but the only thing the waves seemed to say was *Reply hazy, try again.* "Don't help or anything. I've totally got it all," Asher said behind me, bringing in our bags.

"Okay!" I said with feigned gullibility. He rolled his eyes and tossed the last of our bags onto the bed. I let go of the rail and came over to him. "If you hadn't booked us such a long trip, I wouldn't have had to pack so much."

Asher spread his hands. "Well, if you'd just listened to my plan to keep you in here naked the whole time, I feel sure we could have gotten you down to one small carry-on. I kept telling you they have twenty-four-hour room service."

His look—mystified at how I could fail to grasp such logic—made me laugh. He reached for me, and I stepped into his arms. "Think of it, Edie. A two-week trip from LA to Hawaii and back. No snow the whole way."

"Yay, adventure!" I said from the safety of his armpit.

"No. We've had enough of adventure. This"—and he swept his arm grandly over the ocean, like he was Poseidon—"is a vacation."

I hadn't had a vacation in a very long time. The road trips my brother and I had been hauled on as a kid where we'd seen Mount Rushmore hardly counted. I'd had time off before, but I'd never been on a *real* vacation.

And Asher was right about adventures. I didn't need any more of those. I'd spent a year of my life knowing too much about the underworld of our hometown, being involved in what could charitably called hijinks or more reasonably Machiavellian death plans orchestrated by the vampire, werewolf, and shapeshifter communities.

All of that had ended when I'd started dating Asher seven months ago. In a way, the past seven months with him had already been the best and longest vacation in my whole life.

Asher spun me and I yelped in surprise. We both landed on the bed—all white linens, with mountainous amounts of white pillows—and Asher pulled me closer to him. "Imagine it. Two weeks, no patients, no MRSA, no vampires—just you, me, and the sun."

I propped myself up, put my chin on his chest, and squinted at him. "No norovirus?"

He laughed. "I may be a doctor, but I'm not God. No guarantees."

His warm smile lit up the whole room. I was so in love with him. I thought about telling him then, blurting out that I was late—but what if it was nothing? Or—what if by saying something, I jinxed it? Would that be a relief? I didn't even really know yet if I wanted to be pregnant, or even if I was. I was sort of happy, sort of scared, and everything was still sort of imaginary. But we were on board this ship for two weeks—I'd know by the end of our trip. My uterus would have to declare itself one way or the other by then.

He reached out and smoothed my brow with his thumb. "I love you. Everything's going to be perfect."

Yeah. It would be. Either way. I had him, and he had me. I tilted my head to kiss the inside of his palm. "I completely believe you."

The boat, or ship, whatever it was supposed to be properly called, left the dock with a lurch and began to rock beneath our feet. We gained speed as we left the harbor and I heard the sound of waves slapping against its metal sides. It made noises like an older building in a strong wind.

Asher rolled out of bed and started to industriously unpack.

"Can't we go look around first?" Our luggage wasn't going anywhere, and Asher was right, I had packed a lot of stuff. It wasn't my fault there were two separate formal nights on board. Formal nights required a lot of extra provisioning.

"Hang on," he said, while pulling out a stack of jeans, shorts, and swim trunks. "There's a safety lecture coming up that we have to go to." He started putting his clothes away into the drawers beneath the desk diagonally across from our bed.

"How do you—" I was asking when a five-note chime crackled overhead from an intercom I hadn't noticed in the ceiling. Captain Ames introduced himself and welcomed us aboard at incredible volume, and then a scratchy recording instructing passengers to report to their designated safety zones began.

"I just know," Asher said, answering my unfinished question when our instructions were over. "But after this, we can take a tour. I promise."

I just know was Asher's polite way of telling me he *knew,* knew. From before, when he'd been a full-fledged shapeshifter.

Despite us dating for seven months, there were all sorts of things I didn't *know* know about Asher. Things I might never even have the time to find out. As a shapeshifter, he wasn't just the summation of his own memories and experiences, he was the combination of the knowledge and form of everyone he'd ever touched. Anyone he'd ever had skin-to-skin contact with before this past summer was inside him, and he could make himself look like them, and have access to everything they knew. Up to and including me.

Back in July he'd almost gone insane because of it, like all shapeshifters approaching their mid-thirties. He'd been saved from his fate by Santa Muerte, whom we'd been helping at the time; she'd stopped his descent into madness. Afterward, Asher could access old forms and memories, but not take on any new ones. Which was nice because it

meant he didn't always know what I was thinking anymore when he touched me. But it was still strange when
he *just knew* things for no good reason.

And it was one of the reasons why I'd sort of assumed
we couldn't have kids, much to my mother's dismay. I
knew enough science to know about interspecies dating.
Maybe Asher and I would have a liger together. I snorted.

"What?" Asher asked from inside the closet, where he
was hanging up his suit jackets.

"Nothing! Hey, can you hang up my dresses for me?"

"Sure."

I watched him from my position sprawled across the
arctic-white bedspread. When he was done he came over
to stand beside me on the bed, the red formal gown that
I'd bought specifically for this trip hanging down in the
open closet behind him.

"Hey," he said quietly. "What's wrong? Are you sick or
something?"

His question was maybe a little too close to the truth. I
stood up quickly. "Just jet-lagged. Sorry." I smiled at him
like I was carefree. "I'm ready now. Let's go."

And my heart melted when he smiled back at me.

He led us down the hallways without stopping to look at
any signs, and I wondered if he or one of his other personalities had been on this same ship before. I held his
hand but trailed behind him, as the hallways weren't very
wide.

I concentrated on the warmth of his hand as he held
mine. He had a normal body temperature, which I liked. I'd
dated zombies before, and they were cool, while were-
wolves could be too hot. If I were Goldilocks, Asher-the-
shapeshifter was just right. Apparently my uterus agreed.

We reached the entrance to a grand banquet room

together. There were multiple hand sanitizer stations right outside its doors.

"Look, it's like we never left home!" I let go of his hand to cup mine beneath the automatic foam. Asher snorted but followed my lead. It was easy for him to blow things off; he never seemed to get sick. But he grinned at me, and I found myself grinning back.

The cruise employees inside the banquet room's entrance checked our names off their list, and Asher led us to the table that corresponded to our room number.

The room itself was huge. Strange to think that such a big space was confined inside a ship, itself another big space. And that together, we, with those spaces, were hurtling over the ocean. I hadn't really gotten a sense of our movement yet, and I looked around for cues. The chandeliers overhead were brightly colored ornate glass affairs, like the tops of tropical trees, complete with glass flowers and glass birds, all fixed so as not to swing, and the chair Asher pulled out for me to sit down on felt stable against the low carpet underneath. So far the only indication I was even on a ship was the waves I could see out the window, three tables down.

A crowd of people pushed in and slowly filled every chair. Kids too young to be back in school just yet, a few lucky though sullen teenagers whose families were letting them escape school for enforced family bonding, a lot of older adults who could afford to take two weeks off work, and lastly us. I felt very sympathetic toward the teenagers just then.

An older man with short gray hair and wearing a suit jacket pushed a woman up in a wheelchair to join us. She had a blanket covered in pink-and-purple paisley tucked around her legs. He was barrel-chested, one of those old men who'd managed to hold on to his bulk as he aged, betrayed only by the pull-tabs of his hearing aids just barely poking out of his ears. But she had aged even better than him, with bright eyes darting behind her librarian-style half-lenses and short hair smartly styled. Everyone ages, and as a nurse I was forced to be more aware of my mortality than most, but I also knew that some few are lucky enough to age well, and it was clear she fell into this happy category.

He positioned her at the table, put on the wheelchair's brakes, and then sat down beside her. I inhaled to ask her why she was in a wheelchair, then stopped myself and gave her a big camouflaging smile. At my job, being nosy was practically mandatory. But in real life, asking random people rude questions about their health doesn't make you many friends—and makes you seem a little creepy.

Despite my attempts not to stare awkwardly at her wheelchair, she smiled. "Car accident."

"Oh. I'm sorry." I backpedaled—this was a vacation, after all. "Is this your first cruise?"

"No. Yours?"

"Yes. I'm kind of nervous about it." That'd be a good excuse for my rude behavior, and it wasn't that far from the truth. "I don't really like the sea."

The cant of her left eyebrow rising over her glasses' frame said she thought this was an odd vacation choice for me, but age had also given her more tact than I possessed. "We've been going on one a year for the past forty-five years. On our anniversary."

"How nice," I said and gave Asher a side-eye look, hoping he could rescue me from myself, only to find he was looking at something over his shoulder and not currently paying attention. He'd seemed so pleased with himself when he'd planned this trip for us. I couldn't help but wonder just what traditions we'd create together or where we'd be in the next forty-five years.

Asher stood suddenly and gave me a tight hold-that-thought smile. "I'll be right back," he said, and he walked quickly across the room without another word.

"Are you all newlyweds?" the wheelchair woman's husband asked. I flushed bright red.

"Um, no . . ." Even though I might be pregnant by him. Way to stay classy, Edie. But people made mistakes, and besides, if everything worked out, it wasn't a mistake now, was it? Just a happy accident. That was okay, right? This wasn't 1887 anymore. Or even 2007.

"Hal—" she chastised.

"If we're at the same table here our cabins are probably next door. I just want to know if I should take my hearing aids out at night is all," Hal went on, giving me a knowing look.

I caught his gist, with horror, and felt myself turning a Technicolor shade of red.

"Hal, shush!" she said with a laugh at my rising discomfort. She leaned over to pat my hand. "You'll have to ignore him. Lord knows I do."

And to think I'd thought I had the lock on awkward questions. "Ha ha," I forced out.

She leaned forward and gave me a confessional look. "Don't let anyone ever tell you not to have a good time when you can, dear. Married or not."

"Thanks. I'll remember that." Anything to not discuss my sex life with the elderly. "I'm Edie. My erstwhile boyfriend is Asher." I resisted craning my head around to look for him, so he could help get me out of this mess.

"I'm Claire and he's Hal," the woman replied. Hal gave me a nod and a jowly smile.

"Nice to meet you all," Asher said, returning to the table. About time.

An Indian family of four sat down in a rush at the far side of our table before I could ask him where he'd been.

The couple was a little older than Asher and me, but they had their acts more together, as evidenced by their two children, a boy, ten, and a girl, maybe eight. The girl was wearing Coke-bottle glasses over wide-set eyes and her face was cherubically round. Both the girl and the woman had long black hair—the mother's was up, expertly coiffed, showing off large diamond earrings, while the girl's trailed down her back in one thick jealousy-inducing braid.

"I hope we didn't miss anything—" the man said as they sat down.

"No, they haven't started talking yet," Claire informed them.

A life-jacket-wearing cruise employee did a silly dance to attract our attention. He was joined by two other staff, and they mimed rowing across the stage. Oddly, their levity didn't make me feel any safer.

"Have you ever had to do any emergency procedures?" I asked Claire in a whisper.

She smiled indulgently, and I noticed that for an elderly woman she had very good teeth. "Only once, dear, a long time ago. But everything worked out."

Hal leaned in, overhearing. "Don't worry. This cruise line has a stellar reputation."

Asher elbowed me gently. "See? What'd I tell you?"

I gave him a look. He wasn't the one dealing with being scared of the ocean and pregnancy and old people listening to us having sex. But—he was dealing with something. Asher could camouflage his emotions more than most people, but I'd learned he had certain tells. The small crease between his eyebrows was one of them. Had he seen someone else he knew here? If so, I didn't want to think about how he knew them. I was leaning over to ask him what had happened when a person with a megaphone started the safety lecture up front. Asher gave me a pensive look, but shrugged. His problems must not have had anything to do with the integrity of the ship, seeing as he wasn't herding us toward the life rafts. I figured I should listen first and ask questions later.

In the "unlikely" event of any problems, we'd meet in this room again, get life jackets handed out to us, and then be guided to the lifeboats in an orderly fashion. The demonstrated life jackets were low-rent affairs that you had to breathe into to inflate. I wondered if the adjustable straps on them would be able to accommodate some of the larger people in the room.

Our table shook and startled me, but it was just the kids at the far end, playing some sort of hand-tapping tag with each other. As their parents tried to stop them I realized I was the only one at the table even trying to pay attention. Asher's focus was still divided, the parents were pointing and giving their children stern looks, and Hal and Claire were absorbed in thumbing through a tour book for Hawaii, murmuring suggestions and dog-earing pages. Occasionally Claire would glance up and over at the children, giving them a wide grandmotherly grin.

In a way, our little table here was the complete circle of human experience. Asher and I, together, maybe having a kid; that other couple with their handsome if fidgety children; and finally Hal and Claire, with matching short gray hair and wrinkles, aging gracefully. If I was pregnant, it would be weird . . . but we'd be doing what thousands—no, millions—of people did every day. Plunking our little car token around the game board of Life.

I should probably just relax. About everything. No matter what happened, baby, no baby, everything would be fine. There was no reason for it not to be.

The safety lecture was wrapping up. Our vacation had begun, and we were going to have a good time. I reached underneath the table to take Asher's hand, feeling serene— and found his hand balled into a tight fist.

CHAPTER TWO

Asher's hand relaxed and fit easily into mine, but it was too late: The tension I'd felt there relit the fears I'd been trying to smother. I found myself holding my breath as people started filtering out of the room.

Hal stood and took the brakes off Claire's wheelchair. "Don't worry. This is the safest way to travel. See you all at dinner," she said with a smile, waving as he wheeled her away.

Voices rose as people chattered about their plans. There were a few high-pitched kid-squeals, coughing, conversations, laughter—normal life. I looked over to Asher as our table cleared.

"We're still on vacation, right?"

"Of course," he said—but I knew he was lying. We stayed seated, his eyes scanning the crowd. When the room was nearly empty, he rose at some cue I couldn't read, and I followed his lead.

This time I paid attention how to get back to our room. The ship had picked up enough speed for me to feel it beneath my feet, engines straining somewhere deep within the hull.

I waited until the cabin door closed behind me before asking, "What happened out there?"

He sat down on the bed, and I took a spot across from

him, at the desk chair. "I thought I saw an old friend was all."

I waited for him to go on, and when he didn't, I did. "Which part of that is the lie?" I held up my hands to make air-quotes as I spoke. "The 'friend,' the 'old,' or the 'thought' part?"

He made a face. "I used to be a better liar."

"No, I just used to let you get away with it more," I said. He snorted then looked away. I did my best not to look pained while I waited for him to share. I knew that the man I loved, the father of my potential child, had not always been a good man—but he was now, and that's what counted, right? And everything I was imagining while he waited was probably worse than the truth would be. "So come on. 'Fess up."

"I'm not entirely sure and I don't want to worry you over nothing."

I'm surprisingly sympathetic to that right now was what I wanted to blurt out, but I managed to smile and shrugged one shoulder in an encouraging way. "Well, tell me who you thought you saw, and we'll be prepared for the worst together."

Asher's lips twisted, and he gave me a bittersweet smile. "It'd been a while since I'd seen him. I wasn't sure at first."

"But now you are?" I prompted after another pause.

Asher nodded, slowly at first, and then certain. "Yes. Unfortunately."

Which answered the good-past/bad-past question. I didn't want to give up yet, though. "Even bad guys take vacations," I said, trying to make light of things.

"Yeah, they do." He snorted with irony, and then fell silent again.

"Hey now." I moved over to sit beside him on the bed, and shouldered him. "I don't mean you."

Asher sighed and held out both his hands. "Are you sure?"

"Of course."

I could see the muscles in his jaw working as he grit his teeth in thought. "You don't ask many questions about my past, Edie, and I appreciate that."

"I don't need to. I know who you are." I caught one of his hands in my own, nervous that he wasn't looking over at me. It wasn't that I was scared of what he'd say—Asher could take a thousand different forms, but I knew I knew his heart—it was just that hated to see anything cause him pain.

"The thing is, there was a time, when I was young—when I did stupid things. When I didn't care about the consequences, or who I hurt."

"You mean like every kid, ever." I knew his prior shape-shifting abilities lent themselves to spying and corporate espionage. And when he'd been working under the assumption that he'd soon be dead or insane—the fate of all shapeshifters eventually—what was the point in having a conscience?

He shook his head, unwilling to let himself off the hook. "Older than that. Old enough to know better. It's complicated—" he said, and then there was another long pause.

"There's nothing you can say that's going to scare me away from you." I nudged him again with my shoulder. "So spit it out."

"He hired me to acquire some data for him," Asher said, still looking at the ground.

"You mean steal?" I didn't want him to lie to me—or to feel like he had to anymore.

Asher sighed. "Technically, yes."

"About?" I prompted.

"Synthetic blood."

I almost rolled my eyes. "What's so bad about that? There's a huge market for it. Whoever figures it out is going to make a jillion dollars."

"But not many research groups are being underwritten by vampires. Or doing drug trials on unwitting human subjects in countries with no patient protection laws."

That shut me up. "Oh."

"Yeah," Asher agreed, then sighed again.

"And he's here? Like just on board?"

"Apparently."

My brows furrowed in thought. "Did his research succeed? It can't have, otherwise we'd be knee-deep in vampires and living in caves."

"No—I reported him. To the Consortium." Asher twisted his lips sideways, still looking at the floor. "I reported him after his check cashed. I knew he was evil—I touched him, Edie, I knew who he was, and what he was doing—and I waited a week to make sure his money was good. Plus—" Here Asher's voice drifted, and he shook his head again. "I didn't want him to know it was me. It's not like I had any protection, or a private army."

"What happened next?"

"I don't know. I checked up on him after that—at first, all the time. I was waiting to see an obituary. When that didn't happen, I checked less. Honestly, I thought they'd wiped him off the map. But eventually he resurfaced, his name on a few medical patents that were genetically based, back when that was really starting to break out. He must have made millions on some of them."

"So the Consortium didn't do anything to stop him?"

"I don't know. You don't get to ask the Consortium about things like that. You don't even want to know what I had to do to get in touch with them. They want you to think they're always paying attention, but they're not."

The Consortium was some sort of loose governing

group for paranormal creatures. I'd only ever met one of their members, when it'd briefly taken up home in my old charge nurse to reprimand us after a war.

Now I was staring at the carpet too. There were a hundred different questions I wanted to ask him, but only one that really mattered now. "Does he know this version of you?"

This Asher was the one Santa Muerte had given me when she'd saved his life. Sandy-blond hair, blue eyes, and lips that quirked up at the corners half a second before he smiled.

Asher finally turned toward me and gave me a bemused look. "No. No one else knows this me but you, our neighbors back home, and your silly Siamese cat."

I gave him a hopeful grin. "She's cross-eyed. She has no idea what you really look like." He forced a smile back.

This wasn't the first time this had happened. His prior abilities—what I called *the strange,* in my mind—limited as they now were, still affected us, usually at intervals just long enough apart for me to forget that he had them. He'd change into looking like Hector the Doctor for work, and we'd take separate trains in, and then at work we'd pretend to be coworkers. After the first few illicit-seeming months, it hadn't really been that hard. The shapeshifting itself wasn't the strange part—it was all the other things. Instances when he'd made us leave diners after he'd recognized someone back in the kitchen, or him changing banks after a merger. Once he'd gotten out of a speeding ticket by reminding a cop about taking a bribe. As much as, like any girlfriend, I'd wanted to pry into Asher's past—pasts, even, heavy emphasis on the plural—I hadn't. Moments like this were why.

I wished I could open the doors to our room's balcony, let in the sea air, and let it chase out the strange. Every time I thought I'd gotten used to it, I realized I hadn't really—I'd just gotten used to hoping the bulk of it was behind us. Sitting beside him, though, I realized there was no way we'd ever completely outrun it. It was who he was, who he'd been. It followed him wherever he went, like a tail. And right now he looked so alone. I squeezed his hand harder.

"Well, everything's okay now," I said, with the same comforting tone I used on patients all the time.

"You can't just let me off the hook, Edie."

"Why not? It sounds like you've been carrying this around long enough."

"He's not the only person I worked for. None of the rest were as bad as he was—but there's a four-way tie for second place. And you don't want to know how many people are in the running for third." He carefully took my hand off his and released it back to me. "As evil as I know he was, what he was working on—with data I gave him— I can't help but wonder what working with him once makes me."

I took his hand back fiercely. "It makes you someone who changed. That's not a bad thing. I love you." Suddenly I didn't want him to tell me anything else about his past. It was behind us, and it could stay there, forever, where it couldn't hurt us ever again.

He swallowed and stared down at my hand, covering his. "I know you love me. But sometimes I think back on all the things I've done, and I can't see why."

This wasn't the brash devil-may-care Asher I usually knew. I leaned up and kissed his forehead, where wrinkles were starting to show. "I can't speak to all those other Ashers. But the one I love saved my life a few times, and he takes care of people who need him. I love him quite a lot."

A soft smile took the edge off his serious face. "I love you, Edie."

"Not to mention, he brought me on this excellent vacation," I went on.

He gave me a wry look. "I thought you weren't completely sold on the ocean?"

I elbowed him. "I'm trying to make you feel better. Stop making it hard."

He laughed, turning toward me and taking me in his arms.

CHAPTER THREE

Sex was always easy with Asher.

Being with him had always been the kind of hot trouble that normally only strangers can get into, the fearless kind that makes you demanding and loud, both people fighting to take control, neither stopping until they'd been satisfied.

And this time was no different. Arms still around me, Asher's mouth found mine at the same time his hands reached for the button of my jeans.

Just like that, I was ravenous for him as well. Mouths dueling, I returned his kiss with aggression, as he growled low in his throat.

My hands yanked off his shirt, reveling in the feel of his skin against mine, soft and warm, rippling over muscles. I ran my hands down his tightly muscled back and down into his jeans, pulling him close. At the feel of my hands, he shuddered and broke our contact, pulling back to free himself from his clothes, and then to pull my clothes off me.

Returning to me naked, cock erect, he lay down on top of me, forcing his legs between my own. I wrapped my legs around him, trying to urge him farther, desperate for more. But just when I thought he was going to ram inside me, he paused, hot and heavy against me. To prove he could control himself, and that he was in charge of my desire.

"I hate it when you do that," I whispered to him.

"No you don't," he whispered back.

Slowly, he lowered himself so that the smooth underside of his cock ran against me. I shuddered as he began to kiss my breasts and throat. He rubbed himself against me, soft, then hard, but never entering like I wanted him to, instead teasing me, making me wait. I knew if I asked for it I'd get it, he just liked to hear me beg—or make me so hot I couldn't control myself anymore.

Suddenly I needed to be in charge. I pushed him back, off me, to one side, rolling him onto his back. He fought me only for a second then went with it, watching me rise up to straddle him, all of us touching, but still separate. Now it was my turn to grind, chastely, against him. He laughed, pleased to be beneath me, his hands tickling up the insides of my thighs.

"My turn," I announced, reaching down to set the tip of him inside me. His hips arched and I rose to deny him what he'd been denying me. "Tell me that you'll always be mine," I said from above him.

He stopped playing around, sensing the solemnity of my request. "Of course."

"Say it."

His hands slid down my back to rest against my buttocks. "I'll always be yours. Assuming you'll have me."

I grinned down at him, showing teeth. "Oh, I'll have you all right." I shifted my hips as I rocked back down, his cock sliding home. He hissed with the sensation, and I let out a low moan.

After that, there were no more words; we moved as one. I leaned over him, my breasts against his chest, and his hands on my ass to trap me there, as his cock pulsed up and into me and my hips rocked downward to meet him. We found a rhythm together, one that matched the rocking of the boat and the sound of the waves, sweat soon drenching both of us like the sea spray outside. I took his cock deep inside me, arching my whole body forward until it found that secret place deep within that only this position hit. His hands clenched at my ass, pulling me closer, forcing him in deeper, the skin above his cock grinding into my clit—I knew we were both on the edge of coming, that any second now one of us would be thrown overboard and we'd take the other with us when we went. I fought it, I didn't want release yet, I wanted us to stay here forever, the head of his cock rubbing that spot inside, making me feel electrified.

Asher's breathing was ragged now and I realized I'd been moaning with each of his strokes, trying to hold on and not let the moment go. His eyes met mine, dark, wild.

"You're mine," he said, his voice thick.

If any other man had ever said that in the entire history of my sexual career I probably would have laughed him out of bed. But right then I wanted to be Asher's, I wanted him to be right, I wanted it to be true. His motions became exaggerated, sliding all of himself into and out of me. The third time he buried himself inside me, his thick cock rubbing that spot and him grinding against my clit. I screamed, arcing forward against him, as I finally let myself go.

He rode me through my spasms, my body grabbing him tight. And then it was his turn. His cock rock-hard, his thrusts trying to find the deepest part of me, almost desperately. I watched his face as he suddenly let go, his last thrusts quick and sharp, making one low moan of my name.

I didn't want to be the one to break the bond between us, so I lay down on top of him, with him still inside. My hair spilled over his chest, and he raised one hand to absently stroke down my back.

"I love fucking you," he said quietly, almost to himself.

I grinned into his neck, where he couldn't see me. "I can tell."

CHAPTER FOUR

Sex had swept our room free of the past, for now. I heaved myself off Asher, and he complained. He liked snuggling even more than I did. Plus, he was almost asleep. Truth be told, after a day of travel, jet lag, and vigorous sex, I could be almost asleep too.

"Hang on. I have to do girl things."

I went into the bathroom and cleaned up. No blood.

As I stood in front of the mirror, I couldn't help but examine my belly. Despite not having any proof, I was 80 percent sure I was pregnant. Crap. Yay? Crap . . . yay? I poked at my stomach, which looked exactly the same. "I hope we didn't shake things up in there too much for you. Also, sorry about the sperm. Just kick them out of the way or something," I said. Maybe the fetus had hung an OCCUPADO sign up outside my uterus already, and the sperm were milling uselessly around outside. I laughed aloud at the idea. "Sorry, boys."

Asher knocked on the door. "Did you say something?"

I gave him an innocent smile as I emerged. "No."

As tired as we both were, we made a pact to stay up later. If we went to sleep now we'd only wind up awake at 3 A.M. We reluctantly hauled ourselves out of bed and unpacked. Just as I reached the end of my bags and began thinking maybe we could revisit the staying-up-until-a-decent-hour plan, another set of bells chimed overhead and Asher got one more of those looks on his face.

"They're starting a going-away party upstairs now. We should go up and give ourselves a tour."

"Or, we could just stay here?" I said with hope and exhaustion.

"We could . . . or we could go upstairs where people will be dancing and drinking. And make a lap around the boat. So that we know where things are tomorrow."

I crossed my arms in an accusatory fashion. "You seem to know where everything is already."

He made a face at me. "I will admit to having touched more than one cruise employee in my past."

"Touched?" I said, feigning indignant surprise. "Or touched-touched? Like, with your penis?" My voice rose in horror, teasing, as I crawled back out of tickling range on the bed.

"Hey now!" he protested, coming after me. "I can't help it that I was a man-whore!" He paused and looked off into space dramatically, owning the moment. "Wait. That sounds wrong."

I started giggling as he caught up to me on the bed and held himself over me on one arm. "You know I have a troubled past, Edie," he said solemnly, like a movie-trailer announcer. "But from here on out, I swear, my penis only has eyes for you."

I lost it and laughed so hard I snorted. Which made him laugh in turn, falling down to land beside me. I re-gathered myself first, gulping in several large breaths of air. "Okay, okay. If I say we can go on a tour, will you never tell me about your penis having eyeballs again?"

Still naked, Asher got a silly look on his face. "But, Edie, he's nearsighted. What if he needs to see you close up?"

"Oh. My. God." I rolled out of bed and threw the sheets at him with a laugh. "You've won. I'm going. I'm gone. Get up, or you'll have to meet me in the hallway." I reached down to haul on the clothes I'd been wearing before as he sprang out of bed and bowed, using the sheets like a cape.

"We, fair lady, are at your service."

I opened my mouth to say something else, and then I shook my head and clasped my bra. "I don't even want to begin to encourage your use of the royal *we*."

He grinned challengingly, and I beamed back. This was the man I was in love with. The silly, sexy man of the now. Past or no past.

I finished pulling on the clothes I'd been wearing earlier so as not to get anything clean funky. I could shower when we got back to the room. We held hands in the elevator on the way up to the top deck, and I could see my bed head from several unflattering angles on the elevator's mirrored walls. I'd blame it on the sea air or something, if anyone asked. It didn't matter really—I was with Asher. He smiled at my reflection, and I smiled back.

An expanded version of the *Maraschino* in map form covered one wall. There was a tiny red cross indicating the medical center on the bottom-most floor. I'd look there for a pregnancy test tomorrow, first thing. I'd figure out some way to ditch Asher to do it—and I'd put off worrying about anything baby-related till morning time. I deserved one night of vacation at least.

The elevator doors dinged and opened into a small landing on the ninth floor. The entrance to Le Poisson Affamé—which Asher had informed me meant "the famished fish"—was off to one side. It was a fancy restaurant where we had reservations later on in the trip—no way we could get in there, looking like this, tonight. Saloon doors on the other side led out to the deck. We walked through them, still holding hands.

The deck outside wound around smokestacks, interrupted only by herds of deck chairs and an assortment of shallow pools. There were bars at frequent intervals, with people already partying nearby, drinks in hand, as hidden speakers pumped out music with a salsa beat.

Asher and I wove through the people and walked the perimeter of the deck. Railings were reinforced with clear plastic walls to cut down on wind and potential lawsuits. The night breeze smelled like good ocean, clean and salty, not the stale scent of decay that Port Cavell had down by the docks.

Asher wound his arms around me as we looked back at the receding land. It was as if it were ebbing away from us, a reversal of the tide. And as much as I didn't trust the ocean, it was hard not to feel safe. The *Maraschino* was immense, and Asher was at my back. What more could a girl need? Assuming we didn't meet any stray icebergs between LA and Hawaii, we might actually have a fabulous time.

He squeezed me closer. "Want a drink?"

"Nah. If I do, I'll fall asleep where I stand." It was as good an excuse as any for not drinking and not far off from the truth. I turned around inside his arms. "You should if you want, though." The sooner he felt like falling asleep, the sooner I could too, guilt-free.

He thought about it. "Maybe. It is our first night here, after all." I nodded in an encouraging way, and he unlooped his arms around me, gave me a winning smile. "Wait here for me. It's a big boat."

"Aye-aye, Cap'n," I teased, and held on to the railing as he took a step back. The land had entirely disappeared, and the volume of the music turned up as if in triumph. It was as if it were just us—the four thousand or so of us on board—and no one else. No neighbors to complain, no police department to call. We were on a floating city, and out here it felt entirely possible there was no one else left in the world.

A crew member tried to get people to do a coordinated dance on a nearby deck, the Macarena, the refuge of the rhythmless and their children. Parents bobbed in time with the music as their toddlers waddled along. Maybe Claire was right—this wouldn't be such a bad tradition to have.

Asher returned with a blended drink in hand, and I eyed its unmanly pinkness. My boyfriend usually drank Manhattans. "It's tropical," he informed me, offering me a sip. I snorted and demurred.

A child broke from the pack of dancers and ran toward us, followed by a tiny brunette woman.

"Thomas? Thomas!" She raced after him. Luckily, she was already wearing a pink velour jogging suit. "Thomas, get back here!"

It was the sort of thing that had always made me question having children in the past—even though I'd nursed enough kids to know they were unpredictable. But I found myself grinning at the thought of racing after one of my own. There wouldn't be *much* racing, because mine would be better behaved, of course—then I realized that probably all expectant parents lied to themselves about that sort of thing.

A man followed the woman at a distance. Wind struck up, stronger now as the sun was down—but I knew I'd heard Asher's sharp inhale of surprise at seeing the other man.

"That's him," he whispered, then handed me his drink

before moving quickly to intercept the racing child. "Whoa! Hey there, kiddo!"

The man approaching was *him,* him? Evil personified?

It was hard to be scared of him when seeing Asher hold his kid made me queasy inside, in a good way.

"Hey, hey—" Asher repeated, like he was soothing a dog, as the kid fought and squirmed. The woman caught up, swooping her child up into her arms, and smiled sheepishly at us.

"Thank you so much!" she said, making a *Q* of the *you.* "He's so fast, he gets into a lot of trouble."

"It's no mind," Asher said, his accent a subtle imitation of hers that he hadn't had a second ago. I'd seen him do it before at the clinic. I didn't know if he did it on purpose or if the strange just came to him without thinking, but it put people's minds at ease. Who better to be your doctor than someone from your hometown? It wasn't even entirely a lie. He'd touched someone from nearly everywhere, and held a set of their memories inside himself. He only needed to hold up a tag like a dry cleaner's employee and wait for the appropriate past to slide itself forward for him to wear.

The man from Asher's past, presumably her husband, caught up as well. He was more frightening the closer he got. It wasn't his sharp nose or his prominent widow's peak, going gray at both temples. It was the way he took in all of us, emanating an air of disgust at the entire situation. Seeing him be cold to his own overwhelmed wife, child, and randomly helpful strangers made Asher's story all the more believable. While the Consortium might have censured him somehow, they hadn't taught him any lessons.

"Thank you," he said, as if it was a complaint, and he was accent-less. Asher gave him an ignorant smile, but it was hard for me not to stare. Testing fake blood on humans—who knew how many deaths this man had caused?

"Oh, no problem. We're trying to have one ourselves," Asher went on, lying completely, his accent still on. Ironic, seeing as he didn't know my period was late. "Hoping this romantic sea air will help things out, you know?" Asher overshared, as I began to want to die. "I'm Kevin—" Asher went on, leaning forward with his hand out. The woman shook it first.

"I'm Liz—and this is Nathaniel," she said.

"Nathaniel Tannin." Nathaniel introduced himself more formally, with no clue that Asher already knew him. I felt fractionally relieved, but not much.

As Asher took his hand, Nathaniel looked a little pained by the common touch. Like he thought someone who looked like Asher did currently, and who, farmer-like, talked about impregnation at the drop of a hat, might also have barbecue sauce or semen stains hidden on his palm.

When Asher didn't let his hand go, Nathaniel's eyes narrowed.

"And I'm Edie." I introduced myself with my actual name, because I'd never manage to keep a fake one straight, and so I could stop Asher from somehow giving himself away. "What's his name?" I asked Liz despite the fact that I'd heard her shouting it after him, even over the increasingly obnoxious music.

"Thomas. The third," she answered, and her eyes darted to Asher-Kevin, who'd just finally let go of her husband's hand. Nathaniel not-so-discreetly wiped his hand on his leg.

"I have an uncle named Thomas!" I said. Asher turned to blink at me.

You're not the only one who can lie, I tried to say with a well-timed squint. "You remember him, right, Kevin?"

I smiled at the woman. "He's my favorite uncle, he's just a lovely man. I'm sure your son will be lovely too."

"Awww, I'm sure. Thank you. Again." Liz hefted her son up, still squirming, and gave us another shy smile as Nathaniel took her by the elbow and guided her away.

"What was that about?" Asher asked me as soon as they were out of earshot.

"I don't know. You tell me," I said.

I expected him to have some witty retort or explanation. When he didn't, my eyes followed his gaze; he was still watching Nathaniel blend in with the crowd.

My stomach sank, just as the sun had, and everything came into focus. "You didn't try to read him, did you?"

Asher nodded quietly, and when I stared at him aghast he shrugged one shoulder. "It didn't work."

I was stunned.

We didn't get rules when Santa Muerte stopped Asher from going insane. There were no guarantees on her services, no promises that he couldn't fuck things up by trying to be what he once was. Asher had never pushed things before—there'd been no need, we'd been living happily, normally. That he'd do it now, and risk himself, over a ghost from his past? It was unthinkable. I'd almost lost him once before. I wouldn't watch him do it again.

"And what if it had?" I pressed.

"Then I'd know why he was here. And what he was up to."

I pointed back the way they'd come. "He's on a vacation with his family. Like you told me we were on. Remember?"

"He has a daughter who's your age. There's no way that's his wife, or his child." Asher shook his head, denying what we'd seen.

"Oh, so he'd be the first man ever to marry his secretary?"

He frowned. "I know he had a vasectomy—"

"So? Those can be reversed. Or he could be a stepdad. Or that kid could be adopted." I was sputtering now. "I can't believe you were willing to throw everything away—"

I could see on his face that he wasn't going to apologize, he was going to try to explain. "Edie," he began, his voice low. "It didn't work."

"What if it had? Or—what if it hadn't, but you'd broken yourself again? Over nothing?"

"It didn't work!" he protested.

"We're a family now! You can't go abandoning us like that!" People were staring and I didn't care.

"And you don't know him like I do!" Asher shouted back. "Edie, I didn't abandon you—"

"I know that he's here with his family," I said. "And you need to act like you're here with yours."

CHAPTER FIVE

The sun was gone now, and the night was becoming as cold as the untouched drink I still held in one hand. I handed it back to him. I was sure we looked like *that* couple, the ones who tied one on at the airport lounge, and on the shuttle, and in their rooms, and again on the deck. Whatever.

"I'm going back to the room," I said.

"Fine."

There wasn't anything left after that but to huff off. Of course we were on a boat, so I couldn't really *go* anywhere, but I didn't want to be *around* him for at least a little bit. And he knew me well enough to know that he shouldn't chase me—I only left when I really did want to be alone.

I found my room key in my pocket, and used both of the hand sanitizer stations I passed by on my way to the elevators, like I could somehow wash his betrayal off me.

The room still smelled a little like sex when I got there. I wondered bleakly if Claire and Hal had heard anything earlier, or if they'd hear anything again on this whole godforsaken trip. I still needed to take a shower. Now was my chance.

How dare he try to throw everything away? It might be one thing, under controlled circumstances, to test it out.

Safely. Back home. Just to see. But to do it on a boat, here, in a rush, without even warning me? What if he'd broken himself again somehow and died, and left me to raise our child alone?

I shuddered in fear and rage, then shed my clothes before going into the bathroom with the shower. The tub-shower and the toilet were in two separate rooms inside our cabin, like in an old Victorian home. I stepped inside the shower and turned on the water, then held on as the boat took an alarming turn. Between the small size of the tub, the slipperiness of the water, and the motion of the boat, I wondered how many elderly guests broke hips on board. I was careful to brace myself against the wall. If I hurt myself in here while I was hate-showering, I'd never hear the end of it from him.

By the time I was done washing my hair, I heard the outside door open and shut. I finished my shower, trying to think of everything I was going to say, but the second I stepped out with a towel wrapped around my chest, he spoke first.

"What's with all this 'family' stuff?"

"Like you care" came out of my mouth in an instant, and Asher looked snakebit. I wished I could take it back so hard I said so. "I'm sorry." I heaved an apologetic sigh. "I didn't mean that."

Asher still looked hurt. "Edie, of course I care."

"It didn't look like it up there, to me." I pointed in the direction of the decks above us.

"I'm sorry. I never should have done that, not without talking to you first, at least. That was a huge mistake." He seemed earnest as he said it, but he also looked confused. "But what's gotten into you?"

"Um. You did? A couple of weeks ago." I tried to sound lighthearted. I hadn't sat around and thought about how this conversation would go, but even if I had, this wouldn't have been how I pictured it. His face was still blank. I sat down on the bed. "For someone who has at least one doctor's worth of knowledge inside him, you are very very dense."

He frowned, and then realization slowly dawned. "Wait. Are you trying to say you're pregnant?"

"I don't know. Are you trying to hear it? I missed a pill." I made a face at him, then sighed. "And I don't know yet. I just know my period is late."

His frown deepened, and he raised a querulous eyebrow. "That's not possible."

"Wow. Thanks," I said, as sarcastically as I could.

"No, Edie. It is literally not possible. Shapeshifter and human DNA don't mix. Believe me. It's one of the reasons shapeshifters can be so promiscuous. We're never in danger of having children with humans. We also don't get sick."

"Well, that knowledge would have saved me a trip to the clinic for an STD check last year. Thanks for letting me know."

He looked from my stomach to my eyes. "Do you feel pregnant?"

"I have no idea what being pregnant feels like. How would I know? All I know is that my period should have started, and it didn't, and—"

"When were you going to tell me?" he jumped in.

I made a helpless gesture. "After I could scam a pregnancy test from somewhere. I was going to go to the medic for one tomorrow morning. I just didn't want to worry you before I knew anything for sure."

"But you think—"

I cut him off. "I don't know what to think. My uterus isn't always clockwork. And neither am I."

"You should have said something."

I made a face at him. Considering what he'd just done without any warning up above—"You are one to talk."

He shook his head. "That was different."

"Really?" I said, with even more sarcasm than usual.

He relented with a sigh. "Okay, no. Not really." He looked again from my stomach to me. "You should have told me sooner, though. The instant—"

"There's nothing to tell yet," I interrupted, starting to chew on my bottom lip. "And I'm sorry, but I've never done this before. I don't know the rules for this. I'm making it up as I go along."

Was it really impossible? How would I feel about things then? I'd sort of maybe liked to think it was real. If only to get my mom off my back, which as everyone knew was a really good reason to have children.

"You're sure it's impossible?" I asked him, hoping-not-hoping for him to be right.

Asher's brow furrowed in contemplation. "A year ago, yes. But . . . I'm not as positive as I used to be. Shape-shifters living into their mid-thirties is pretty impossible. Santa Muerte changed me. Maybe she did more than I know."

I wrung my hands together in my lap. "Just once, I'd like to know everything for sure, you know?"

Asher snorted softly. "Me too."

There was a long pause between us during which I wished he'd magically say the right thing, while at the same time knowing wishing that was epically unfair. "Is it okay?" I asked, my voice small.

He looked surprised. "Yeah. Why wouldn't it be? Unless you don't want it. Then—" He made a mysterious gesture in the air.

I twisted my lips to one side. "So you're ambivalent about it, is what you're saying?"

"I've had less than five minutes to think about it. It's still a maybe. What more do you want from me?"

If he'd said that with the wrong tone, I might have lost it. I'd had a very, very long day. But he was earnestly asking what else, if anything, he could do, and I was wise enough to know he meant it.

"Let's figure it out for sure tomorrow. And then we can celebrate, or celebrate, depending," I said. "It would be celebrating, right? And don't say what I want to hear because you know already. That'll just piss me off."

Asher looked as stunned as I'd been feeling for the past fourteen or so hours. "I never thought I would ever be a dad. I never wanted to be one. After my dad leaving us . . . I couldn't ever imagine bringing a kid into the world."

It felt like a lead fishing weight was dropping down my throat while he talked.

"But—" He took my hands in his, and calmed their wringing. "I can see doing it, with you. I've never thought about it before now. I just assumed we couldn't, ever. But if I was going to have a kid, I'd want it to be with you."

I squinted at him. "You're not just saying that because I threatened you?"

"Not in the least. I sort of figured eventually your mom would wear you down and we'd adopt or something."

"Really?"

"Yeah. Why not? I've seen you. You're good with kids. You like them. I wasn't going to deny them to you. I just never thought they'd be from me." He inhaled, held it, and then carefully spoke again. "What if . . . it's part shapeshifter?"

I knew what he meant when he said that. What if it'd be like him, and have to grow up outside of society for his, or her, own protection, until it was old enough to deal with the strange. And if it was shapeshifter, even in part, what would happen to it when it aged? Would Asher and I get to have any grandkids? Could ligers breed? Or would it lose itself in the sea of personalities inside, like Asher had almost done?

I shook my head. All that was too far away. We didn't need to go looking into the future for things to worry about; we had enough options in the here and now. "I don't know. We'll figure it out. If it's real. Tomorrow."

"Tomorrow," he agreed.

I crawled backward onto the bed. "What are we going to do about dinner? It's been a long day—I don't feel like leaving the room."

"This, I'm prepared for." He reached over to his bedside table and got the room service menu guide for me. "Twenty-four seven. As promised."

I hadn't eaten all day—what with traveling, sex, and exhaustion, everything on the menu looked good, and I said so. Asher got a clever-looking smile, and I shut him down. "Don't you dare make some lame joke about me eating for two."

After the arrival of two club sandwiches with a side of french fries, we arranged a picnic on our bed, and our conversation continued.

"So it didn't work. Not at all?" I asked, shoving around ketchup with the edge of a fry.

He shook his head. A little too hard. Was I being hypervigilant, or was he overprotecting me?

I pressed on. "What were you hoping to even accomplish?"

"Other than ruining everything?" he said, brows raised, sort of teasing, sort of not.

"Yeah."

He heaved a sigh. "I just wanted to see. Maybe if he'd become some great humanitarian in the last few years. Or if a lot of bad things had happened to him, if karma had won out."

"And what if neither of those things had happened?"

Asher snorted. "I don't know. It's a big boat. I bet people fall overboard all the time."

The fry I'd been raising to my mouth paused in midair. "Did you just hear yourself say that?"

He made a face at me. "Oh, come on, Edie, I was teasing."

"It's only teasing if you've never done anything like that before." I carefully set the fry with its burden of ketchup back down. "If you have, then it's kind of a threat."

Asher groaned and swung his gaze to look up at the ceiling, pondering it for a moment before looking again back at me. "I'm not that person anymore. Honestly."

"It isn't that I want you to change, Asher. It's just that—" The words hung between us as I tried to think of a phrase that would prove my point, because I really, really really, did want him to change, or at least pretend that killing people wasn't okay, no matter how awful they might be.

"You don't want to be in love with a murderer," he said, cutting me off with a resigned nod. "I get that. It's fair."

I gave him a halfhearted grin and tried to lighten the mood. "You know I can't take time out of my busy schedule to visit you in jail. When would I get my nails done?" I looked down at my hands—I had gone and gotten a rare manicure for this trip, scheduled it yesterday after work, when I'd be safe from my own overzealous hand sanitizing habit. The red nail polish was already chipping a little bit at the edges, where only I could see.

"When indeed," he said drily, and poached a fry off my plate.

CHAPTER SIX

After our picnic, we crawled into bed. Asher slept soundly and I envied him. I wanted to, but couldn't. I missed my Ambien prescription. Ironically, I could get Hector MD to write me one, but I felt stupid needing it now that I was supposedly on a day-shift schedule. I hadn't thought about the stresses of jet lag, finding out my period was late, and discussing whether my morally ambiguous boyfriend should kill someone, even if he was a really bad someone, on my vacation trip. Oh, well, I didn't know if Ambien was safe for indeterminately pregnant people, either.

I was too keyed up to sleep. My mind was an angry dog, chasing after endless cars.

Would Asher make a good dad? I thought he would. Then again, his own dad sucked. But what better excuse to overcompensate than to fix your own past?

Would I make a good mom? Oh, God, who knew. I knew I'd be full of good intentions—just like the proverbial path to hell.

I threw the sheets off me and walked across the room to the balcony, unlocked the doors, and stepped outside into the night.

The *Maraschino* put out too much light pollution itself for me to see the stars. But the newly waning moon was overhead. I knew all weres were safe from its pull for now. I leaned against the railing, looking out at the water.

Was it even safe to bring a kid into this world? One that I knew had vampires, and weres, and a hundred other things that could go bump in the night in it? If we did have a kid—ours, or adopted—and it was scared of something under the bed, would I honestly be able to tell it that things would be just fine?

"Edie?" I heard Asher's voice from the room behind me and turned around. There were no lights in the room; his disembodied voice was coming from the dark. "Come back to bed."

I walked back into our cabin, blindly. I didn't lock the balcony doors behind me, because really, we were six floors up and in the middle of the ocean. It wasn't like we were expecting a visit from Batman. I took three steps in—and then I turned around and walked back and did lock the doors, because, well, who knew.

When I slid back under the sheets Asher moved to spoon me. "Why're you so cold?" he murmured, and threw an arm across me to pull me close.

In the morning, the ship was bucking against the waves. I didn't know if this was normal or not, but it felt as if the ocean were trying to throw the *Maraschino* off, and it was making me seasick.

Asher was already awake, reading a book beside me. "You ready?" he asked as I wiped the sleep out of my eyes.

"Not really. But let's go." I knew that you were supposed to use your first pee of the day for pregnancy testing, and I didn't want to wait too long.

We got up and dressed, and the elevator we rode down

was full of people. Many of them got off and immediately went to queue up at the guest services station, where I could see them handing out seasickness bags. Maybe somehow we'd gotten contaminated with norovirus, like I'd privately feared, after all those shows about "my cruise ship tried to poison me" on the news. Whatever it was, I was glad to know I wasn't the only one who found the current motion disconcerting.

We reached the first floor alone, although I realized when we got there the ship was actually deeper than this—there must be floors underneath that were all engines, laundry, and rooms for the crew. The medical center was down the rightmost hallway. I walked through the open door into a small waiting room, with another open door beyond, and I peeked into it. There was a short examination bed, a desk, some cabinets, and a chair—and a man sitting in it with his back to me. I went back to Asher. There was only room for one of us in the medical room, really. "I appreciate the moral support, but you can stay here."

"I'll be right outside."

I knocked on the doorjamb and took a step inside. "Hello?"

"We are not open yet," the man said curtly, without turning around. There was a clock fastened to one wall; it was 7:45 A.M. ship time, which made it almost noon back home.

I didn't want to wait, and more important I wasn't sure how much longer I could not pee. "I just need a pregnancy test."

He made an irritated noise, spinning around in his chair to look at me. He had brown skin, and an accent, and he made a pointed look at my ring finger. "Where is your husband?"

"Does that matter?"

He didn't answer me.

I knew from having worked with people of different ethnicities that certain cultures had ways of acting, talking, or gesturing that could be perceived as rude from the outside when compared with one's own cultural norm without that being their intended gist at all. I'd learned to look past a lot of that, because I knew it wasn't personal, and because I realized it was mostly in my head.

However, as both a woman and a nurse, I could also identify a judgy doctor at twenty paces.

"Is it an emergency?" he asked archly, looking me up and down, as if I were unclean.

"No."

"Then can't it wait?"

"Look, I can pay you for it. I'd just like to know."

"So you can drink," he said, and I had a feeling it wasn't just me he hated, but possibly his job, and possibly all Americans. I bet he did see a ton of alcohol poisonings on these trips—were I in his likely Muslim and abstemious shoes, that might bias me, too.

"Nope. Mormon," I lied. Super-lied, come to think of it, seeing as I was asking for a pregnancy test, and I clearly wasn't the Virgin Mary. "Look, I just want to know."

He started going through the drawers of his desk. When those didn't produce what he was looking for—probably a card with a disappointed-looking face that said YOU SHOULD HAVE WASHED YOUR HANDS BETTER! in twenty languages—he started looking in the cabinets above his desk, where the contents of each shelf were held in with slide-stoppers and/or bungee cord.

He produced a pregnancy test at long last from the back of one of these. If it was possible for one to expire, I'm sure this one would have. I'd seen less wrinkled packaging emerge on strips of gum that I'd lost in my purse.

"Do you know how to use it?" he asked again.

"Pretty sure I just pee on one end."

"That might be the last one I have. So don't come back here looking for more."

"I won't. I swear."

He snorted to let me know what he thought of that. And then swiveled back around on his chair.

I emerged in the hall to find Asher speaking something that sounded like German to a crew member with a crew cut. He wrapped up their conversation quickly when he saw me, and the crew member gave me a courteous nod before leaving.

"Did they have one?" he asked once we were in the elevator, alone.

"Yeah. Was that German?"

"Nope. Afrikaans." I hadn't known that Asher spoke Afrikaans. That was my boyfriend, perpetually full of surprises. "How'd it go?"

I made a face. "I wish I'd taken you in with me instead."

"Yeah—Marius was telling me the doctor was a prick. On the downlow, you know, countryman-to-countryman."

"Well, he's right. I almost had to promise him our first-born to get this." I held the test up. The wrapper was illegible. "What language is this in, polylinguist?"

Asher inspected it. "Cantonese?"

"Great."

Asher grinned at me. "Even people in China want to know if they're pregnant, Edie. I'm sure it's fine."

I inhaled deeply, girding my loins in a metaphorical sense. "Let's go back to our room and see."

* * *

I went into the bathroom alone. For having had to pee all morning, my bladder was now suddenly shy.

"It's too late now," I told myself. "Come on. Let's just know already." It was weird knowing that Asher was listening in outside. I leaned over and turned on the faucet.

My bladder couldn't hold out forever, thank goodness. I did what needed doing, and then set the stick on a dry washcloth on the counter while I pulled up my clothing and washed my hands. And then I came out to show it to Asher. "It has two lines. What does that mean?"

"Wǒmen yǒu yīgè yīng'ér," he said, looking smug.

I squinted at him. "Does that mean what I think it means? I'm going off the smart-ass look on your face, since I have no idea what you just said."

Asher's grin got even wider. "We're going to be parents."

"Oh, my God." I leaned back against the closed bathroom door behind me. I'd sort of been hoping I was, but part of me was also hoping the other way too, just because I didn't think I was ready to be a mom yet.

But maybe I was. I looked at the test again. "Oh, my God."

"It's good, right?" Asher looked at me, still grinning.

I looked at him beaming, so happy for me—for us. We would make it work somehow. I nodded wildly.

He laughed and engulfed me in his arms. "I never thought this would happen for me, Edie." He kissed the side of my head and pressed me to him. "It's crazy."

"I know," I said into his neck. This was it. We were going to be a family. The three of us. Asher inhaled to say something else, and the ship lurched to one side. So did my stomach. I put my hand on his chest. "Hold that thought."

* * *

Morning sickness cinched it. Or seasickness that over-lapped morning sickness. Either way, I was left wishing I'd smuggled Zofran on board.

By the time I felt better-ish, which was a good fifteen minutes of hurling and general nausea after I began, I was ready to face my mom. When I explained what I wanted to do, Asher was less sure. "Shouldn't you wait? There's a lot of spontaneous abortions early on—"

I gave him a weary grin. "Here's the doctor I know and love." The ship kept rocking—I needed to hurry, or it'd be too late. "Look, if it's good news, she'll be pissed off if she wasn't in on it from the beginning. If it's bad news, if things don't work out because our DNA has a chromo-somal imbalance or whatever, I'll be sad and need some-one to talk to."

He frowned, but nodded slowly. "If you say so."

"Not that you're not awesome, but sometimes having backup is better, just in case. Trust me." I picked up the cabin's phone. "Now, if I can only figure out how to call her."

Dialing off the ship was like making an international call. But reading the instructions in the manual while the ship was hightailing it across the sea was like trying to read in the passenger seat of a car, which had a history of making me ill. By my fourth time through—looking, I'm sure, increasingly green—Asher shook his head. "Screw it." He rummaged in his bedside drawer, unlocked his cell phone, and tossed it to me. "Roam away."

It was already afternoon back home. My mother picked up the phone, her voice unsure because she didn't recog-nize Asher's number. "Hey, Mom? It's me. Guess what . . ."

She started screaming before I could finish my entire sentence. She heard "baby" and let loose—which was good because right after that, the phone cut out. "Mom? Mom?" I tried redialing, and found I couldn't; there was no connection. I handed Asher back his phone. He tried again, and when it didn't work, he shrugged.

"We're probably too far out."

"She heard enough—she'll probably be waiting for us at the dock." Holding a diaper bag and a list of distant relatives she wanted to invite to our baby shower.

"I could hear her from over here." He grinned and sat beside me. "How are you feeling?"

"Apart from the sick thing, good. I think." I spent a moment checking in with myself. I was going to be a mom. A mom . . . I looked at him, eyes wide. Oh, my God. It was real.

Asher watched me panicking. "You're sure?"

"Yeah. I think." The world around me was narrowing, though. I felt like I was in a tunnel, and the distant exit was getting smaller.

He wrapped an arm around me and held me close. "It's okay to be scared. But everything's going to be just fine."

"How do you know?"

He beamed down at me. "Because it's too early for you—for either of us—to be able to screw anything up. It's not even worth worrying about now."

"But what if I still do? Or—things later?" The enormity of eighteen years of responsibility, and beyond, stretched in front of me like open road.

He made an absurd face. "That's not going to happen, Edie."

"But what if it does?"

"Then you'll have me around to help you unscrew it," Asher said, and I nodded slowly, forcing myself to agree with him. I knew he meant it. But I also knew my propensity to mess things up. "Are you seriously worried about that, this early in the game?" he went on. "Don't make me start chalking things up to hormones this fast."

I inhaled deeply and held it for a second too long to

buy myself time to think. "You knew I was naturally paranoid when you started dating me. Not just knew, but knew-knew." I wiggled my fingers between us to indicate *the strange*.

"I did," he agreed. "It's oddly charming, though completely unnecessary."

"What if I suck at this?" I poked at my stomach, like the creature inside there could poke back.

"Are you being serious?" Asher pulled away to look at me like I might be coming down with something.

"Completely. What if I mess up their life? What if they hate me?"

"Edie," he said, dismissing me with a head shake, his voice low. "There is no possible way that will happen."

"You know me. I mean, you really know me, Asher. It wouldn't be the first thing I'd screwed up—" There was a swelling under my breastbone, and I didn't know if it was more nausea or stomach acid. I put my hand there, to press it down.

Asher's hand followed mine, interlacing his fingers. "No one gets any guarantees. And while you *are* reckless—I know you try harder than anyone. If anyone can make this work, it's you and me. We're a team. Okay?"

I nodded quickly, as though I was trying to convince myself, and took several deep breaths. "Thanks."

"I love you." He stood suddenly, pulling me up after him. "I never actually loved anyone before I met you."

"That's because you were too busy using them," I said aloud with my outside voice. Asher looked pained, pressing his lips together tight. "Oh, God. See? That was it. I do that. I don't mean to do it, but I do that. Sometimes. It's like I can't even help doing it. I'll be doing that all over PTA meetings. For the next eighteen years."

The pained look was replaced by soft exasperation,

and then he laughed aloud. "And somehow I still love you. In spite of it. Maybe because of it."

I bit the insides of my lips before I could say anything else. He sank to his knees in front of me. "Edie, let's get married."

CHAPTER SEVEN

My lips became unglued. "What?"

"You heard me."

He was kneeling in front of me, looking up expectantly. I stared at him like a deer in headlights. The longer I was stunned, the wider he smiled.

"Say yes. We're on a ship for two weeks. We'll get the captain to do it somehow."

I blinked. "Yes." He stood immediately and I shoved him lightly before he could kiss me. "I can't believe you're not even nervous! About anything!"

Asher laughed and swooped me up. "Of course I am. I'm just better at faking being calm than you."

And then he kissed me, one of those sweet kisses you see on diamond jewelry commercials on TV, except it was me. The girl who just got everything she ever wanted, mostly. When we came up for air I was beaming.

"Someone should pinch me," I said. With an evil grin, Asher did. "Hey!"

"Just following orders, ma'am," he said, innocently.

I laughed. His hand rested where he'd pinched, then moved up underneath my shirt. I extricated myself, still laughing, and stretched out on the bed, and he moved to lie beside me. I snuggled him.

"Will your mom get mad?" Asher asked, a possessive arm around my waist.

"No. It'll be easier this way. Assuming we can swing it."

Asher shrugged. "We'll swing it."

Of course we would. If it wasn't allowed, or there wasn't time, he'd just bribe whoever he had to until rules were broken in our favor. Asher was the type of man who made things happen—betrothals or pushing people overboard. For better, or for worse.

But getting married on the ship would be easier on everyone. There'd be fewer hoops to jump through, and I wouldn't have to worry about getting all my family in one place at the same time, fight-free. And this way my mom wouldn't get the chance to ask questions about where Asher's absent family was.

"Are there any shapeshifter traditions I should be aware of?" I imagined myself throwing a grenade instead of a bouquet.

There was a long pause. "Live fast, die free?"

"All this time we've been dating, and you never told me you were secretly in a motorcycle gang."

He snorted. "We don't do this that often. You're supposed to find someone like yourself to settle down with. Have a few kids, fast. Raise them up to fend for themselves in time."

"How old were you when . . ." My voice drifted, unsure what I was asking him.

"When all the adults in my life abandoned me?" he filled in. "Fourteen."

"You've been on your own since then?"

"Yeah. Of course."

"Wasn't it hard?"

"Not really. It wasn't fun . . . but it wasn't hard, either." I twisted back to see him better, caught him staring at the ceiling thoughtfully. "It was mostly lonely."

I found his hand wrapped around my waist, with my own, and his fingers twined with mine. "Not anymore."

Asher looked down at me. "You're really going to be with me, a misfit shapeshifter, for the rest of your life?"

I smiled up at him. "Yeah. I think you're pretty much stuck with me now."

"Good." He nodded, and kissed my temple, and then held me as the ship rocked back and forth on the waves. We were quiet together, and I wondered what he was thinking. I managed not to ask him, though. I closed my eyes and just let the moment spin. When I opened them again, he had a questioning look on his face.

"Sleeping? Food? Or other things?"

This really was a vacation. I really didn't have anything I had to do for fourteen whole days. I couldn't remember the last time I'd had that long off. Maybe the summer break before I got a job, back in high school.

I stretched beside him. I was hungry; my stomach was still on the other coast. "Food. And then we'll see about sex, fiancé."

Asher grinned. "I like the sound of that."

It was in between breakfast and lunch, but there were certain restaurants on board that never closed. We made our way to one of these on the third floor, the Dolphin, through an indoor bar and promenade, with leather chairs facing huge portal windows showing a deck and, past it, the choppy seas outside. If I looked just right, I could see the orange belly of a lifeboat hanging down. Good to know. I wasn't sure which was making me more green, the motion of the ship or my pregnancy, but I was fixated on getting pancakes. If only I'd had a day or two longer to get sea legs under me before everything else.

"Are you sure you want to risk it?" Asher asked solicitously.

"Yes." I might learn better right afterward, but I was set on learning the hard way. "They're spongy. They might help." I wished I'd listened to all my pregnant coworkers back in the day. I'd always tuned out their pregnant-lady talks before. My current ignorance served me right. "At least the syrup might be fast calories? Maybe I can absorb some without throwing them up."

Asher didn't look like he thought it was a good idea, but he shrugged, willing to let me learn for myself.

This time of morning, the restaurant was mostly empty, except for the dolphins painted on the walls chasing one another. The maître d' seated us near a window. Asher began to tell him to move us, but I quickly shook my head. "It's nice to see outside." Maybe if I could see the waves, I'd begin to get a feel for their motion, and separate them from my stomach. The window was bubbled out, giving a view in all directions, dark waters below, sun ahead, and behind us fast clouds pushing in.

As the waiter took our order, Asher sized up another uniformed cruise employee near the door. "Be right back."

I didn't have to ask what he was doing to know. I'd seen him do it at least a hundred times. He reached the man and started talking to him in his intuitively congenial way. Asher could make anyone like him. I watched him with a mixture of jealousy and awe, and the realization dawned that I was engaged to, and impregnated by, a hustler. Not that that was a bad thing, at least not in Asher's case. But it was . . . a thing. Something I'd never had to deal with before.

Asher laughed and the man laughed and they were laughing together—I shook my head in bemusement, then let my gaze wander the room. This restaurant had an under-the-sea theme, with walls covered by splashing ocean waves and happy denizens of the sea swimming underneath.

I spotted the family we'd sat through the safety lecture with, the Indian couple with their kids, and I waved at them so as not to seem creepy, as the mother caught me staring a second too long. She absentmindedly waved back, clear she had no memory of me from yesterday. As a mom, this was probably like a working vacation for her. They might not be at home, but she hadn't gotten to take a break from her mom-job.

I watched her out of the corner of my eye, trying to put myself in her shoes and failing. Her boy was scarfing down a huge plate of scrambled eggs, and her daughter was studiously drawing on a place mat with crayons. That was going to be me. Give or take eight years.

Asher returned to his seat, disrupting my reverie. "I know who to talk to now. I'll go out after this and move things along."

I smiled at him and snorted. "Wow, if you're fast enough, this may be our only breakfast as fiancés."

"I hope so, because that word sounds weird."

"How shotgun is our wedding going to be? Am I going to have to find a white dress somewhere on board?"

He laughed, and just like the man he'd been conversing with, I found myself wanting to laugh with him. "Only as shotgun as you want." He beamed at me. "I don't care what you wear, as long as you show up."

This week might be the last week I fit into the red dress I'd brought along for formal nights for a while. "I'm going to wear red then. I've already got that outfit, and it's easier this way. Especially seeing as it's just for us, and whatever witnesses we have to rope in for it to be legal."

He grinned, then gave me a sober look. "You should get your hair done, though. And your nails. Whatever other fun things women do. I don't want you to miss out on all of that just because I'm rushing you."

I inspected my nails. My manicure might hold well enough for a few more days, seeing as there wouldn't be any dishes for me to do, if I could avoid my natural inclination to use All the Sanitizer. But getting it redone just because I could was tempting, too. Wasn't that how vacations worked? "You're not rushing me, honest. I wouldn't want the hassle of planning everything anyhow. This is saving me a ton of stress." Avoiding sending out invitations, check. Avoiding endless discussions with my mother about colors, flowers, or dresses, double check. Not having to wonder if my brother's going to show up or not, high or not, or being the worst-sister-ever again if I didn't invite him to avoid that entirely, super-check.

Our breakfast arrived, and Asher waited until the waiter left to speak again. "Well, I'd still like it to be romantic. Even if it is practical."

"It will be. It's with you." I grinned at him over my pancakes. They smelled so good—my stomach flipped a coin, and hungry won. I ate a few bites, and things held. I sank back into my chair, relieved. "What about rings? I'm not really a ring wearer—" Work gave me the opportunity to touch too many gross things.

He quickly shook his head. "Rings are too complicated."

I blinked, as I realized he was right. People at work didn't know I was with Hector—they'd only ever met me dating some blond guy named Asher, who just happened to never be around when Hector was. Same with my brother and folks. There would be no way to explain things at work, and the second either of us showed up wearing a ring—people there might not put us with each other, but there'd be questions to answer for sure. It would be easier without them, less chances to screw up.

"I'm sorry," he said.

"No, it's okay, I understand." I set my fork down and

held up my ring-free hands for illustration. "I don't like them anyway, and besides, I'd be worried about it falling into an abscess all the time."

Asher's eyebrows rose in mock horror. "Please tell me you wear gloves when you change dressings."

"I do, but—" I mimed taking off a glove and then a ring flying off and over, to land into Asher's scrambled eggs. He made a face and then laughed.

"That's disgusting."

"My ability to be disgusting and still eat is kind of why you love me." I leaned over and forked a bite off his plate by way of demonstration.

He grinned at me. "There are more reasons than that, but that is definitely one of them."

I snickered and then leaned forward to kiss him across the table—something I realized I might not be able to do in a few months when I'd gotten a belly—and he leaned forward to kiss me back, and that's when I heard it. The sound of someone choking.

CHAPTER EIGHT

You don't actually hear the sound of someone choking. The hallmark of choking is that the chokee can't actually make any sounds. If they can talk, they can breathe, and they just need to cough things out.

What you do hear is the screams of other people's panic as their tablemate turns blue.

"Someone help! He can't breathe!" shouted someone with an Indian accent.

Asher and I both looked over. The woman was standing and her son was facedown in his eggs. Her daughter watched her brother, openmouthed and terrified.

Asher leaped up and raced over, and introduced himself by his occupation, not his name. "I'm a doctor."

I was close behind him. He circled the boy, braced his hand around his waist, and popped his fists up underneath the boy's sternum. The mom was still shouting for help, but she was wise enough to stay out of the way.

A plug of eggs popped out of the boy's mouth on the third blow, and he started coughing violently.

"There you go—" Asher set the boy down on the chair beside his mother, and he promptly threw up. I reached over to the next unoccupied set table and grabbed all the napkins fast to put over the mess.

By then, the ship's doctor had arrived, the same one I'd

gotten the pregnancy test from this morning. He started looking over the boy as Asher and I faded back. He seemed competent from afar; maybe this morning I'd just caught him off guard.

The rest of the crew brought in a wheelchair and took the boy away for observation. His mother looked back at us on her way out the door. "Thank you so much, Doctor," she said, still breathless from her ordeal.

Asher took it in stride and waved like a prom king.

We sat back down at our table. "Oh, Doctor," I said to Asher, quietly, mimicking her intonation.

He snorted as our waiter returned and thanked us, his hands clasped nervously in front of his chest. "You were so fast! We have protocols, practices, but we don't use them very often. Is there anything I can get you extra? For your help?" He looked from Asher to me.

My nurse's stomach had withstood the onslaught of someone else's emesis, but the pregnant portion of me was now rethinking everything else. I pushed my half-eaten plate of pancakes away. "I think I'm good. Thank you, though."

"Oh, no, no, thank you. So many people sick on board," he said, shaking his head. And then he blanched as though he'd said too much. "But it's not us, it's the waves. We're racing a storm. All the waves' fault."

"I believe you," Asher said, with just the right tone to calm the man.

"Thank you, thank you," he said again, waiting for an extra second in case we changed our minds, and then backing hurriedly away.

"Are you okay?" Asher asked me, looking worried.

I smiled at him, trying not to look at the table or smell anything. "Yeah. I'm fine. You should eat, though."

"Maybe later." He smiled, pushed his plate away, and

stood to offer me his arm. "Let's go on a walk. After all, my job here is done."

I made it until we were outside the restaurant, and out of earshot of everyone. "Oh, Doctor—" I teased again, in fair imitation of the boy's mother. "Save me, Doctor!" I pretended to faint against him.

"You realize you're not too pregnant yet for me to spank?" he chided.

I stood a little straighter and took a step away. "I just like how you get to be the one to save people's lives, and even on vacation I'm the one that gets to deal with the biowaste."

He gave me a thoughtful look, then shrugged. "Well, now that you put it like that, being a doctor does sound sexy."

We walked past a cruise employee furiously wiping down handrails with cleaner. I felt for the man. He, at least, understood how germy people could be.

There were saloon doors in front of us, and someone pushed through them, letting fresh air in from outside. "Oh, that's nice."

Asher stopped and propelled me forward. "You go out—I'll catch up with you. I have someone I need to meet."

I was about to protest when I realized he meant Operation Shotgun was under way. "By meet, you mean bribe?"

He broke into a wolfish grin. "If that's what it takes."

"That's my fiancé."

He raised my hand to kiss it without the least hint of irony.

Outside, it was brisk and turning gray as the clouds caught up. I'd brought precisely one sweater for this trip, and luckily

I was wearing it now. I'd packed with our destination in mind—Hawaii, lush and green, all short sleeves and sunblock—and hadn't planned for this. This *was* better than Port Cavell, though, where it snowed all winter long. There was something to be said for being outdoors without a thick coat.

Besides, this weather was nice in its own way. The air tasted like salt and storm, wild. I walked to the end of the deck and stared over the edge with my hands on the railing, and I found myself a lot less fearful of it than I'd been at the dock. The sea here wasn't pretending to be calm, and I liked it better for its honesty.

I leaned over and watched the bow of the ship cut through the waves, spray shooting up like a running horse's mane. A side gust caught me, the kind of wind that made you feel like you could grow wings and fly. It took my breath away—and my nausea. When I couldn't feel my nose anymore, I turned and walked the perimeter of the deck.

There were fewer people out here than there'd been the night before, what with the weather. But even if there'd been more, the person in the wheelchair up ahead still would have been recognizable. Claire's paisley blanket was higher now, shielding her from her shoulders down. She turned and caught me looking at her, then waved me over, her hand peeking out from underneath her cover.

"How are you doing?" she asked as I arrived.

"I'm slightly more convinced about this mode of transportation than I was yesterday."

She nodded, like I had just learned a valuable lesson. "I love it out here. You'll need a thicker coat, though, especially for the Alaskan cruises."

"I'll get one." I hugged myself, standing still.

"Would a walk help keep you warm?" she asked.

"Sure, uh—" I looked at the brakes on her wheelchair. To wheel, or not to wheel, was the question.

"You look pretty strong. Plus, I'm warmer this way," she prompted, shrugging her blanket.

"Ha. Okay." I leaned over and undid the brakes. "Hey, you know how Hal asked us if we were newlyweds yesterday?" She nodded as I pushed her. She was heavier than she looked, but her wheelchair made an excellent windblock. "Well, Asher proposed this morning. So we almost are." I ought to get to share my second piece of good news with someone. My mom would be fine with an out-of-wedlock baby, having long since given up on my timeliness, but she might never forgive me if she didn't get a chance to host a wedding shower.

Claire turned to look back at me. "Oh, congratulations!"

"Thanks." I beamed. It felt good to tell someone.

She tilted her head and pierced me with one bird-like eye. "What about the baby? Does he know?"

I stopped abruptly, and the ship rolled, sending her wheelchair back to run up against my foot before I caught it. "What? How did you—"

"I'm an old woman," she said, as though that were answer enough.

Well. Since I'd already outed myself anyway. "Um, yes. He found out about the baby before he proposed. Not that he wouldn't have anyway, eventually—he was just really excited about everything."

She smiled and nodded. "He's a stand-up man."

"I like to think so." And despite the fact that I'd asked for it, I felt a little overexposed and desperate to change the conversation. "Do you have kids of your own?" If she did, they'd be my age—or my mother's.

Claire shook her head sorrowfully. "Oh, no, that was never in the cards for Hal and me. I do like children, though."

"Me too. I think." I waited a bit. "I hope."

She laughed melodiously. "I'm sure you'll catch on," she said, and leaned out of the wheelchair to point. "Can we go over there? That's where I was supposed to be, before I started wandering." I started to push her across the deck, impressed she'd been able to roll herself that far. Her upper body was probably stronger than mine.

"So where are you going next, after this?" she asked me.

"Back to the room?" I guessed, like it might be the wrong answer.

She shook her head. "No, no. I mean after this cruise." She braced herself on the wheelchair's arms underneath her blanket and craned back at me, seemingly oblivious to the rocking of the waves. "You shouldn't finish one trip without having another one in mind. It's the secret to staying young—always having something to look forward to." She gave me a conspiratorial smile. "You've got to see the world while you can, preferably while you still have your original knees."

I grinned at her. "How old are you? If I can ask, that is."

"Well, I'd tell you that bullshit line about ladies never revealing their age, but let's just say I'm pushing eighty-nine. Or you are, since you're back there."

I snorted. We'd almost made a full circle of the deck—on this side, we were protected by structures on the deck from the wind. We passed by a few people determined to be tropical, huddling shoulder-high in the hot tub, and a few kids racing around the kiddie pool under shivering parental supervision.

"It's like they don't have any nerves," Claire said from the warmth of her blanket.

"Or they're a different species," I agreed. It was hard not to stare at them and think too hard. Would that be me out there in a year? *What will she look like?* I thought, half a second before I realized I desperately hoped we'd be having a girl. I'd never thought about that before. Ever.

Claire looked back up at me, expectantly. I'd stopped without warning. "Sorry," I apologized, and started walking again.

Please please please, may it be a girl, I prayed fervently, to anyone who could be listening, with a smile.

"We have to go now, Thomas." The wind carried a voice I recognized over to me, and I looked back to see Liz scooping her arms toward her child, who began crying.

He was fighting her, reaching back for the water she was pulling him away from. "Stop that, honey. Come on, it's time for lunch."

He went into full-on tantrum mode, and she was having none of it, folding in limbs as fast as he could free them while he fought her to stay.

Then came a moment when he stopped fighting her and went limp. I could see him accept defeat, tears streaming down his face. And then he looked at me, looking at him—and beyond, to the ocean at my back. I could almost read his thoughts. If he was being made to leave one body of water—so what, when there was a much bigger one nearby? His hand slipped out of hers and he barreled toward the nearest railing, twenty feet away from Claire and me.

CHAPTER NINE

"Claire, hang on." I trusted her wheelchairing skills to save her as I let go and raced to stop him. It was silly really, he was just a kid, and I was so much bigger. I beat him easily and swooped down to catch him just as Asher had the night before. He barreled into me, let me pick him up, and then tried to climb over me, to use me as a launching ramp to get out to the sea.

"Hey!" I tried to pry him off me while he fought like a monkey to stay on and climb higher. The ship rolled with a wave and I fell to the deck with a yelp, taking Thomas down. He knocked my breath away as he landed on top of me; it was all I could do to breathe and keep him still.

"Thomas!" Liz warned at full volume. He didn't stop fighting me until she was near enough to cast a shadow over us both, like a passing hawk.

"Woman, restrain your child!" Claire chastised, wheeling over.

"It's okay—" I let go of Thomas carefully, like passing a baton, only releasing him when I knew Liz had a firm hold.

"It's not okay. What kind of mother are you?" Claire went on, squinting up at Liz. "Who lets their child do that?"

"Edie?" Asher arrived just as I was managing to stand.

"That monster knocked over your fiancée." A bony hand emerged from under Claire's blanket to point at the offending child.

"I'm so sorry. I have no idea what's gotten into him lately," Liz said. I could see she was on the brink of tears—and I heard Claire inhale, to give her no quarter.

"It's fine. Honestly. It's fine," I said, trying to cut things off.

Asher looked me over, his eyes dark. "You're okay, right?"

"Completely." I gave Liz as warm a smile as I could. It wasn't her fault that Thomas was unruly; kids his age were just like that. Toddlers were supposed to be scared of strangers and new things—being on a cruise ship must be terrifying for him.

Not to mention his dad being some kind of cold scientist. That had to be rough, on both of them. "I don't know what would have happened if you hadn't been there to catch him," she said, shaking her head, Thomas clutched near.

"He probably would have run into the railing, like a bird into a windowpane, is what," Claire said.

"Yes, exactly," Liz agreed, trying to smile us into liking her again. It was working on me. I gave her another smile back, and she seemed fractionally relieved.

But Asher was looming nervously, worried about me. She shied away from him in a skittish-horse kind of way, spinning Thomas to her other hip. "Why don't you come to dinner with Nathaniel and me tonight? It's the least I can do." She asked me, not him.

"Oh, that's okay—" I began. I felt bad for her, she seemed genuinely nice and a little lonely, but I didn't want to volunteer to spend my free time with her husband.

"Sure," Asher butted in, calmly. "What time?"

Liz smiled even more, all of her even white teeth showing. By us accepting, her child's behavior would be forgiven, and calm would be restored. Something about the way she held herself, her facial expressions, the place she stood—I'd seen this eggshell walk before, and it made my heart bleed a little for her. *Oh, Liz, you're definitely too good for him.*

"Seven. At the, uh, fancy one on the ninth floor," she said, not willing to try the French.

"Thanks. We'll see you there," Asher answered for both of us. Freed to leave, Liz carried Thomas away.

"If I'd had a child, he would never, ever, act like that," Claire said, and rearranged her blanket carefully back over herself. I didn't say anything—but I didn't think I'd ever get to be as freely judgmental as Claire again. In a few years, *that* kid might be *my* kid, no matter how hard I tried. At least Asher wasn't Nathaniel, though.

Asher was quiet while I pushed Claire back to where Hal was now waiting.

"I can't believe you conned this nice couple into pushing you around," Hal said with the kind of over-enunciating that hearing loss sometimes brought on, as if by making himself more clear, the world would return the favor.

"Only the one. Him, I'm not so sure about yet," Claire said, pointing to Asher, who manufactured a good-natured grin. "Don't try flirting with me, young man," she warned. "I'm a taken woman. It will get you nowhere."

Abashed, Asher laughed and smiled for real.

"That's better, boy. I can tell when people are faking," Claire said, and then turned back to me. "Thank you for the lovely walk. See you at dinner soon, I hope."

"Thanks. You too." I waved as Hal pulled her away.

The second they were out of earshot, Asher turned to me. "Are you really okay?"

"Honestly. I'm fine." We walked off the deck and caught the next elevator. As soon as we'd stepped inside, he started touching the arm I'd fallen on, for medical purposes. I hissed, and he frowned deeply.

"You didn't fracture it, did you?"

"No. It's just a bruise." I swung it around to prove to him I still had my full range of motion.

"And . . . your stomach?" he said tentatively.

"Is currently fine too." The doors opened, and we walked without talking down the halls until we got to our room. "You're not going to try anything out again at dinner, are you?"

"Probably not." I blinked at him, and he half shrugged. "I thought you'd appreciate my honesty, rather than me lying and disappointing you again."

I stared at him flatly. "You're a better study of human behavior than that."

He held his hands up. "Oh, come on, Edie, I was teasing. I won't touch the man. But there's no rule against talking to him, is there? I mean, there's probably a reason his kid keeps running away."

"I think we're a little far for a children's protective services call out here, Asher." But I had seen that cowed look on Liz's face. I couldn't just ignore it.

"Besides, I was just being polite," Asher went on. "And the opportunity presented itself. I'm an opportunity taker." He took a step nearer me, as though an opportunity were around. I frowned.

"This is currently not super-sexy."

He got a devilish gleam in his eye. "What if I told you we were getting married next week?"

I squinted up at him. "I'm listening."

"On a secluded beach in Hawaii," he went on, his voice as smooth as a late-night radio host.

"Did it involve bribery?"

"It leaned more toward highway robbery. But it looks

beautiful in the pictures they showed me. I didn't think you'd mind."

I wrinkled my face in disbelief. "Married on Hawaii. That's even more frivolous than I'd previously thought."

"Too late. It's done. We just have to show up."

He did look hopeful. He wanted my approval—even if he was still going to take chances. In the end, he was who he was. I wasn't going to be able to change him.

I sighed. "It's a good thing you're handsome."

"It is, isn't it?" he agreed. And he leaned in.

Our clothes were off and we were on the floor together in no time. I didn't know what he was thinking, but I knew how I felt. Our future was barreling down toward us like a bullet flying out of a gun. I was looking forward to it, yes—but I also knew it was going to hit me.

Sex was a way to press PAUSE, to stay in the here and now, and now, and now.

The top of Asher's back was against the side of the couch, and my legs were wrapped around his waist. He was curved up, and I could play my hands down the flatness of his stomach. I could feel his muscles flex when he pushed into me, and I tried to settle deeper into his lap. We hadn't said a word since we'd started; we didn't need to.

Then the intercom overhead chimed so loudly I squeaked in surprise.

"This is Captain Ames speaking—"

I stopped what I was doing, although Asher didn't. He was able to ignore the captain—who was sharing the fact that we were trying to outrun a storm. And while the outbreak of nausea among passengers was directly related our speed, it would be a good idea if we all washed our hands. He started singing the "Happy Birthday" song to show us how long we ought to wash our hands for, by way of demonstration.

I couldn't help it. I laughed out loud.

"You'd think this would turn you on," Asher teased. "I know you're a fan of hand washing."

"This is the least sexy song on the planet."

"Then don't listen to it," he challenged me, still sliding himself incrementally in and out of me.

"I can't help it. He's so loud," I said over the captain's singing voice. "Stop it, Asher. You're perverting 'Happy Birthday.'"

"So?"

"Is nothing sacred?" I asked him.

A completely wicked look passed over his face. "Never."

And suddenly he had my full attention again.

CHAPTER TEN

When we were done there was that awkward moment there sometimes is when you realize that you're human. Like when the clock strikes twelve, or the hourglass runs out—the magic of the moment is gone and suddenly you're all flesh and bones and silly parts.

"Here." Asher, oblivious to my existential plight, fished in the pockets of his cast-off jeans. "While I was out, I got this for you." He held up a gold necklace with a small amethyst pendant dangling from the end.

I reached out for the stone. "Oh, it's lovely—but why?"

"Because I didn't think you'd wear a diamond." He let the necklace fall into my hand. "Even if we can't have rings—you should have something for the occasion. To prove that I proposed. The two of us will know what it means." He nudged my hand. "Go on, put it on."

I fastened it around my neck, and the stone hit at the V of my throat. I felt slightly more magical, even though I was still minus clothes. Asher smiled at me.

"Too bad we have to go out tonight."

"What?" I'd completely forgotten about our dinner plans. "Oh, no—let's just stand them up."

"That would be rude," he said.

"So? We wouldn't be the first rude people on vacation." I wished that Liz's kid hadn't run into me today—or that Claire had had functional legs to chase after him, instead.

"Do you really think I'll misbehave that badly?"

"Yes."

He gave me a look.

"Not entirely," I adjusted. "But I know you."

"I'll be good. And you need to eat something," he said, standing up and then offering me a hand. I took it and tried to pull him back down, but he wouldn't let me. I sighed and let him help me up.

"I can't imagine what we'll have to talk about. You'll ask him about his vasectomy, and I'll ask her where she gets her teeth bleached, and then where will we be?"

"We can pretend we're private investigators," he said, walking over to the closet to flip through hangers.

"Ugh. Please say you're not suggesting we do role-playing outside the bedroom. Seriously."

"Okay, I'm not. You just keep her and Thomas busy, and leave him to me." He pulled out a blue shirt and set it on the bed.

"When you say that, what do you mean precisely?"

"There's no harm in asking him a few questions, Edie."

"Uh, yeah, there is. What if he figures things out and remembers you?"

Asher gave me a look. "I'm a shapeshifter. Deceiving people is my forte."

"But it's not mine. What if I let something on? What if I act weird and—"

"Then it'll be different from any other time we go out to dinner how, precisely?" he said, cutting me off.

I stared at him with dagger-eyes. "You are soooooooo funny."

He chuckled, and then sobered. "Seriously, Edie. It's

important to me. Can't that just be enough? It would be nice if I could go into my new life with you with a clean conscience."

"And what if you can't?" I asked his back as he started picking out a tie.

"Then nothing's changed, has it?" he said with a too-easy shrug. "Indulge me and my personal curiosity, Edie. Please."

Which was as close as he might get to admitting to me how much this mattered to him. It was hard to be mad at him while he was naked, too. "All right. But after tonight—promise you're going to cut it out. If I'm not allowed to worry about the future, you can't keep chasing down your past. I want the whole rest of this trip to be about us. You, me, and the baby."

He gave me a beatific smile. "Deal."

There was no way to hide the bruise on my elbow from the incident that afternoon. But the dress I was wearing was black, so hopefully it matched. The rest of me was cute at least—being on vacation meant having time to do crazy things like blow-dry and curl my hair. It was nice to blow-dry my hair for fun, not so it wouldn't freeze when I stepped outside.

And Asher was pulled together, as always. We made a dashing pair. If my recently purchased makeup primer packaging was to be believed, we might even stay looking this way all night.

Asher didn't change until we were alone in the elevator. Not into another person, like I knew he could, reverting to someone he'd touched before he'd been saved, but overall. His shoulders slumped a little, and the way he held his head seemed like it became less sharp and more likely to nod and agree. He pulled at the crisp collar of his suit so that it looked more wrinkled than it was, like it hadn't been tailored specifically for him.

"Remember, I'm Kevin tonight," Asher reminded me.

"Got it. Kevin . . . Private Eye, Kevin," I agreed, trying to lighten the mood. He smiled and his hand squeezed mine.

Liz was watching for us at the door of the restaurant and flagged us down as soon as we arrived. The décor in here seemed tasteful, at least as far as I could tell from watching HGTV shows. Subdued lighting, muted colors, staff in crisp suits. Lovely exposed beams across the ceiling that any Realtor would have commented on. I was glad I'd tried so hard to dress up nicely; otherwise it would have been more than just my bruised elbow making me feel out of place.

Liz sat by the shark-faced man we'd met the prior night. His suit was impeccable, and she was wearing a yellow designer dress with a pearl necklace. Even Thomas was adorable in a little three-piece suit, although he looked uncomfortable inside it.

"Nathaniel, this is Edie and Kevin. You remember them from yesterday, don't you?" Liz prompted her husband.

He stood at our arrival with formal manners and looked over at me. "Of course I do. I hear you rescued our little boy this afternoon," he said, without a change in tone. Nathaniel had a flat affect, with fish-dead eyes. It'd been a long time since I worked with vampires; I wasn't used to being stared through anymore.

"Oh, well, you know, he ran into me," I said with a shrug.

"No, you saved him, I saw. He gets into trouble like you wouldn't believe," Liz said, gesturing to the empty chair beside her, which I took, and we all sat down.

She was too sweet for him by a factor of ten—and I

realized that despite the money she was flashing casually here, she hadn't discovered she could buy friends yet. She still thought she had to be nice to get them.

That, or Nathaniel creeped out anyone who tried to get too close.

"So what do you two do?" Asher-Kevin said, with the same tone anyone trying to get to know anyone else casually would use, as the waiter came up and pressed menus into our hands.

"Investments," Nathaniel answered flatly, then turned the question around. "You?"

"I'm a doctor," Asher said.

Nathaniel's chin jerked up subtly at this. "What kind of doctor?"

"What kind of investments?" Asher asked back, with the right teasing tone and a self-satisfied aren't-I-funny laugh. "No, really, I do hospice care. But I used to do oncology."

Well, I had no doubt that there was probably at least one oncologist inside of Asher that he could draw on.

"Oh, isn't that sad?" Liz asked, voice full of genuine concern.

Asher changed to faux suave for her sake; being a doctor got him a lot of play. "It is, but someone has to do it."

I could see Nathaniel writing "Kevin" off as a show-boat. Maybe that was Asher's plan.

"And, you know," Asher went on, "that's where I met Edie. She's a nurse."

Liz turned to me, delighted by this less grim turn. "You two met at work? Just like on TV?"

I had the sudden urge to pick a spoon up off the table and stab myself with it. It sounded so trite when he put it like that. I felt like by dating Asher, who could occasionally be a doctor, I was letting down all nursing-kind, most of whom wouldn't touch doctors with someone else's used

Foley catheter. But I realized I wasn't going to have to role-play as a PI tonight; I just needed to pretend to be nice-Edie. "Yeah. Something like that," I said, through slightly gritted teeth. "What do you do?"

"Oh, I stay at home," Liz said. "Watching Thomas is a full-time job. He's a little hyperactive."

You could say that. Thomas was the process of un-tucking his dress shirt. Poor kid. I gave her a comforting grin. "We're having one too. We just found out this morning."

"Really? That's marvelous! Congratulations!" Liz said, clapping her hands.

"Thank you," I said, grinning a little at her cheer.

"I'd order us champagne," she went on. "But you know that's off limits now."

"Yeah." I grinned at her infectious excitement and looked over at Asher—and I could see from his face that he was displeased. We were supposed to be getting information from them, not sharing it. Whatever. I gave him a shrug.

For his part, Nathaniel was still watching all of us with disdain. I wasn't sure which he was more disappointed in, Liz's cheerful interest in me, or that Asher and I were breeding in an age without eugenics.

"So when are you due? Is it a boy or a girl?" Liz latched on to this safe conversational thread. "Have you thought of any names?"

I'd inadvertently opened us up an encyclopedia's worth of safe small talk, and I gave Asher a look that made it clear I was abandoning him to his own devices at the manly side of the table. "Oh, we just-just found out. Like this morning. No ultrasounds or anything yet. I'm not even a month along."

"I'll cross my fingers then for you that it's a girl. Because boys are just too much," she said, leaning over Thomas to tuck his shirt back in.

Dinner arrived, and I found myself liking Liz more and more. She and Nathaniel lived a few hours away from us, in the next biggest city over, a fact I pretended to be surprised about. It gave us even more safe topics of conversation to have. I couldn't tell how Asher was faring, which was fine. He could make it on his own.

Thomas was good for his part, if messy. Liz was wiping spaghetti sauce off his face when he shook his head violently. An experienced mother, she followed with her napkin—only he didn't stop shaking, and his arms and hands followed.

"What's happening?"

"Seizure," I said just as he threw his head back stiffly.

Liz gasped, and Asher rushed in, pulling Thomas gently to the floor. "He's burning up."

"What's happening?" Liz repeated. She looked from Asher to me. I kept hold of Thomas's side so he wouldn't flop around like a dying fish.

"He's just having a seizure is all," I said, trying to sound calm.

"What a shame," Nathaniel said, his voice actually calm, no pretending. He squatted beside us, taking in the situation clinically. Asher gave me a worried look.

Liz's mouth dropped in horror. She looked from Thomas to Nathaniel and then back again, and then reached over and shoved Nathaniel, hard. He fell back off his heels, onto his ass.

"You!" she exclaimed, stood abruptly—and then ran off.

I looked over to Asher for explanation, but he looked as bewildered as I was. He didn't need me here—he was, after all, a doctor. I stood and chased after her.

"Liz? Liz!" Luckily, I'd worn flats. I dodged around the same people she had, the crowd that seemed to spring fully formed around any medical emergency. She drew up short outside an opening elevator door and rushed inside. I waved my hand to hold it just in time and followed her in.

"Are you okay?" I asked her, panting. We weren't the only ones inside the elevator, just the only ones out of breath.

"I've got to get his pills," she said, but her face was completely panicked. She looked flushed, beyond what the run should have done; sweat was showing through her dress's armpits as she repeatedly hit the button for her floor.

"Pills for what?" You didn't give seizing people pills.

She opened her mouth to tell me, then closed it resolutely again.

"I'm a nurse, remember?"

"You don't understand." She hit her floor button a few more times, like it would speed the elevator up.

I decided to try a calming tack. "Look, seizures happen all the time. Kids just get them. Sometimes no one even knows what causes them—and they go away on their own."

Her head began shaking halfway through my explanation, as she held down the button for her floor. "It's not that. You don't understand!" she said, in a pleading voice.

"Then tell me—what's going on?" I got the feeling it was something bigger than just Thomas's illness, but whatever it was, it was no excuse for this. "Your son is back there. You need to go be with him. He needs you."

The elevator rose, stopping on floor after floor, people shoving inside with us, our loud conversation and her radiating crazy making them regret their choice. "This isn't right, Liz—" I put a hand out to stop her from holding the button down. "If you're scared, don't be—"

The elevator settled onto her floor and I tried to block the door bodily. "Let me go! You can't help us!" she protested.

"I can if you'll tell me!" I wanted to spill it all then—
what I knew about Nathaniel's past from Asher—but I
didn't dare. "Liz—"

She gave me another torn look, but she didn't respond—
and there was nothing else I could do without restraining
her physically. I moved out of her way before she could
elbow me aside, and she began running down the hall.

"You'll regret this!" I shouted after her. Because how
could she not? What mother in her right mind would
leave her sick child behind? I shook my head in disbelief
and dismay. "What the—" I began, ready to curse. Then I
saw another woman looking traumatized at the back of
the elevator, with her child smashed protectively in the
corner behind her. That was more like it. And then I realized between the two of us, Liz and I must have been a
frightening scene.

"Sorry about all that," I apologized, and hit the button
for my own floor.

CHAPTER ELEVEN

There was no point in going back to the restaurant, so I walked down the hall to our room. Just what the hell had happened back there? With Liz, with Nathaniel, and most especially with Thomas? Was he okay? I assumed by now he was in the medical center, getting treatment. I thought about things that would cause a sudden seizure in a child— most of them were not good, and some of them were contagious. Meningitis was the worst, and fever and seizure were its typical presentation in children.

I walked by another housekeeper on doorknob-wiping duty. When I reached the far end of the cart, I grabbed one of the extra spray bottles of cleaner dangling by its handle and held it up to my chest to hide it as I walked quickly past.

When I got up to our room, I washed my hands so long I could have sung "Happy Birthday" three times. And then I carefully got out of my dress and hopped into the shower to wash off the rest of me.

Asher opened up the door an hour later, with a bottle of cleaner also in his hands. I pointed to mine on the table. "Great minds think alike. How's Thomas?"

"Rough. What happened with Liz?"

"I have no fucking idea." I'd been trying to work it out

in the shower as I washed all of my makeup primer and
hair spray down the drain, hopefully along with whatever
germs I'd been exposed to. "It was like she was scared,
but I'm not sure what of. She said something about getting him pills. What happened once I left?"

"The doctor came. This time I got to see him in action.
He has no bedside manner, but he seems competent."
Asher was holding his hands out in front of himself as if
he were scrubbed in for surgery. "Mind getting the door
for me?" he asked, nodding toward the bathroom.

I opened it up, and it swung shut behind him. I cleaned
off the handle he'd used to enter the room with one of the
bottles of cleaner. He spent as long in the shower as I had,
and when he emerged he was wrapped in a fresh towel,
holding his clothing with a washcloth to keep it from
touching his newly washed skin. "Let's set it all out to be
cleaned."

"Sounds good to me." I held the laundry bag up, and
he deposited my dress carefully inside as well. "What
happened with Nathaniel?"

"Nothing. He was concerned, but only in a clinical
way. He didn't try to comfort Thomas, or soothe him, he
didn't even follow the stretcher all that closely."

I frowned at the thought of a little boy all alone on a
gurney. I'd been right to try to get Liz to go back downstairs.

"It was like he didn't even know him. Cold."

"Was he like that all the time?" I asked, well aware
that Asher had a copy of Nathaniel's older-self somewhere inside him.

"No. That's the strange thing. He loved his daughter,
back in the day. Her and money were the only two things
he loved." He sat down on the edge of the bed, which
housekeeping had kindly made up during the brief time
we were out. "What were the pills for?"

"She wouldn't say. But not for seizures—if he had a seizure history she'd know better than to give him pills." Sticking your fingers in the mouth of someone who was seizing was a good way to get bitten. I sat on the bed beside him. "Fevers, seizures—what's a little meningitis between friends?"

"That is the obvious choice, isn't it? Or something else. Worse."

I made a face. "What're you saying?"

"I don't know yet. Only that I know what he's capable of." He turned toward me suddenly. "Edie, we wouldn't have been there—you wouldn't have been sitting across from him—if it weren't for me."

"I work at a freaking public health clinic with you. And you know I've seen worse—been bled on by worse—before."

His hands kneaded the edge of the mattress. "It's just that if anything happened to you because of me, I'd never forgive myself."

"Which I'll admit is sweet, albeit in a twisted way," I said, reaching out to put my hand on top of his nearest one to stop its wringing motion. "But I'm safe, so everything's fine."

His eyes rose to meet mine, gaze somber. "You'd better stay that way."

"Or what?" I challenged, ludicrously imagining Asher miniaturized, going into my blood vessels to punch out germs by hand.

"Or else," he said, leaving his threat to the universe hanging in the room.

Neither of us wanted to go to sleep. I lay pressed against his side, my head on his chest, as he flipped through TV stations. At home we didn't really watch TV, so it was something of a novelty, even the commercials. We eventually settled on an old vampire film. It was hilariously inaccurate—all the vampires were sexy and incompetent, instead of disgusting and deadly. I found myself wishing we had popcorn to throw at the screen.

"Are you ever upset that shapeshifters don't get TV shows?"

"No. It proves my kind's better at hiding their tracks."

I thought about this. "Vampires do live longer. Presumably that means they have to work harder at hiding it. Plus, they have to drink blood. Your kind can just go to Burger King."

Asher's eyebrows raised, but he was still watching the show. "Yes, but they can mesmerize people into thinking they weren't there."

"But you can do that, too. Blending into a crowd, changing form—"

He made a thoughtful noise; I heard it rumble in his chest. "True. I think their real problem is that eventually they all get greedy."

"Probably." One of the vampires on screen did an awful job of chasing a hapless victim whom I was pretty much at this point hoping would die. "Anna offered to change me once."

"Really?"

"Yeah. When I was stabbed." I gestured to my stomach. I still had the scar. I hadn't thought about it in a while, but now I wondered how big it would stretch as my stomach did, and if I'd have to get a C-section due to the residual damage inside. The way the vampire who'd stabbed me had been going, I was lucky to still have a uterus at all. "I still wonder how she's doing sometimes."

"Anna's immortal. I'm sure she's fine." He pointed at the woman who'd just tripped on the screen during her escape. "Why can't she just run? Our kid is taking track."

I gave him a nervous grin he didn't see. That was the first time either of us had said anything explicit about my pregnancy since our decontaminatory showers. Joking about things was the first step on the path to normalcy. "She can't run because they couldn't afford a bigger set."

The woman on the screen was screaming louder now as the vampire neared. At least the on-screen vampire was hot. He looked winded from having chased her, though, in a way that a real vampire would never be.

Asher suddenly clicked off the remote. The screaming didn't stop.

We both sat up. "It's close," he said.

In one move he'd stood and was pulling clothes out of the drawers on his side of the bed. I followed his lead on my side, and he looked over at me.

"What?" I asked.

"You're staying here."

I frowned at him while latching my bra closed. "I'm not like that, Asher." I tugged a T-shirt down over my head.

"Please. For me."

I stood there, caught between action and inaction. I wanted to go. I wanted to help. I felt trapped by motherhood, though I wasn't even showing yet.

The screaming went on—and Asher wasn't the only one with a stubborn past. He sighed. "If there's trouble, promise me you'll leave."

"Done," I said, and quickly yanked pants on.

I tucked a room key into my pocket as I followed him outside. There was already a stream of people traveling down the hall in assorted disarray, robes and pajamas, bare feet and slippers.

"I need a doctor!" Our next-door neighbor was in the

hallway, holding his door open with one foot, looking out at the growing crowd. "Is anyone here a doctor?"

"How convenient," I muttered as Asher elbowed forward. I imagined someone walking in on their loved one in the process of having a heart attack. Given the median age on this ship, times the ample buffets—then I realized I recognized him. It was the father of the two kids from our safety lecture the other day, the one with the boy who'd been choking this morning. He looked haggard now, but his eyes lit up in hope at seeing Asher. "Come in, please, hurry, he's in the bathroom—"

Asher pushed past him and I followed. The mother was crouched over her son in the tub, her hand covered in blood.

"He had a fever, he wanted to take a bath—" she explained. Her hand was clutched her to chest, and she was sobbing big tears. Pillows were wedged in on either side of her boy, and everything was wet. "It's you. From this morning—" she said, recognizing Asher. "What's wrong with him? What's wrong with my son?"

This was more how I thought Liz's fear should be. "Let's wash your hand off." I knelt down and pulled her up and away, to make room for Asher to see the boy. She held her injured hand to her chest like a baby bird.

The woman and I jostled against each other in the short hallway to the other half bathroom. I got her hand underneath the sink and went into autopilot. "What happened?"

"His fever, it was so high. They gave me Tylenol downstairs, and I put him in the tub, and ran cool water on him like he wanted, and then he started to shake—like he was having a seizure—I didn't want him to swallow his tongue so—" That explained the pillows, and the nasty gash on her hand. Too bad so many people still believed that old myth. She hissed as I scrubbed in soap.

"This'll hurt," I warned, too late.

"I don't want to leave him—" She began pulling her hand away from the water flow. It was clear she was in some kind of shock. Not the blood-loss kind—her kid had been kind enough to miss any arteries—but at being bitten by her own child. No wonder all she'd been able to do was incoherently scream.

"I know. But we need to give them space to load him up, okay?" I said, pulling her back to finish my scrub-down.

There came the clattering of a gurney past our door, and then the three–two–one as medics coordinated their efforts to get the child smoothly onto the board. I wrapped the mother's hand in a clean towel and we emerged from the bathroom after seeing the gurney pass back out into the hall.

"I'm going with him," the mother demanded.

It was just as well—she needed stitches, and iodine wouldn't hurt. "Hey—" I reached out and grabbed the last medic in line. "She's his mom, and she's cut her hand." No need to announce in the hall that her own boy bit her.

It was Marius, the Afrikaans man Asher'd spoken to this morning. His haircut said ex-military, but his face was kind. He nodded curtly. "Come along," he said to her, and then "Make way! Make way!" to the still-growing crowd outside, with a booming voice.

Together, Asher and I watched them leave, running with the boy down the hall, his mother in tow. The husband stayed behind with his terrified daughter clinging to his leg, her glasses making her wide-set eyes look even bigger than they were. The crowd slowly started to disperse now that the show was over. Asher looked to the man once the medics were out of sight.

"If anything happens to either of you, fever, seizure, dizziness, anything strange—call them immediately. And we're right next door." He pointed at our door.

"You think it's contagious?" the father asked, his face pale.

Asher gave me a dark glance. "I don't know."

CHAPTER TWELVE

We were quiet on the short way back to our room, where we performed another elaborate hand washing and showering ritual. When I finished my shower, he was waiting for me outside. "You're on room arrest."

I wanted to fight him. Two patients were hardly a data set. And yet—

"He's behind this somehow."

From the look in Asher's eyes, he believed what he was saying completely. While I wasn't convinced, I didn't want to disagree. "Okay. But behind what, precisely?"

"I don't know. Yet."

"If there is an outbreak of meningitis or whatever this is"—I pointed behind me toward next door—"don't you think they'll turn the ship around?"

"Possibly. Or helicopter people off. I don't know." He started pacing, and I sat down on the edge of the bed in our last towel.

"Should we warn other people about it?" Not that I had any clue how to even begin warning people without causing a riot on board.

Asher dismissed the thought with a shake of his head. "Everyone with a paper cut would rush downstairs. They'd be swamped before they even got to the real cases, and the crowding would help with transmission."

"If there even are any more cases."

"If." His lips thinned in contemplation.

"If he is behind it, what's the point? Giving kids seizures is sad and all, but it's hardly aerosolized bird flu." I leaned forward, contemplating the worried face of the man I loved. "Is the answer inside you anywhere?"

"No. I've spent more time thinking about him and sifting through his memories—" Asher shuddered like someone had walked over his grave, and I wondered if going through other people's pasts was like putting on dead people's clothing. "He always thought big and courted danger, but nothing about anything like this. Not back then. I'll have to go down to the sick bay tomorrow and see, doctor-to-doctor, what's going on."

Nurse-to-nurse, I'd been conned onto this boat believing there was a vacation inside. I couldn't fault Asher's humanitarian bent, but I wished all of this weren't happening now. I was hoping everything would turn out to be some sort of dreadful coincidence, even as that seemed less possible with every passing moment or seizing child. I bit my own lip and put a nervous hand on my own belly.

"Things were easier when I could just touch people and get answers," he said, mostly to himself.

"You miss it, don't you?" I said, and he startled, like he'd been caught. "You hide it, but—" I shrugged.

"Sorry," he apologized.

As happy as we both were to be alive after the events of this past summer, there'd been a time afterward when Asher had seemed withdrawn. I'd figured out he was depressed, but I hadn't wanted to ask why—especially when I thought I already knew, and the answer was something I couldn't fix.

"It's okay. You don't have to hide it—or think you're hiding it, which you're not by the way."

He snorted and stretched his hand out, looking at it as

though he'd just been holding something, only he couldn't precisely remember what it was.

"It feels like I'm missing a part of me. It's not just like having my wings clipped. It's like missing an arm. Both arms." He closed his hand into a fist in the air. "It was everything that I was, and then it was gone."

"But you're still you," I said, smiling hopefully at him.

"Hardly." He was still staring at his empty fist. "If I was, I wouldn't be here."

I stared at him blankly while my heart cracked in two.

If I'd said something half a second faster I could have covered it up. I could have glossed over it, and things would have gone on and been fine and I would have learned my Very Important Lesson about Hope and the Girl Who Shouldn't Pry.

But the record scratch of silence between us went on too long to be ignored. He looked over at me, at the expression on my face, and then blanched in turn. "Oh, God. And you think you say the wrong things sometimes, Edie—"

"We wouldn't be a thing if you were still a shapeshifter, would we?" I blurted out before he could apologize. It was too horrible for me to contemplate, and so I hadn't, this whole time. Which was funny, because part of me had always known the truth.

At least now it wouldn't be hanging over me anymore like a sword.

Asher inhaled to protest, to give me the easy answer— but we were past that, weren't we? I looked deep into his eyes, and he let out a long head-shaking sigh. "No."

I nodded, trying to be both brave and understanding, like a woman watching someone she loves go off to war.

"Shapeshifters aren't supposed to make friends with humans, much less fall in love with them. We're like parasites." He was trying to soften the blow by explaining.

"There wasn't any room for you in my past life. Hell, there wasn't even any room left inside me."

And I knew that too. I'd known him back then, back when being what he was almost made him go insane. It's just that despite the fact that I was a completely nonmagical human, I'd always hoped, in some tiny-twelve-year-old part of my brain, that I'd been the woman to tame the monster. That he'd chosen me because I was special. Not that I'd won his love by default.

I swallowed. The next logical question was *Would he give up everything we had here, now, to be a shapeshifter again?* But for once I kept my mouth shut and didn't run toward the spinning knives.

He took my nearer hand in his own and squeezed it until his knuckles were white. "I love you more than anything, Edie. Please, don't let me have ruined that."

I swallowed again, and breathed, slowly. "You haven't. It's okay. I love you, too."

"We're okay?" he asked, his voice tight.

"We're fine." I squeezed his hand back, and then took my own away from him. "Let's just go to sleep. It's been a long night."

It was the truth, and a way out of the tar pit we'd both fallen in. "Okay."

We crawled into bed together, lying side by side. He wrapped his arm around me like he always did, and I snuggled back against him like I always did. Pretending to be fine is half the battle of actually being fine. I was tired, and it had been a long day. I closed my eyes, and waited for sleep.

I'd always wanted to think that love could heal anything. But I realized lying there, eyes closed, listening to Asher breathe, that really love is what happens when you find out that it can't.

* * *

I wasn't sure what time it was when I woke in the morning; all I knew was that I wanted to throw up, and apparently I was alone.

"Asher?" I knocked on the second bathroom door before taking my place inside the first one as nausea hit me. Dammit to hell. If someone had ever explained to me to what extent being pregnant would make me intimate with a toilet, and if I'd been wise enough to believe them at the time, I wouldn't have been on the pill, I'd have been on a freaking IUD. Three IUDs. Twelve. The number rose with each involuntary spasm. My uterus would have been like Christmas Day for copper thieves.

I puked down to bright green bile before I was done, and I wanted to scrub my tongue down with an entire tin of Altoids. I staggered to standing and poked my stomach. "Thanks for nothing, kid, I mean it."

I rinsed with water and spit without swallowing so I couldn't trigger anything else. My morning sickness had better resolve before I got home, otherwise I was going to be having middle-of-the-night sickness, and the thought was too awful to comprehend.

I heard the cabin door open and went outside, catching Asher in the hall. "I didn't want to wake you. Are you okay?" he asked, solicitously—like there wasn't an N95 mask dangling from his hand.

N95 masks were the highest-grade filters you could get. They were only for serious germs like tuberculosis and meningitis, or weird ones, like H1N1 and SARS. When I'd worked at the hospital I'd been fitted for a new one each year. It'd lived in my locker afterward, a worst-case-scenario reminder every time I opened the metal door.

I ignored his question and nodded at the mask. "So it's like that, is it?"

"I'm afraid so." He set the mask down by the spray

bottles of cleaner we'd stolen. "People started dying last night. Let me wash my hands."

"Shit." I staggered back to the bed. He didn't let me touch him as I passed, and he stepped into the other non-puke-scented bathroom. I was still perched on the edge of the bed feeling green when he returned.

"You're sure you're okay?" He tried to put a hand on my forehead, and I ducked.

"Yeah. Just morning sickness. How many people are ill? What's going on downstairs?"

"They're presuming it's meningitis and everyone's in isolation gear now."

"Oh, no."

He nodded in agreement, reaching for my forehead again. I sighed and relented, feeling like a kid trying to play hooky from school.

"No fever," he announced.

"Like I told you." I took his hand back and held it in my own. "Are they turning the ship around?"

"They can't. We're closer to Hawaii than we are to California. And there's still the storm catching up behind us. Their plan is to get as close as they can to land, and have faster medical rescue ships meet us for transfers."

"How many patients are there?"

"Twenty, so far."

I pointed at the mask with my chin. "Where's yours?"

"I've still never been sick. And it's not me that I'm worried about. We've got to get you off this boat."

While I wholeheartedly agreed with his sentiment, it seemed impossible. We were in the middle of the Pacific Ocean. "How?"

"I'm not sure. But you're staying in here until I figure it out." He took his hand back and stood, reaching for the closet doors.

"What are you doing?" I asked as he took his current shirt off, pulled a dress shirt from a hanger, and began buttoning it down. The *Maraschino* jumped sideways, and I felt sick to my stomach all over again.

"It's him, Edie. I know it—"

"What happened to Thomas?" I interrupted.

Asher shook his head without looking at me. "He didn't make it. He died sometime last night. I'm sorry."

It was always a shock when a child died. Even if it wasn't yours, and you were just watching it distantly on the news. There was no way to mitigate a child's death, no bargaining you could do with the universe about luck, fairness, or age. It was just wrong, and everybody knew it in their gut.

"I'm sorry, Edie," Asher repeated, finishing his last button and turning toward me.

"Me too." I was queasy again now, for all the wrong reasons. "Was Liz with him at least?"

"Yes—but she's sick too. It's affecting adults now, and all sorts of people are calling down for Tylenol for fevers in their rooms." He crouched down, his shirt still untucked, and took my hands in his. "I've got to go back down there, Edie."

"To . . . help?" If they needed another doctor downstairs, one who couldn't get ill, I could hardly deny the rest of the passengers that—but I didn't want him to leave. I wasn't normally a scared person, but this place wasn't my home, and I didn't have my family or my cat—Asher was the only safe thing here.

"I have to talk to Liz. Before she passes."

"She's going to die?" I asked, my voice rising.

"You and I both know what death's door looks like. Antibiotics aren't even touching her fevers—she's over a hundred and six. She doesn't have long."

"Stay." I held on to his hands as tightly as I could.

"I have to go down there, Edie. It's the only way I'll know. I have to talk to her while she's still alive." He squeezed my hands back then let go, reaching into the closet behind him for his suit pants.

"Talk to her about what?" I asked, but I already knew, watching him dress. "You're going down there as him. To talk to her."

He nodded and began thumbing his belt through loops.

"Then . . . what?"

"If I can figure out his game—"

I started shaking my head before I butted in. "I don't want you to go. You can't just leave me here."

"It's the only way I can protect you."

"No. No no no." I hadn't wanted to come on this ship in the first place, and I was pregnant by accident—this was going to get to be my choice, this one thing, decided on by me. He could not leave.

But he was already laying his tie across his shoulders.

"So you're going to go down there? And do what, precisely? Comfort her? Doing an impression of her husband?"

"No. I'm going to ask her what she knows. He's here himself, Edie. There's some way he's not getting ill. Maybe she knows how."

"While she's delirious and you're pretending to be related to her?" He ignored me and pulled on his suit jacket. Anger and impotence stirred in my stomach to make a nauseating brew.

"Is this what you miss about being what you were?" I asked. His hands paused over his tie, and I pressed. "All the hanging out with people that you want to push overboard?"

He finished knotting his tie, pulling the tail through with finality. "I'll be back as soon as I can."

"I need you here."

"Edie, I'm doing this to save you."

"Then I don't want to be saved."

He looked at me, his eyes full of sadness, and then his face settled into the shape of someone new: Nathaniel from years ago, back when Asher had still had his powers. More stern than the man we'd eaten dinner with last night. A stronger jaw, a more aquiline nose. I didn't think he realized it, the way the lips he wore sneered down at me. "You don't mean that. And I couldn't live with myself if anything happened to you."

Listening to his words come out of someone else's mouth—only years of attempting to seem unflappable as a nurse saved me from jumping back.

I shook my head again involuntarily, trying to negate everything that'd happened this morning—his shitty plan, this conversation, this trip, all the things I'd found out that I hadn't wanted to know. If I kept shaking, maybe I could rewind back to the part where everything was simple again.

"Edie, I wanted to believe he was on vacation here," Asher tried to explain. "More than anything else in the world. I wanted to believe that he could change."

"Because if he could, you could too," I said. Accusing him. Trying to guilt him into staying.

"I have changed. You know it." He sank down beside me on the bed. "You do, don't you?"

Of course I do, I wanted to say, while being aware it made me sound like one of those hopeless women who fell for serial killers in prison. But if I said yes, then he'd leave me. Although looking into his eyes, even if they weren't the ones I was familiar with, I could tell that if I lied and didn't say yes, I'd break his heart.

"I do."

He swallowed and stood. "Good. I love you—and I'm sorry. I may not have much time. I have to hurry."

Eyes that weren't the ones I loved blinked drily, and he shook his head before speaking with another man's voice. "I'll be back. Just give me twenty-four hours to see this thing through. She may not talk at first, but if she does I'll figure out a way. Order a ton of room service now; you might not get the chance later if it spreads. Choose things that won't go bad."

"I'm not okay with this."

"Just stay inside the room until I get back," Nathaniel's voice commanded. He leaned in to kiss me again, and this time I jerked away from him, unused to the strange face he wore. "I'm sorry," he apologized.

I was so mad and scared that I didn't know what to say—and it was clear he was going, no matter what. I didn't want him to leave like this. I scrunched up my face a second time, and closed my eyes so I wouldn't see him coming in. A stranger's lips touched mine.

"I'll be back in twenty-four hours," he repeated.

"Be careful. You're not as supernatural as you used to be," I reminded him.

"Don't worry about me. I'll be fine," he said, and let himself out the door.

CHAPTER THIRTEEN

This was bullshit. Everything about it was bullshit.

I knew—deep-down bone-level knew—that Asher was different now. But his past seemed destined to follow us. I imagined it indistinct and dark, lurking underneath the waves outside, bigger than the boat, waiting for us to make a mistake and swallow us whole.

How could I love a man who'd facilitated, even for an instant, testing anything on people? Even if he hadn't hurt anyone personally, he'd helped a vampire sympathizer to get ahead.

Then again, I'd saved Anna—which had been the right thing to do at the time, I was sure—but I'd also saved Dren. Who had untold deaths on his hands, maybe more since I'd set him free. It's not like he'd converted into being a vegetarian because I'd been crazy enough to save him. Or like such a thing were even possible for a vampire.

Good substitutes for human blood didn't exist. Red blood cells did too many things that weren't imitable. They were small, they were flexible enough to squeeze through capillaries, and they transported oxygen every-where. Some blood substitutes had managed to be two of those things, but never all three at the same time. Yet.

A bad allergic reaction to the fake blood, or a stroke-causing clot: That would be the end of things, and probably fatal to boot. No one would willingly volunteer for the duty, so who were they testing on? And where? And—under what conditions? If they were paying them, a big if, they'd have to be desperate, either for cures or for cash. How could I love a man who'd profited on other people's sorrow? What kind of person did that make me for loving him—evil once removed?

I couldn't believe I'd let him go, but I didn't know how I could have possibly stopped him. I felt so impotent and abandoned, and that was the worst, knowing there was nothing I would have done differently.

I ordered room service angrily, and sat on the bed like it was an island, and watched piped-in programs on daytime TV. Movies slid by, family-friendly fare, where grown-ups were stupid and preternaturally smart kids saved the day, and I loathed them all.

Including the small traitor part of me that agreed with him. Not about him leaving me, but the staying-in-here-safely part, hiding from all the germs in the outside world. Protecting myself and the baby inside me.

"I hate it," I said, unsure what I was hating precisely—this place, Asher, the baby, me—just knowing that I meant what I said.

I threw up a couple more times, out of anger or regret, and returned to my perch on the bed. The ocean raced by outside the closed balcony doors, waves sharply drawn like carved stone.

When room service arrived I tipped them all the money left in Asher's wallet as a small act of rebellion.

I set the room service trays out—sandwiches and cheese platters and cookies, anything that might possibly sound good over the course of the next day—and left all the silver lids on, so I wouldn't have to smell all of them at once. I carefully tested my stomach's tolerance of a french fry.

My stomach disagreed with everything but the salt. I licked the fry clean, and chunked it into the trash can afterward.

I was licking the salt off another fry when I saw something out of the corner of my eye. A man, splay-legged, tumbling like a snowflake, outside my window. Down to the sea.

I raced to the balcony doors and flung them open. Cold salt air smacked me like a wall. My bare feet slid across the short space to the railing, slick with condensation from the coming storm. I clung to the railing, my T-shirt and jeans not up to the task of keeping me warm, and leaned over, trying to see where he'd fallen. Trying to prove that I'd seen him at all. The churning ocean beneath the *Maraschino* was the color of the mist enveloping us—I couldn't see anything, really.

But I knew I'd seen a man fall.

I closed my eyes, trying to pull up the memory precisely, to slow it down and really see it. I pictured the railing like a microscope's cover slip—and a man falling, like a protozoan darting beneath.

Where did he come from? And why? I leaned out and looked up, in case anyone else was staring down like me, but I couldn't see past the bottom of the balcony above. And no one else was leaning out on my deck, or staring like me, below. I was alone. Again.

I carefully stepped back inside my room and called the front desk.

I couldn't make a decent report, as I wasn't even sure who I'd seen, just that I'd seen someone. I could tell that the person listening to me was trying to be considerate, but I knew I sounded insane.

"I just saw a man go overboard. You need to stop the boat. I'm in room six thirty-one. He fell down from above me somewhere. I think he was older, and he had a green shirt on."

"Please calm down, Mrs. Stonefield," she said. Of course. Asher had booked our rooms under his own name. I had to bite my tongue not to correct her. "We'll be looking into things," she went on.

"He might still be alive—" I said before I stopped to ponder the odds. Could anyone survive the fall? How high up had he started, anyhow? And how much would the water have felt like cement when he hit it? I sat on the bed, staring out at the ocean through the balcony doors, as though I might catch sight of someone else falling there. It didn't look like we were plowing through the waves any more slowly.

"We've already sent out a tender boat—"

"Someone else saw him?" If so, how had they managed to call in faster than me?

"Uh—" The woman paused on the far end of the line.

Either she was lying to me—or she wasn't. And there'd been another reason for a search boat to already be out in the sea.

"How many people have gone overboard?"

The woman cleared her throat. "I'm sorry, I can't tell you official ship's business. Please trust that we're looking into things, though, Mrs. Stonefield, honestly we are." And the line clicked dead.

I tried calling back, but the line was busy and went to hold music immediately. I waited for five minutes and then gave up in disgust.

Maybe they couldn't stop the ship if we were going to outrace the storm and get the sick people safely off. That was better than thinking that they didn't care—or that they were already overwhelmed. I went out on the balcony for a second look.

The ship hadn't even tried to slow down, but even if it had, what would be the point? I assumed cruise ships were like trains: It would take the *Maraschino* miles to decelerate at the speed we were going, and after that, who knew how much longer to turn around? The ocean outside was as wild as it had been the day before, when I'd been pushing Claire. Knowing it had taken someone made it seem worse somehow, more stark and unforgiving, even hungry.

I returned to the warmth of the cabin and locked the balcony doors behind me, pulled the curtains tight, and tried to ignore the fact that the bed I curled up on was far too big for just me.

Had that man been pushed overboard? By . . . Asher? I grimaced and rolled my eyes at the thought. No, he hadn't been screaming on his way down—I would have heard. He'd jumped.

Inside my mind, I made up a whole story for him. He was on board with his only daughter; his wife had died in childbirth long ago. When his daughter got sick, coming down with whatever Thomas had had, and died, he'd flung himself overboard in grief.

It was melodramatic, the stuff of old fairy tales or tragic myth. But I found solace in it nonetheless, because it was a story. And stories had to make sense in a way that it increasingly looked like my life did not.

I didn't remember falling asleep, or even being tired. But sometimes my body shut down under stress, and maybe the pregnancy, or me not eating much but puking a ton, had taken a toll. I woke to a commotion out in the hall as the sun began to set, and looked at the alarm clock on Asher's empty side of the bed: 8 P.M., local time. Not even twelve hours since he'd left.

CHAPTER FOURTEEN

I thought about taking the mask out with me. But if I brought it, there was the chance that people would want to know how I'd gotten it—what was so special about me? I doubted they were like life jackets, one for everyone on board. I'd seen enough mob mentality in the hospital; I didn't want to invite it. Besides, if whatever Nathaniel had set on us was that contagious, I'd probably already been exposed to it. I just wouldn't touch anything or come within droplet range of anyone and trust my nursing immune system to do the rest. I opened up my door and listened—and all the voices I heard were angry. I carefully snuck out and walked down the hall.

"You're kidding me—I've got a dinner reservation at Le Poisson Affamé tonight," someone in a suit was saying ahead, butchering the pronunciation. "I booked it before I even got on board!"

I reached the back of a small group of people who were complaining to two cruise employees stationed at the stairs and noticed that the floor indicator lights above the elevators were off.

"What's going on?" I asked a woman standing near the back.

"They've just shut down all travel between floors," she

said, crossing her arms, face sour. "And I've got late-night bingo plans."

"You will be refunded," one of the employees was explaining to the angry man. "But we need you all to go back to your rooms."

"This is unacceptable," the bingo woman muttered.

"The captain will be explaining things shortly." The cruise employees were burly, but they didn't look pleased to be playing the heavy in the face of so many angry vacationers. "Please go back to your rooms, and stay indoors."

"How long?" I asked, over the crowd.

"The captain will be explaining shortly—" the man repeated, patting the air in front of him to get us to settle down.

Just in time, chimes sounded overhead, and people quieted to hear what the captain would say.

"This is Captain Ames speaking. I'm sure you all have noticed that we are no longer allowing travel between floors. While there is no reason to panic, we need you all to stay in your rooms for a short portion of our voyage."

"How long is that?" one of the angry people asked aloud, as if the captain could hear him and answer back.

"Our legendary room service will continue to be available upon request. If you need anything, or begin to feel ill, please contact guest services immediately. Please be patient, and we'll continue to keep you informed."

The chimes descended in tone, letting us know the captain was tuning out.

"What's that even mean?" complained the man missing his reservation.

"It means you will be refunded for the special dinner you are missing tonight," one of the employees repeated.

"My travel agent's going to hear about this. And the entire Internet. And my bingo club!" the woman complained.

One of the guards tried hard not to crack a smile at that. If guest services hadn't been overwhelmed earlier, they would be now. Maybe that's why people were jumping—they couldn't handle the horror of the bingo club cancellation.

I snorted, and then I realized the captain had stopped just short of calling this what it was—a quarantine. I stepped back, keeping even more space between me and the other complaining passengers.

"You heard the captain. Please go back to your rooms, and this will all be over by morning," the cruise employee repeated.

Which wasn't precisely what the man had said, but I suspected the "guards" here would have changed shifts by then, and his lie would be someone else's problem at dawn.

I hung back in the hallway, not touching the wall nor anyone else around me as the crowd dispersed, and then I approached the two cruise employees, trying to seem pleasant and meek.

"Hi there—my husband was out earlier on, and I'm not sure where he is now." Might as well lie all the way. *Husband* had a weight that *fiancé* did not. "I think he might be trapped on another floor."

"The phone systems on board are fine. I'm sure he'll call your room soon," he said, with an emphasis on the word *room,* with the implication that I wouldn't know if he'd called unless I was back there. "Please don't worry, this is just temporary."

I inhaled to fight him, but I didn't know with what. I could hardly tell him that there was a mad scientist on board. I didn't like being turned away, but I wasn't sure what else to say. "Sure, okay."

I walked back to my room, as pissed off as the bingo-lady and a hundred times more frightened. I heard someone sneezing in their room as I passed by and thought darkly about calling guest services to make a report. I shook my head and opened my room door with more questions than answers, again.

I washed my hands, and then paced. There were no messages waiting for me on the room phone. I pulled out Asher's cell phone and tried to call out, but I didn't get a signal. I hadn't brought a laptop, since we were supposed to be vacationing. And I tried to make an outside call from the in-room phone, only to find that that system had been disconnected as well. Probably so people like my neighbor couldn't already be complaining to their bingo buddies. Guest services got through, but only to hold music, and then a "your call will be answered in thirty-seven minutes" automated system.

The most sensible thing to do would be to wait here for the full twenty-four hours. Asher would come back, or if he couldn't, he'd figure out some way to contact me.

But the small dark voice of my mind whispered, *If he doesn't, what then?*

I didn't really know.

I stared at the N95.

If I had a temperature of 106 for very long it would boil my baby alive.

But if Asher didn't come back, then that would mean something bad had happened to him. Asher didn't say things he didn't mean—and he didn't make promises he couldn't keep. If twenty-four hours passed without him—thinking about it made me feel nauseous all over again. I dry-swallowed and tried to calm down.

There was no point in making any hard choices—yet.

I sat on the bed, pulled my knees up to my chin, and turned on the TV.

An hour of television I couldn't remember later, there was a knock at the door.

"Asher?" I stood, brimming with hope. And then I remembered that he would have a room key. I walked over to the door and peeked through the peephole. "Who's there?"

"I need a favor," a man's voice with a light Indian accent said through the door. It was the father of the family next door. I locked up the chain and opened up the door the six inches it allowed—revealing him standing there, with his daughter at his side, her Coke-bottle glasses peering out fearfully. "My wife's still down there with our boy. I need to check in on them. Can you watch her?"

"Um. Hang on." I closed the door again and undid the latch so we could have a normal conversation. "How are you getting down there? We're all supposed to be in our rooms."

"With these." He held out his hand. His wife's diamond earrings sat in his palm.

"Those are expensive—"

"Precisely." He closed his fingers around the stones. "And I'm not an idiot—there's more than one set of stairs on this floor."

I looked from him to his daughter—I wasn't in the mood to babysit. "I'm sorry, but no—"

"I'll be right back. I just have to check up on them. And I can't take Emily with me." His daughter was clinging to his leg like a barnacle. Ignoring me, he started to pry her loose.

"Look, you really should wait. I'm sure it won't be long," I lied, trying to shut the door, wishing I'd never undone the chain lock.

He craned forward to look quickly around my room, and then nodded, as if making up his own mind. "You're not a parent, you wouldn't understand."

At that, my jaw snapped shut. He grabbed Emily bodily and pulled her off him. "Emily, I need you to stay here with this nice woman, sweetie. I'll be right back, with Zach and Mommy, okay?"

Emily didn't say anything, but she did nod, once. With him so bound and determined, what else could she do? He shoved her at me and handed me a room card. When I didn't take it, he let it drop on the floor.

"I'll be back as soon as I can," he said and rushed out of the room, slamming my door. I opened it, with a *Hey!* on the tip of my tongue, but he was running the other direction from the elevator and stairwell down the hall—and I found I didn't want to get him busted. I swallowed my shout. Maybe his crazy plan would work. It didn't occur to me until then that I should have asked him to check in on Asher, too.

I looked down at Emily and she started to cry.

CHAPTER FIFTEEN

Usually when I had to deal with crying children, I was getting paid to do it, which made it easier. Not only was Emily crying, but she'd face-planted on my bed, with her likely contaminated clothing. Her long thick braid spooled beside her tearful face like rope. I picked up the key to her room and wiped it on my jeans.

"Hey, Emily. My name's Edie." *And I am so not in the mood.* I patted her back awkwardly, fighting down the urge to spray her with housekeeping cleaner fluid like a bad house cat. "I'm sorry, just, stop that. Don't." I pulled the comforter out of her hands and sat beside her. "Emily, is it?"

"I'm Whisper," she corrected me, after heaving a particularly pathetic sob. "Whisper the pony."

"Well, okay then. I'm Edie, the nurse. Nice to meet you." I offered her the remote control in lieu of a hand shake. She took it.

"I want my daddy." Her glasses made her eyes larger than they really were, magnifying long eyelashes sprinkled with tears. Her lower lip quivered as she asked, "Can you make my daddy come back?"

"Oh, honey." What kind of person would ditch their kid with a stranger? "Not yet. Soon though."

"Where is he?" she asked, sitting up to look around the room like he might be hiding somewhere.

"He's very worried about your brother."

She finished her circuit of the room, found me again, and sighed. "They're always worried about him."

"Well, yeah. Some brothers are like that. Believe me, I know." I latched on to an idea. "Hey, so, Whisper—I have a confession to make."

Her teary eyes narrowed. "What?"

"I am terribly allergic to ponies. Can you go wash your hands real good, with soap?"

She made a face that said she knew I was lying to her. "Fine." She hopped off the bed and went into the bathroom.

We were going to be breathing the same air in here. Although chances were, if she'd been hanging around her brother during his contagious phase, she'd have it already, whatever *it* was.

"I'm hungry," she complained when she emerged from the bathroom. From the looks of it, she'd dried her hands on the front of her shirt.

I reached over to one of the room service trays on the couch and opened it to reveal a grilled cheese sandwich. "Bon appétit."

Having a physical child present in the room anchored me. I let her control the remote. She watched children's programming while I watched the clock as it neared midnight.

I found it hard to believe that everyone else was just calmly waiting in their rooms. I peeked outside now and then, and once I saw a room service waiter furtively carrying an overloaded tray into someone else's room. He then emerged empty-handed and walked down the hall the opposite way from the guarded stairwells and turned-off elevators. Emily's dad was right: There must be a service elevator or stairs hidden elsewhere on each floor.

I let the door fall closed. Emily was watching the TV in that fixated way that kids did, as if the programming were an alien transmission meant especially for her, another sandwich half eaten in her hand. That was good at least. I had no idea how I'd manage to listen to the inane chatter in the background all night, but it was better than making conversation with a strange child.

I licked some salt off a fry and drank some water. And then I tried to actually eat a bite. The second it hit my stomach, I could feel the churning begin. Hurlsville.

"I'll be right back," I warned Emily and dashed into the bathroom, barely managing to close the door behind me before I threw up. Was it going to be like this the whole time I was pregnant? Nine months of this was going to be a very, very long time.

I heard the children's programming stop, and there was a tentative tap at the door. "Are you okay?" Emily asked me.

"Yeah. Just hang on." I clung to the sides of the toilet. Maybe it wasn't supposed to be like this. I wished I had the Internet, and then I remembered that there probably wasn't a *What to Expect When You're Expecting a Half-Shapeshifter Baby* book out there. After this I could write one, though. Chapter One: Prepare to Stay in the Bathroom at All Times.

There was another knocking—only not at the bathroom door. "Emily—don't get that—" I stood and wiped the back of my hand across my mouth.

But it was too late. "Daddy?" Emily guessed with hope, and I heard the cabin door click.

"Oh, look at all this food!" said an unfamiliar voice. I opened the bathroom door just as a stranger walked by.

From the back she looked normal, but when she turned I could see her stomach was distended abnormally. Like pictures of starving children from Africa, or people with end-stage liver failure, only she wasn't orange. Emily got out of her way, and she snatched up the sandwich Emily had left behind on the bed to take a bite of it as if it were her own.

"Who are you?" I asked. I waved Emily over, and she came back, walking as far around the weird woman as she could. When the girl reached me, I shoved her into the bathroom behind me and said, "Whisper, lock the door."

The strange woman polished off Emily's sandwich and moved on to the chips that'd come with it, stuffing a handful into her mouth. "I'm so hungry!" she complained around them.

"You need to go," I said, my voice low, trying to sound threatening.

"But you have so much food!" she protested, eyeing my room service buffet.

Food deprivation issues made people do strange things— I'd fished hidden sandwiches out from underneath people's pillows at the hospital before. But that was no excuse for this woman to be here in my room now. I walked around her so I wouldn't be between her and the door— and so I'd be right by the phone.

"Get out—or I'm calling security," I bluffed.

"I will when I'm full!" She began eyeing the collection of room service trays behind me, and took a threatening step forward.

I could go for the phone—or the desk chair. For some reason, the chair felt safer. I hoisted it up and waved it at her like I was a lion tamer. "Get the fuck back. I mean it. Do it now."

She knelt down with a grunt. The collection of fries that I'd licked all the salt off were sitting on the top of the trash. She picked them up and shoved them toward her maw. Just seeing her do that made me want to throw up all over again.

"Get out, get out, get out!" I screamed with increasing volume.

She looked up at me and screamed back, just as loud as I had, a guttural animal sound. Something frothed inside her mouth. Loud knocking started on the other side of our cabin door and a male voice asked. "Is everything okay?"

Emily unlocked the bathroom door and raced out, shrieking, "Daddy!" The strange woman tracked her motion, turning with frightening speed to lope after her, like she was a cheeseburger on legs. Emily opened the door and made it into the hallway, the woman hot on her heels. I threw the desk chair onto the bed and ran full speed after them—and reached the hallway just in time to see Hal step forward and clock the woman upside the head with a cane.

She went down with a crack, and Hal stood over her, ready to wallop her again. When she didn't move, he looked at me as I panted in the doorway. "Are you okay?" he asked with a shout.

I nodded and took in the situation. The downed woman was breathing, but not much else. "Shit."

CHAPTER SIXTEEN

Major concussion? Subdural hematoma? Shit shit shit.

I knelt down. I didn't want to touch her, she was probably covered in germs, but—I folded her eyelids up and checked for blown pupils, then I felt over her head for dents. She wasn't bleeding, but he'd hit her hard, and she'd gone down solidly. She was hot, like the children had been before.

"I said—are you okay?" Hal asked again, interrupting me. He pointed to the side of his head. "My hearing aids are out."

"Yeah, I'm good, thanks." I glanced over to Emily, who was staring up at Hal with a mixture of awe and disgust. "Are you okay, Emily?"

"You're not my daddy," she told Hal with disappointment.

"Nope," Hal agreed. Then he knelt beside me. "Is she still breathing? I hit her pretty hard." He was still overly loud—loud enough for himself to hear.

"She's still breathing." Though not much else. I knew I ought to try to wake her up, to check for brain function—but I couldn't get the image of her rooting in my trash for licked fries out of my brain.

"Claire said she was threatening you, that I needed to get over here." He looked from her to his cane.

I nodded emphatically so he'd know what I meant even if he couldn't hear me. "I'm glad she heard us. Thank you." I wasn't sure I'd be able to explain it in court if this woman was dying now, but Emily and I had definitely been in danger.

He squinted, reading my lips. He probably needed glasses, too. Then he smiled widely. "You're welcome!"

Claire came out of their room, rolling her wheelchair over to us, fighting the rocking of the ship. "How did you know?" I asked her.

"My ears are as good as my legs aren't." She looked down at the woman. "Oh, my."

"Oh, my, is right." With extreme reluctance I patted the woman's rotund stomach. It was taut, but I couldn't feel a baby inside—and frankly, the woman looked too old to have kids. Although these days with IVF, who knew?

"You two get her into her room—I'll go get help from up the hall. Can you help me, little girl?" Claire asked Emily. Emily nodded and started pushing Claire's wheelchair, although I could tell that Claire was doing most of the work.

The woman's room was two up and across from mine, and the door was still barely open; it hadn't clicked fully shut. I ran over to prop it open with a room service tray, trying to ignore the thirty or so she had stacked inside.

Then it took a lot of heaving and hoing—bodies were awkward to move. Thank goodness Hal was strong.

"She's got a fever," Hal over-enunciated to me.

"I'd noticed," I muttered. I was trying not to breathe the woman's air, and ignore that I was covered in her sweat.

"She's very hot!" Hal reexplained.

I nodded again. "I KNOW." I hauled her torso forward until we reached the end of her bed. "Help me get her sitting up." I didn't want her drowning in puke before the cavalry came. *If they came,* more like.

There were food trays all over the room. I wondered if finding out we were all on room arrest had triggered some kind of hysteria in her. I knew my room looked like I shouldn't be one to talk, but this was absurd—and all her trays were empty.

"I've heard of feeding a fever, but this is ridiculous," I said after taking a look around.

Hal grunted, the kind of noncommittal noise that people who couldn't hear well made to keep conversations afloat. He did seem remarkably composed for a man who'd just brained someone into unconsciousness. Did he have a touch of Alzheimer's, or was he just old school? Despite his strength he looked ancient enough to have been in any of the last five major wars.

I stood and my back popped. This was not what Asher had in mind when he'd left me up here to stay safe, and so much for wearing the mask. Hal dusted his hands off and looked to me for direction.

"Shouldn't someone stay?" he shouted.

Technically? Yes. She could have a bleed inside her brain, above and beyond whatever ailment she'd had that'd made her go crazy and attack us. But there was nothing I could do about it right now, and I didn't think the doctor below could even monitor her, much less do any pressure-relieving trepanation that didn't involve a corkscrew or a beer tap. It hadn't exactly been an ICU facility when I'd been down there for my pregnancy test.

And if I were honest, I didn't want to be here when she woke up. Being in her room, trays practically licked clean—right down to tiny ketchup and mustard bottles, emptied—stacked on every available surface, made my hackles rise.

"They're going to send help—but they warned it might be quite some time," Claire said from the hall. Emily was sitting on her lap now, and Claire was running fingers through the girl's long hair, which had somehow come out of its braid. "They said we should wash our hands, and each get back to our own room for the duration of the quarantine."

I snorted. "I bet they did. Did they say the word *quarantine*?"

"No. But what else could this be?" she said sensibly.

I stood over the insensate woman with her weird stomach and her weirder ways. It was stay here and watch her for signs of life like a hawk—and being afraid of her if she did wake up—or take the cruise employees at their word and walk away. I shook my head. I didn't want it to be me who stayed here, but Emily was too young, and Hal and Claire were too old.

There was a lick of froth at the corner of the woman's mouth now. Left-sided heart failure? Or . . . rabies? I frowned.

"Come out of there, you two. You're not responsible for her—and I, for one, don't want to catch what she has," Claire said, absolving us all in one cantankerous swoop.

I put a hand to my stomach, weighing alternatives. *Being in here is not good for you, baby, and that's all that matters*. I quickly followed Hal out the door.

CHAPTER SEVENTEEN

As the woman's door locked shut behind us, trapping us all—or just me—with the consequences of our decision, chimes blared again overhead. I jumped like it'd caught us doing something shameful. Maybe because it had.

"Hello, guests, sorry to wake you. This is Captain Ames again. Just a reminder that we need you to continue to remain in your room, for the safety of yourself and other guests." He coughed a bit and waited for attention. "However, we are in need of additional medical crew. If you have any expertise in a medical field and possess current qualifications, we would appreciate it if you would report to the Dolphin restaurant on the third deck. But be aware that if you do so, you might not be able to return to your cabin, possibly for the rest of the voyage, so please do not leave small children unattended. And remember, volunteering is voluntary!" he said, and chuckled, as though he'd made a hilarious joke. The chimes descended, and the intercom clicked off.

"You look pained, dear. She's going to be fine. And if she's not, well, it's no business of ours."

I wondered if being so personally near death had given Claire a ruthless clarity that I lacked. "It's not that—well, it is, but—I'm a nurse. I should go help."

Claire shook her head with finality. "You're pregnant.

You only have responsibility for one person right now."
She shot my belly a meaningful look. "You owe nobody
nothing. You should go back to your room and rest."

I was a little sweaty from the effort of moving that
woman. But not sick-sweat, I was sure. I sighed. "You're
right, I should." I put my hand out for Emily, and after a
moment's hesitation she took it, hopping off Claire's lap.

When Emily and I made it back into our own room, she
turned toward me. "That lady was weird."

"Yeah, she was," I agreed. I wondered what kind of
person I was for just leaving her over there. It wasn't like
me to panic like that, but she'd scared me and something
more primal had taken over. I'd lost whatever moral high
ground I'd had this morning in the process—but I knew
Asher wouldn't care. He wasn't the type of person to have
problems with what I'd done.

My eyes found the clock. He had less than ten hours
now. I wondered if his interrogation of Liz had been prof-
itable. Whatever that woman had was not meningitis—it
didn't map to any illness I knew. But I had a hard time
believing that Nathaniel could have come up with an entirely novel disease. Genetics didn't work like that. You
based things on other things, borrowed DNA, jumping
genes. So far it was too hard to create anything new out of
whole cloth.

So what mapped with fever, sometimes to the point of
seizures, and weird hunger, with a dash of froth?

Not rabies, given the number of trays in her room—
when you were rabid, your throat constricted and hurt too
badly to swallow; that's why rabid creatures perpetually
drooled. And it would be too effing ironic for me to see
someone with rabies now when I'd already survived being exposed to were-blood on a full moon night.

The left-sided heart failure I didn't want to think about.

There were meds to help it—but if you were so far gone that you were frothing because your heart and lungs weren't talking right, your outlook wasn't good.

Last but not least, there were esoteric genetic diseases that caused strange behaviors. Prader-Willi syndrome caused chronic hunger and disinhibition, which made you want to eat whatever you could. Families with people who suffered from it had to lock their afflicted relatives safe inside houses, and/or strap them down. And Lesch-Nyhan syndrome, a rare illness that made people want to eat themselves. The only solution for that was highly experimental drugs, brain stimulation, or pulling out all your teeth to stop you from eating your own lips and fingers. Just the idea of it made me ill. And I couldn't get away from the image of that women digging through my trash to eat my pre-licked fries.

"Are you going to be sick again?" Emily asked.

I barely managed to nod before I made it into the bathroom to throw up.

This time, no strangers came while I was gone. And I hoped Emily'd learned her lesson about opening the door for just anyone. But I couldn't blame her for wishing her father would return, when I was still waiting for Asher. I wanted him to come back and tell me everything was going to be all right, even if it was a lie.

He'd never broken a promise to me before, and that was the only thing that kept me here now. The hope—as impossible as it was beginning to seem—that he'd be back by morning like he'd said he would.

Emily slept on the couch, limp like a puppy, completely passed out. I threw a sheet over her, and then I tossed and turned on the bed, not even trying to sleep, just thinking What-If thoughts. Every flicker of the show Emily had left on seemed like the shadow of the door opening, and I got up periodically to touch her forehead and make sure she wasn't getting hot.

At 5 A.M., she threw the sheet off. I stood up to check on her again, and if I hadn't been listening so hard for my own door I might not have heard it—the sound of the next door over clicking open, and then sliding shut.

Was her dad back? With news? Had he seen Asher? And would he take Emily off my hands? I pulled Emily's room key out of my pocket. Even though Asher would know I wouldn't leave a child unattended in our room for long, I felt compelled to write him a note with the stationery on the desk.

Next door. Be right back! I signed my name underneath, like he wouldn't know it was me if he returned while I was gone.

I tiptoed next door and knocked softly. I didn't want to interrupt anyone doing anything private, but I did want the girl off my hands. I knocked a little louder, but hopefully too quiet for Emily to hear, just a wall away. After long enough, I gave up and tried the lock with my loaned key.

"Hello?" I called out quietly.

It was dark inside. I reached out for a light switch. Maybe I'd only imagined the sound.

The light illuminated Emily's father, sitting in the dark on the edge of their foldout couch.

"Oh, my gosh." I clasped my hand to my chest, startled. "You're back. Is your boy okay?"

He slowly turned to face me, and his eyes blinked as though they were unused to the chore. "He's dead."

That gut punch of a child's death again. "Oh, no. I'm so sorry."

He didn't shake his head, or hunch over to cry, or anything else that I might have recognized as grieving.

"Did they let you back up here? Is the quarantine off?" I hadn't heard any obnoxious chimes overhead, and there's no way in my current state I would have slept through them. He didn't answer me.

"Should I . . . go get . . . Emily?" I said, uncertain of my place here. I backed up against the door. Would he want some time alone with his grief? I could get that. If anything had happened to Asher, I'd need to be the fuck alone too. "Where's your wife?"

"She's dead too."

"Oh, I'm so sorry," I repeated, like it would help.

He ignored me and turned his gaze back out to the ocean, back to where I realized he'd been looking before. "I'm so thirsty."

"Would you like a glass of water?" I could see into the bathroom from where I stood, glasses from last night's room service at the ready.

It happened in the second I looked away. One moment he was seated, apparently morose—the next he was standing and walking toward the balcony doors.

"Hey—" I took a step away from the door as he stepped outside.

From there it was only a long step and a half to the railing. I'd started to run, but he climbed up like he was mounting a horse, swinging over one leg at a time, and without hesitation he leapt.

This time was different from the man I'd seen go before. We were still six floors up, but the night was clear, and the moon was bright. I raced outside after him, hands reaching, too late. My hands clung to the railing as I looked overboard.

CHAPTER EIGHTEEN

He'd splashed—not like an Olympic diver, but like a kid, cannonball-style, disappearing beneath the waves. Everything had happened in silence. I hadn't screamed. Screaming would attract attention—it would wake up Emily, and then where would I be? Explaining that her father'd just flung himself overboard?

But I was screaming on the inside. I watched the ocean in horror, biting my lips. I stepped back from the balcony's edge and into the room, backing up until my knees were caught by the foldout couch where Emily's dad had just been.

That wasn't right. It simply was not right. He'd been here, and then he'd just thrown himself overboard—why? Grief? Panic? Why?

I took two deep breaths, and then I picked up the phone to dial guest services for whatever good it would do. I was sent to a messaging service, and I set the receiver down without leaving one.

I crept back to my own cabin, and touched Emily's cool forehead again, just in case. How would I tell her? Should I? I generally wasn't in favor of lying to children, but if I didn't tell her, who would? Everyone else in her family was dead. It could wait until morning at least; she deserved one more night of sweet dreams.

She was alone in the world now.

As for me . . . I wrapped my hand around my stomach, where Asher's hand was supposed to be. Was he, in some small distant way, partially responsible for all of this? I didn't know. I could figure how to deal with that later.

For right now, I just wanted him back.

I would have cried but I was too tired and too frightened. Crying would have been like admitting defeat. So I didn't, I just lay down and watched Emily dream.

I must have gone to sleep after that. Too much crazy, not enough to eat—I woke up and didn't remember anything for a blissful second and then, ushered in by the sound of Darth Vader breathing nearby, it all came rushing back.

I opened my eyes and found Emily three inches from my face, with the N95 mask on.

"Jesus Christ!" I yelped. She jumped back, as startled as I was.

"I found this!" Emily explained, her voice muffled. "It's like a bridle!"

"It is," I agreed with a pant—and I remembered that I'd seen the last remaining member of her family float away the night before. God.

"You look sad," she said.

"I'm just tired is all." I sat up, blinking, and checked the clock. It was 10 A.M. Emily had watched TV quietly and helped herself to another sandwich while I'd slept in. Asher hadn't returned. My note to him last night sat tented on the desk, mocking me.

I rocked back in bed and nodded to myself. This was it. He'd had his twenty-four hours and more. I was going to have to go look for him.

"Neeeeighhhh?" Emily said for attention, pawing at the ground with a foot like a horse.

I gave her a half smile. "Here, let me show you how to wear your bridle right."

I folded the mask's metal bridge around her nose. It wouldn't seal—it was the wrong size for her. But she still didn't have a fever. I didn't think she'd contract whatever had taken the rest of her family down, due to either luck or natural immunity. While I tied the elastic bands to fit tighter around her head, I looked around the room.

All of my belongings that I liked were in this room with me, with the exception of Minnie, my cat, who was being boarded back home. The silver cuff Asher had given me a Christmas ago, to help protect me from vampires. The glamorous shoes I'd bought on super-sale that I'd carefully broken in, that I'd been waiting to get the chance to dance in. The blue shirt that I'd worn on our first real date that had felt like a date, a normal date, just us going out to see a movie, like normal people do. I had the feeling if I left this room I would never see any of it again.

And that was okay, as long as I found Asher.

"Are you going to be sick again?" Emily asked, her voice hushed by the mask. Her glasses fogged up with her breath.

I shook my head. "There's no time for that anymore."

I took Emily out into the hall and knocked politely at Hal and Claire's door, trusting Claire's ears to hear us. I heard a grunt behind the door as Hal spotted us through the peephole, and noticed when he opened the door up that he'd set down his cane nearby. All the better to beat us with.

"Hi again," I said, and he nodded, letting us into their room. I looked from him to Claire, who had an expectant look. "I need to ask a big favor of you."

"What?" Claire asked.

"Can you watch Emily?"

"What?" This time Emily spoke. Her voice rose, and she grabbed for my leg. "Nooooooooooooooo," she began yelling, in an air-raid-siren squeal.

"I'm sorry, Emily. I've got to—"

"What's changed?" Claire asked, with a sideways glance toward my nonshowing belly.

"He said he'd be back by now. He's not." I realized that for anyone who didn't know Asher or me, what I was going to say next might sound foolish, but—"My fiancé. He's never made a promise he didn't keep."

Claire frowned. "It's probably not safe yet, dear—"

But who was it safe for? Waiting around wasn't going to change anything, not while people were acting crazy and flinging themselves overboard. And if the captain was really going to do something about it, there'd be a fleet of helicopters overhead by now, airlifting us off.

Somehow Nathaniel was using the *Maraschino* as his personal petri dish—and Asher's attempt to stop him hadn't worked. It was up to me, first to find him, and then to figure things out.

"I'll be careful," I said, before she could dear-me again. I held my room key out to her. "There's plenty of food in my room still. I ordered up at the first sign of trouble." Emily was still sobbing, sliding down my leg.

"Why does everyone always leave me?" she yelled, each word louder than the last.

She didn't know the half of it. But I steeled myself. I couldn't go back in time and bring her family back—I needed to find the other half of mine.

Claire watched Emily's meltdown then sighed. "All right. I'll keep the girl here." She reached out and took the key from me. "But you should take Hal with you. He's good in a tight spot."

I was shaking my head before she could finish the

words. "I believe you, but I'm sorry—I can't. I need to do things in a rush. I appreciated your help earlier and your help now, but—"

Claire frowned—she was unused to being told no. All the same, I wasn't going to take a lumbering elderly man with me who might slow me down on my search. "Your loss," she warned. "Do you at least have a plan?"

I nodded. As plans went, it wasn't a great one, but it counted. "I'm going to go volunteer."

Emily's screaming was awful. Even though I knew it wasn't so much at me as it was at the continuing and escalating unfairness of her situation, it made me feel bad.

Not bad enough to stop and console her, but bad.

I let myself out of Hal and Claire's room and walked down the hall. Asher had gone down to interrogate Liz—he might still just be trapped down there by the quarantine for all I knew. But given that Emily's dad had been able to come up somehow, and that Asher was who he was—the chances that he'd been stopped by mere guards was very, very low. Something must have happened to him. The medical bay was as good a place as any to start figuring out what.

I reached the stairway, where two new crew members were stationed outside. "Hi. I'm a nurse. I came to volunteer, like the captain announced last night."

The crew member nearest me gave me an unsure look. "Why didn't you come down then?"

"I thought I might have whatever it was. But I'm fine now, it was just allergies." I tried to give the man a trustworthy smile.

It worked. He smiled back as the other coworker radioed down asking if they still needed help. He leaned forward so his voice wouldn't carry far. "I don't want to worry you, miss, but I wouldn't go down there if I were you."

The radio in his coworker's hand crackled to life in response. "Send them down."

I gave the first man an apologetic smile. "Too late."

I walked down the central stair unescorted, although at each landing crew members/guards waved me on, until I reached the third floor.

"The hospital's down that way," one of them told me as they let me pass.

I would have guessed from the smell. My stomach lurched, and I pressed a hand to it to calm it. *Not now, baby.* Luckily no one else was there to see me waver.

There was a chance that in doing this I was making a big mistake. What if I did come down with whatever it was? I'd trusted in my nurse's immune system before and it'd failed me. I didn't want to catch anything, and I certainly didn't want to hurt our child. But if Asher hadn't come back, something was seriously wrong.

I knew from getting my pregnancy test that the medical office was on the first floor, and I also knew from that short trip that there'd be no way they'd have been able to fit everyone who was ill downstairs. As the smell got stronger, my path became more familiar, and I remembered that the medical staff had commandeered a restaurant. The Dolphin. Where Asher and I had eaten breakfast just two days ago.

The entrance to the restaurant was partitioned off with freestanding curtains like they use in waiting rooms so that people can privately change. They created a small room and blocked the view of the restaurant beyond, but they couldn't keep out the smells or the sounds of people groaning and crying.

There was a table in the curtain-room, and the doctor I'd seen for the pregnancy test sat behind it, papers scattered everywhere in front of him. He had highlighters and pens out and was making copious notes—he looked like a cop near the end of a serial killer TV show: frantic, about to break.

"Name and room number?" he asked, without looking up.

"Edie Spence, room six thirty-one," I said.

The doctor found my name somewhere on his list and checked me off with an orange line. "And you're sure you're not sick?" he asked, finally looking up at me. His eyes narrowed in recognition.

"Not yet, no."

"And the results of your test?"

"Negative," I lied.

He grunted. "Good. Why are you here?"

"To help. I'm a nurse." There was a groan from the far side of the curtains that startled me. Asher said he couldn't get sick—but what if he was wrong? He'd said I couldn't get pregnant, and look what'd happened.

"Well, I hope you got in enough drinking before all this," he said with a snort. He leaned back, pulling the curtains behind him aside enough for him to shout through. "Raluca!"

A short dark-haired woman wearing a cruise-themed polo shirt emerged through a gap in the curtain-wall. "Did you figure it out?"

He shook his head. "Not yet." He snapped his fingers at me. "She volunteered to help."

She looked me up and down. I looked healthy enough, so far. She nodded. "What's your medical expertise?"

"Clinics and hospitals. I used to be intensive care."

"Good. What you're going to see—do not judge us, okay? We are doing the best we can with limited resources." Her voice was slightly accented in an Eastern European way. I nodded to encourage her. Whatever it would be, I'd have to have seen worse already, back on Y4.

She pulled back to let me through. I realized the curtains were set up so that gawkers in the lobby, if there were any, wouldn't be able to see in.

As I rounded the bend myself, I realized why.

CHAPTER NINETEEN

The restaurant was like a hospital floor in a wartime film with a big budget, but nothing here was special effects. There was all the chaos with none of the sterility or equipment. It looked like a primitive insane asylum, the kind they'd kept people in up until recently, even in our own "great" United States. People were tied to the undersides of tables with tethers of torn sheets, lashed like so many Odysseuses to masts. That didn't stop them from moaning, though, or puking, or shitting themselves from the smell.

"Oh, God," I said, before I could stop myself.

People like me—healthy volunteers—gophered up to see who I was before sinking back down to the tasks at hand. I saw them feeding people carefully, offering sips through straws, passing pills, wiping away the excretia as best they could.

"I know how this looks. Like one of your horror films." Raluca shook her head. "You probably think us inhumane. But if we did not tie them down, they would run outside and fling themselves overboard."

It took me a second to be able to answer her, even though I knew she was telling the truth. It was just that the room was so horrible, so far beyond anywhere I'd ever had to nurse anyone before. My head started shaking again. "No—I believe you. I saw a man go over myself." I could tell my admission relieved her fractionally. "How many people are here?"

"Total? Two hundred. Fifty well, a hundred and fifty sick. A hundred have already passed."

A hundred deaths on Nathaniel's hands. "Do you have any idea what's causing it?"

She shrugged. "Dr. Haddad is working on that still. We're treating the sick people as best we can in the meantime."

I wondered if the woman Hal had clocked was down here—and found myself dearly hoping that Asher was not.

"What are you treating them with?"

"Restraints, ice—and Tylenol, Valium, Cipro." She ticked off the medications starting with her thumb.

Cipro explained all the shit, literally. Nothing like one of the world's strongest antibiotics to clean out your intestinal flora. And the people underneath the tables couldn't warn you when they were going to go.

"Where do you put the people who get better?" I asked, still staring around at the horrors of the room.

Her lips thinned into a line. "No one has gotten better, yet."

A young man moving between the patients lashed to tables stood and waved. "Raluca—we're out of Valium over here."

She frowned again, reached for her keys, and headed back to the curtains at the front of the restaurant. "Please, show her how to get ice. I will return," she said, and then disappeared.

I was left in the care of a teenage boy with black jeans and a black T-shirt with hair clearly dyed to match. He was like the teenage version of a poison dart frog—*Don't touch me.* Raging acne scarred his pale face, and his expression was not kind. He took me in and shrugged a shoulder. "Come on—the ice machine's this way—"

I hadn't finished looking around the room yet. Too many of the sick people were facing away from me. A few still had attentive relatives or friends nearby, but a lot of them were alone. None of them looked like Asher from here, but I needed to get closer to be sure.

"Can you wait just a second?" I asked him.

"Why?"

"I'm looking for a friend."

He gave me a look that said that he didn't have time to explain all the ways that I was dumb. "If they're here, it's too late. They're already a zombie."

"These people aren't actually zombies." I'd been in love with a zombie before. I knew what zombies were like.

His chin twitched up in challenge. "What the hell else can they be?"

I didn't have an answer for him. "I don't know."

He gave me a teenage snort, unsurprised by my idiocy. "Yeah, well—let's go on the tour."

We canvassed the room quickly in all its depressingly repulsive glory. The healthy people, volunteers like me or people who'd been trapped when they'd arrived with relatives, had looked haggard. They'd seen too much too fast with too little preparation. It was one thing at the hospital where eventually you became inured to horrors and had coworkers' support to fall back on; no one, could have warned these people what would happen on their cruise. Even in nursing school, they'd babied us a little at first. These poor people had gotten steamrolled.

Their number included this boy, who, despite his bravado and his penchant for black, was clearly out of his depth. I was sure on Xbox Live he had a lot of swagger, but nothing in his video game world had prepared him for this much actual death.

Most of the volunteers ignored me, too tired to care. A few shot me dirty glances as I hunched over to look into their relatives' faces to make double-triple sure that none of them was Asher.

One of the volunteers I surprised accosted me. "What are you looking at?" He had a wig cap and makeup on from a prior night. He moved to block my view of his friend, who was slouched over and also had fading makeup, but who looked much worse for the wear.

"I'm searching for a friend of mine is all. Sorry." I waved my hands to defuse the tension.

He deflated a little, lined lips pursing. "Me too." He reached down to brush a sweaty lock of hair away from his friend's forehead. "For your sake."

I nodded and stood. The boy at my side was still sullen. "Did you find them?" he asked, despite the fact that he'd been with me the whole time.

"No."

"Lucky you," he said sarcastically.

CHAPTER TWENTY

I followed the boy down an empty staff hallway at the back of the restaurant. "Where's the crew? Aren't any of them ill?"

"Raluca's got them quarantined separately down below where there's no windows or decks to jump off."

"Good idea," I said and got no response. "My name's Edie," I told the back of his head.

"Rory," he said without slowing down.

"Who wrangled you onto this boat, Rory?" I knew he hadn't made the call to go anywhere tropical—he had even less of a tan than I did, and with his lack of vitamin D he must have been approaching rickets.

"My parents. Who became zombies and died horribly," he said completely deadpan. "They wanted to get me out of the house. Any more awkward questions?"

"Nope. Sorry."

"Whatever."

He pushed through another set of saloon doors, and we entered a huge industrial kitchen. Rory led me around countertops and tables, all shining stainless steel, until we reached a massive ice machine at the back. He rummaged off to one side and returned with an empty trash can, which he handed to me. "Only take as much ice as you can really carry. It gets heavy by the end of the hall."

Without gloves, we reached into the machine's belly and scooped the ice out by hand. It wasn't long till I couldn't feel my hands anymore, which was good because then it didn't hurt. Scraping out handfuls of ice, hearing the sound of it drum and settle on the bottom of the cans—my actions fell into a rhythm with my thoughts. I was glad Asher wasn't here—but where else could he be?

Rory touched my arm with an icy palm before whirling and startling me.

There was a shadow behind us—I saw its reflection in the ice machine door.

"Hey!" Rory shouted as I turned more slowly.

"Hey yourself," the shadow shouted back. A man stepped out from behind a rack of dangling spatulas.

My breath caught in my throat. Nathaniel. I put a nearly frozen hand to my face.

His eyes narrowed at the sight of me. "Good to see you again—Edie, was it?"

I kept my hand in place as it froze me. This Nathaniel was the older one with the slight belly, the weaker jaw—not the younger specimen Asher had imitated perfectly on his way out yesterday.

"We ate dinner together the other night. Before this nightmare began," he clarified for me.

I put my hand down slowly. "I remember you." I wanted to say more, but I wasn't sure how. *Have you seen my boyfriend? The last time I saw him, he was imitating you,* didn't seem feasible, no matter that it was true. "How's Liz?" And a second later, when I remembered I wasn't supposed to know that Thomas had died, "And your son?"

"Died. Both of them."

"Why're you here?" Rory asked, staring him down.

"I got trapped down here, with everyone else," Nathaniel answered, with an irritated tone.

"You weren't eating back here, were you? Like the others who're getting sick?"

"No."

"Then why aren't you out there helping?" Rory demanded.

I decided to cut in. "Do you know anything about this? About what's going on?" I tried to sound confused, hoping he'd let some small clue drop.

"Of course not," Nathaniel said.

What were the chances he'd just come out and tell me about his nefarious plans? He wasn't some villain by way of Scooby-Doo. I wanted to confront him, but I didn't want to blow my chance at it—I didn't think I'd get more than one shot.

Rory looked back and forth between us and then stared at Nathaniel again. "So what were you doing back here?"

"I was tired. They wouldn't let me back upstairs. I was taking a nap." Nathaniel pointed behind himself and off to the side.

"With everything that's been going on—you've been taking a nap?" Rory said, his voice rising. He had a lot of anger and no place for it to go.

Nathaniel took offense and spoke in clipped tones. "I had a long night."

I placed a cold hand on Rory's arm to hold him back, just in case. Rory was tense a second more then shrugged me off.

Nathaniel patted down the collar of his jacket and then straightened his tie. I didn't have proof of anything, and I couldn't let on about anything that Asher'd told me. Before I could think of what to say he jerked his chin at me. "Where's your doctor fellow?"

To lie, or not to lie? Given what Asher'd been doing, I probably should lie—but my hands weren't the only thing that were numb. I decided to answer honestly. "I don't know."

Nathaniel's lips pursed at this, and his brows rose. "Well, well."

"Have you seen him?" I blurted out. I felt like a little kid asking *Have you seen my puppy, mister?* minus a handmade sign. I hated myself for putting him in a position of power over me—but if I didn't ask him, and if it somehow managed to be just this simple, I'd hate myself even more.

"No. Why would I?" He yawned and shook his head, as though he was still waking up.

At the yawn, Rory snapped. "I don't know if you noticed, but everything's going to shit and the rest of us aren't getting to take naps." Rory pointed up the hall like he was chastising a dog. "Go back in that restaurant and ask Raluca where you can help."

Nathaniel gave Rory a cold smile. "Make me."

A moment passed between them like gunslingers in an Old West showdown, and I would have bet all my money on Rory, his anger lashing around him like a whip. Maybe sensing this—that Rory's irrational heat was sharper than his cool pride—Nathaniel subtly backed down and snorted dismissively before walking away.

He was rumpled, but not distraught. I believed that he'd been napping, yes, but not that he'd seen two loved ones die. Whereas beside me Rory's loss was etched on his face and held in his hands, clenched into fists at his sides.

"When you caught him behind us—those were some insane video game reflexes right there," I said lightly, trying to calm him down.

"Thanks." He grunted and shrugged, apparently his preferred method of communication, and I could almost feel him swallowing his anger down, folding it away. And in case I might forget that he didn't like me, or anyone else in the world right now, he added, "I guess."

We hauled the half-full trash cans back to the restaurant's floor, where Rory had me hold trash bags open to catch the ice as he poured. And when we were done, with ten separate trash bags half full, he picked up one. "Find the hot ones that are still alive."

I picked up two bags and walked around. A weeping woman gestured me over and then had me apply the cold bag to the man beside her. Nearing, I could see that he was a boy. Presumably her son. He wasn't much older than Rory, if that, and while Rory was an example of nerd-life, her son had been a shining testament to model boyhood with a sunny tan and a sleek quarterback's physique—and a fever of at least 105. She glanced over at me and then over at Rory walking past us with ice for other patients, and I could see her thinking that it was unfair.

"I'm sorry," I said, because I didn't know what else to say.

"I'm thirsty," her son responded.

She focused back on him. "I know, honey, I know." She held up a cup of water and a straw. In a second, he'd sucked the whole cup down.

"I'm still thirsty," he complained with cracked lips as she took the cup away.

"You have to wait a bit first. You can't drink as much as you want, you're not right in the head now, okay?" the woman patiently explained, holding back tears.

"But I'm so thirsty—" the boy complained, his voice raw.

I didn't know if I should stay or go. What would I do if it were my child under there? I heard the ice in the other bag I held clink as it settled, melting, which gave me an excuse. I made a gesture with it to the woman to explain my leaving, and I backed up and stood. I looked away because I had to—and caught Nathaniel, leaning against a wall of the restaurant, not helping in the least, watching me.

I stared back. If he had done this, I would come up with a way to make him pay.

"Hey, ice lady." The man with the wig cap on snapped his fingers to get my attention. I went over to his side as he stood.

"Here." He held up a half-melted bag of ice to me. Not knowing what else to do, I took it. "It shouldn't go to waste," he explained with tears in his eyes. I glanced down. Beneath the table, his friend was slumped forward. No chest rise.

"I'm sorry," I said again, for all the good it would do.

The man stood and held his hands to his face, beginning to cry. I set the bags of ice down and patted his back gently, trying hard not to be a sympathetic crier. Rory was right—this room was full of zombies. But they weren't the sick people, they were all the living ones left behind.

Raluca returned through the curtains, the Robin Hood to our not-so-merry crew. "Hello everyone. I've got more Valium, and it's time for another round of Cipro."

"I'll take some of that over here." The man beside me reached up and pulled off his fake lashes savagely. "The Valium, not the Cipro."

CHAPTER TWENTY-ONE

The man set his false eyelashes down on the table, where they looked like lost caterpillars. Then he knelt down and began undoing the knots that had tied his friend.

Rory came over to take the ice from me that I was doing such a shitty job of distributing. He looked down, shaking his head. "I don't want to move another corpse."

Calling this man's friend a corpse in front of him seemed harsh. But then I hadn't been through what Rory'd been through.

"I can't go back there again," Rory went on. It took me a second to realize where he meant—the morgue. Or wherever they were keeping all the bodies. And I realized what I had to do, just in case. If Asher wasn't here, there was still one place worse he could be. I frowned and looked up. Nathaniel was still watching.

"I'll go," I volunteered.

Rory nodded with increasing speed, picked up the bags of ice, and took them away.

"Help me then?" The man unfurled the sheet his friend had been tied with, preparing to use it as a shroud.

"Sure." I knelt and grabbed the corpse's feet, and together we rolled the man over and onto the sheet, which made a hammock-like gurney for transport.

The man hefted his half up easily. Mine came up with a grunt. "Let's go."

We walked down the same hall Rory and I had with the body dangling between us, but past the kitchen doors. I was glad that he was the one walking backward down the hall into the unknown instead of me. The hall bent, and then we took a freight elevator down to the first floor.

I had no idea what I'd do if I found Asher's body up ahead. None at all. There was a growing knot of fear inside my stomach even contemplating it. It seemed unlikely, but unlikely wasn't the same as a zero percent chance. I heard a small puppy-sound and realized the man holding up the other end of the sheet was crying. I'd been too self-absorbed to notice. I bit my lip. What to say?

"I'm so sorry for your loss." As generic as a sympathy card. Dammit.

He nodded and whimpered again. It was the part of the time with families when I'd normally hug whoever was crying—but I couldn't here, I'd drop half of his friend. The elevator opened and he walked backward out of it, walking and crying, until he reached a lull in his tears.

"The worst part is that our act was finally doing so well. We were finally going places together, just like we'd always dreamed."

Talking was better than crying. "What was it?" I asked him.

"We were the Two Chers on South Deck," he said with a long sniffle. "Just another Steve and Eve show—you know, two drag queens, high heels and higher wigs, trying to make our way in the world." He said it all very tongue-in-cheek before sighing. "We were the late-night entertainment two nights a week. Raunchy comedy and karaoke favorites. Stefano did a mean Cher. I did a nice one." Interpreting my silence for the confusion that it was, he continued. "You know—he was very 'Dark Lady,' I was more 'Believe in Life After Love.' Except that he's dead now, and after the shit I have seen today I don't believe in fuck-all anymore."

"I'm so sorry," I repeated.

"Thanks. I'm Jorge." He lifted and wagged the body we held. "This is Stefano. Was Stefano."

"I'm Edie." The stupid part of my brain latched on to the only Cher song I knew. "If I could turn back time—"

Jorge shot me a dark look. "Don't even."

I bit my tongue too late. "Sorry. Very, very sorry."

He snorted, defused. "Stefano always liked bad puns."

The farther down the hall we went, the more it smelled like flowers. Then we started passing them in the halls, piles upon piles of flowers, like a parade float had beached here to die, and I realized they must have repurposed the floral freezer for the morgue.

Jorge said. "You planned it like this, didn't you?" It took me a second to realize he was talking to Stefano. "You knew I'd be too cheap to buy you all these flowers otherwise."

Treading upon bruised petals, we walked through the freezer door.

It was less horrific than the restaurant in here by a factor of ten, but twenty times more sad. When I saw the bodies spread evenly on the floor, I felt a huge temptation to just drop his friend and run away. I'd been around carnage before, but I'd never seen so many bodies all at once—and I still had to see if any of them were Asher.

I concentrated on helping Jorge at the moment; I didn't want to drop my end of Stefano. Jorge looked over his shoulder and shuffled backward to Tetris in Stefano's body at the end of the fourth row. When he was done, he folded the end of the sheet over Stefano's feet.

I did some quick math. There were ten rows of ten bodies here, minus an incomplete row here or there, but at least ninety corpses. Some were clearly women and children, but others were men in suits. I shivered and tried to tell myself I was just cold.

Jorge straightened out Stefano's limbs and stood quietly, looking down at his friend. Maybe lover. It didn't matter that I didn't know. "Did you want to say something?" I asked him. "Or I could, if you wanted." It wouldn't be the first time a family member had pressed me into oration.

Jorge shook his head. "This might be the first time I've ever been speechless. Stefano would like that. He always said I talked too much." He knelt down and touched his friend's forehead. I waited quietly for my turn. I didn't want Jorge to see me rifling through the other bodies. After a moment more, he stood, resolved, and covered Stefano's head with the other end of the sheet. Then he headed for the door and held it open for me.

I gave him a sad smile. "Sorry. I'm still looking for my friend."

"Oh." He gave me a compassionate look. "If you don't mind, I'll wait outside."

"Sure." Then the door swung shut, and ninety or so bodies and I were alone.

The freezers overhead were running at full blast, dialed down from chilling orchids to frozen dinners. Standing and looking at the contents of the room, I realized Raluca would have to use another freezer soon, or we'd have to start stacking bodies two-deep.

I didn't know what person had started covering the corpses with the corners of their sheets; I'm sure they thought at the time it was kind, so that people coming in with new ones wouldn't have to stare at so many dead sets of eyes. But now it meant I had to go around to every man wearing a blue suit, just in case.

I made my way to the first one in the farthest back corner, determined to make a scientific effort of it and go row by row. I had to pick out visible floor to step on in between the bodies, bouncing from patch of cement to patch of cement like a CrossFitter doing a monster-truck-tire-run. Eventually I found myself at the first contender and stood awkwardly on either side of his head. The older bodies had a layer of frost on them, like frozen dinners left in the freezer too long, and the sheet was stuck to the corpse's face. Holding my breath, I yanked on it until I pried enough off to know that it wasn't Asher. Just some other poor person. For all I knew, it was Rory's dad.

The corpse's chin waggled. "How's it going, Edie?"

I gasped and fell backward onto my ass on the corpse's cold chest, my hand unfortunately planting into the man's crotch.

"Down here. And get your hand off my cock."

"What the fuck—" I teetered to standing, wiping frozen-body-Popsicle off my hand.

I only knew of one entity that would think of joking at me from inside a corpse. I punched the body in the chest. "That's not funny, Shadows."

The voices coming from the mouth of the dead man laughed.

The Shadows were awful creatures located underneath my old hospital back home, where they lived off the pain and sorrow dripping down from above. I hadn't seen them since July, when Asher'd been saved. After that, they'd offered me my old job back, and I'd refused them.

"What the fuck is going on here? Where's Asher?"

"Shhhhh," they warned me, from the darkness inside a dead man's mouth. "Keep your voice down."

I don't know why I listened to them, but I did. "Where. Is. Asher?" I asked, my voice low.

"We don't know. He's not hiding in here with us."

In with the dead bodies, in the dark. Where there'd be a continual stream of sad people to feed on. Of course.

"Then what good are you—" I said, standing.

"Don't you want to know why you're on board?"

I slowly sank back down, still straddling the corpse.

"That's more like it. Listen close—we don't have much power here, unless you'd like to cry for us."

"I'm listening."

"We sent you here."

"What?" I'd never been so tempted to strangle a dead man.

"We'd heard rumors, so we decided to send you in. You've got a nose for trouble and a knack for staying alive—not to mention a shapeshifter bodyguard."

"But Asher picked out this cruise—"

"Oh, it was nothing to convince him," they said, interrupting my protest. "So easy for us to plant a few ideas inside his overstuffed head. Plus, this mess is partially his fault—it was the least he could do to help us clean it up. He owed us, and the Consortium."

"So why aren't you out there fixing things?"

"We're not omnipotent, and we have to stay in the dark. Plus"—the voice receded, as if it was speaking from deeper inside the dead man's throat—"we're in hiding."

"From?"

"You'll see."

I pounded another fist against the man's frozen chest,

and hoped to hell no one else would come in the morgue just then to see me. "Is there anything useful you can tell me?"

"Yes. Try to stay alive. You'll see. Oh, Edie, you'll wish you'd come back to us by the end of this. Working for us will seem like a distant dream—" they said, and then their voices abruptly stopped.

"Dammit, Shadows!" I yelled. All I got in return was silence.

"You're all insane." I stood and nudged the corpse with my foot. It felt just like kicking a cement block would.

There was a knock at the freezer door, and this time I managed to whirl around without falling. Jorge was at the door, a bouquet of flowers from outside in his hands. "Everything okay?" he asked. I nodded, and he came in to set the flowers down on Stefano. "Don't get me wrong, but you sounded a little crazy there. Talking to yourself in other voices. It's not like I haven't done the same thing, but usually when I do I'm getting paid."

"I'm fine." I hugged myself and realized how cold I was getting. All this excitement probably wasn't good for the baby, either.

"Was he here?" Jorge asked.

I looked down. I hadn't made it past this first man in a suit, because of the Shadows. I surveyed the rest of the room. I wanted to believe what they'd told me—not that things would end badly, but that Asher wasn't here. If Asher was in here dead, wouldn't they show me his body so I would grieve and they could feed? I had to believe they would have.

"No. He's not," I answered Jorge with a head shake.

But if Asher wasn't in the restaurant-sickroom or in the floral-storage-morgue, where else could he be?

What had Nathaniel done to him?

And—as I knelt to replace the sheet over the man the Shadows had violated—what was there in the world that the Shadows could possibly be scared of?

CHAPTER TWENTY-TWO

My head was swimming with too many questions and not enough answers as we walked back to the restaurant. I asked the simplest one of Jorge. "How did you know it was a he?"

Jorge shrugged. "Trouble is almost always a man."

We entered the sick floor just as Raluca was mounting a chair with a megaphone for an announcement.

"Remaining volunteers—I have good news. The doctor has just informed me that the medical ship is on its way."

Maybe twelve hours ago that would have been good news. But right now all the enthusiasm those standing could muster was a sarcastic "Hooray" from Jorge. I heard Rory's matching snort from across the room.

Undeterred, Raluca continued. "I've put out rations for anyone who wants them. You have to take care of yourself, so you can take care of your loved ones. Remember to wash your hands. That is all."

She clicked off the megaphone and stepped down.

The volunteers who were mobile staggered up and queued to go outside, and I followed them. I needed to break free from here and look for Asher—or find Nathaniel and get him to tell me more. I scanned the room for him and didn't see his sneer.

Outside, we walked past the food table en masse. Grilled cheeses all around. My stomach turned green. Without thinking, I sagged forward, bile rising, and Jorge caught me.

"Hey—hey." He set me upright as I looked for something nearby that I could puke into. "You're sure you're not sick?"

I waved away his concern. "Not like that, no. The ocean. It gets me."

"Raluca's giving out Dramamine like candy. You should take some," he advised.

"Thanks, but—" I began.

It was too late; he'd already started to wave for her. "Raluca, she needs Dramamine—"

There was nowhere to hide. What was the worst that could happen—she'd take me into the next room over and tie me to a table?

Raluca came over to give me the nursing once-over—I recognized it, nurse-to-nurse, in her eye. I tried to pretend that everything was okay, for the currently low values of okay we all shared, as she touched my forehead with the back of her hand. I thought I still felt like an icicle from my time in the morgue, and I could tell from her face relaxing that she did too.

"Where did these come from?" I gestured to the table.

"There's still healthy people crewing the last kitchen, as best they can. We can't let everyone starve."

Which begged the most obvious question I hadn't asked yet. "How many people are left on board?"

She inhaled to answer me, then paused, and I saw my opportunity.

"You don't know, do you?" I asked. It was hard not to sound excited.

Raluca shook her head. "We haven't gone room to room yet—"

"So there could be sick people up there." I pointed above us, to indicate the rest of the rooms. "Too sick to call."

"We're overwhelmed as it is—"

"But what if the medical ships come, and they don't take everyone? There could be hundreds of people, feverish in their beds, trapped."

Her eyes narrowed, and she gave me another look, nurse-to-nurse. "Just how big do you think the medical ship will be?"

Not big enough. "But shouldn't we know?" I pressed. "Maybe we could move them down, or put *X*'s on the doors—something." Anything that would get me permission to do a room-to-room search. I would pull the entire ship apart to find Asher if I had to.

"If you don't authorize it, I'll go do it anyhow. You can't stop me." My voice rose as Raluca frowned.

"I'll go with her," Jorge volunteered.

Dr. Haddad emerged from behind his desk at the commotion and eyed us all with equal displeasure. I had Asher's word he was competent, but I doubted the man had ever had a decent bedside manner. Raluca leaned over to whisper something in his ear, and he sighed. "Five people can go." He held up two fingers and pointed at Jorge and me. "The troublemakers. Then—" He began to look around. "Her." He pointed at the woman whose son was Rory's age—I assumed he'd passed by virtue of being away from him—"and him, and you." He jabbed his finger at a man with a startlingly bad self-tan, and at Nathaniel, who'd been standing in the back. I felt a silent thrill at his being included in our number. Maybe I'd get a chance to talk to him alone.

"I want to go too," Rory volunteered.

"No." Raluca shook her head immediately. "We need you here."

And I realized what the doctor was doing: giving us people he, or Raluca, wanted gone.

"Don't I get a choice?" the tan-man asked.

The doctor narrowed his eyes. "I caught you trying to steal Valium." He looked around and spotted someone. "Marius—you're in charge of this mess. Take a master key and a radio. And this." He disappeared back into to the curtained room, returning with a paper list that he handed to Marius. "Check the manifest as you go. Putting X's on the doors is not a bad idea," he said, glancing at me with a grunt, then turning to our small group as a whole. "The medical rescue ship will be here in three hours. That's all the time you've got. Wash your hands before you go."

Then the doctor darted back into his room like a moray eel. Raluca gave our group a pained look. "The medical team's on radio station five. Good luck," she said, and walked after the doctor.

I gave Marius a sympathetic glance as the rest of the volunteers followed Raluca back inside, grilled cheeses largely uneaten. He shrugged. "The doctor's always disliked me. Where is your man, my countryman?"

I shrugged back at him and tried to look competent, but with a side of damsel in distress, just in case it helped my cause. "I'm not sure."

"Ah. So that's why you want to do this," he said, and then turned to address all of us. "We'll go up and search room-to-room, breaking up into groups of three and doing both sides of the floor simultaneously." He started making hand gestures to indicate what our plan of attack would be, which sealed my assumption that he was ex-military, and began directing us down the hall. "Head out."

Marius opened up a door that said STAFF ONLY and loaded us into the freight elevator behind it.

"I can't believe we have to do this," said the tan-man who'd been roped in. The woman was still sobbing quietly beside me as Marius pressed number 9.

"No one's holding a gun to your head," Nathaniel said, then after a dramatic pause, "yet."

Tan-man leaned forward, pressing the crying woman back, until she stepped on my shoe.

"If we have to do this, we'll be doing it in an orderly fashion," Marius said before a fight could start. "We'll use *X*'s for rooms that we've cleared, *O*'s for rooms that are empty, and *S*'s for ones with people who are sick." He paused to look around and make sure we weren't all idiots. "Knock first—give the guests a chance to answer. Some of the fancy rooms are big, and some of the guests are slow or deaf. Then, if no one answers, go in and look around. Clear from room to room, including bathrooms, closets, and balconies. Okay?"

"There's only one master key?" Jorge asked.

Marius nodded. "And it's mine. I'm in charge of this expedition."

The elevator doors opened and we spilled out onto the ninth floor's very nice carpeting. "Outside rooms—you, you, and you." He pointed to me, the other woman, and Jorge. "Inside rooms, us three." He pointed to himself, Nathaniel, and Tan-man.

"Boys versus girls," Nathaniel said with a shark-like grin.

"Quite," Jorge said, aligning himself on our "ladies" side.

Marius looked at the sheet the doctor had given him. "You all have the Averys. We've got the Steinmetzes. Start knocking," Marius commanded, leaning in to unlock our door and rap loudly on it while doing so by way of example.

Jorge clicked his heels and saluted him ironically.

* * *

Our door didn't open all the way; there was still a latch closed at the top. That was good, I guessed—it meant someone was still inside.

"Hello?" I called through the gap as Marius's group disappeared into the room behind us.

"What's your name?" Jorge asked the crying woman.

She sniffled some. "Kate."

"Okay. I'm not getting fresh or anything, but if you need to, you can hold my hand," Jorge said, offering it out. Kate shook her head and gave him a sad smile.

At that moment, I would have gladly held Jorge's hand. It would be nice to find some human comfort in all this mess. But there was an entire ship to search and only three hours to do it in. "Hello?" I asked the gap between the door and doorjamb again. "Mr. and Mrs. Avery?"

"Who are you?" A woman's startled face appeared on the other side.

I wasn't entirely prepared for someone standing and well. "I'm—I'm Edie Spence. I'm with the medical team. We're here to check in on our guests. Is there anyone here needing medical attention?" I tried to sound official. I think Marius would have approved.

The woman's eye searched me up and down, and then the door closed and reopened fully, latch undone. When she saw Jorge and Kate standing outside she frowned and clutched at her chest. That would be just great, if she were fine up until the point where seeing our trio gave her a surprise heart attack.

"Mrs. Avery?" I said, holding up my list, trying to seem official. "Are you and your husband okay?"

She got over the shock of seeing us, and composed herself quickly. "Of course we are. Why wouldn't we be?"

"Can we see your husband too?" Visual confirmation was best.

"You're kidding, right?"

"Ask 'em why they're here!" someone shouted from the back.

"They want to see us," she shouted back.

"Ask them why room service is running slow!" yelled the distant voice.

The woman looked archly at me. "Well? Why is it?"

The ship swung to one side as a wave hit it. The ocean was getting rougher as the storm neared. I inhaled sharply. Jorge took my nausea-induced silence for anger and stepped in. "We're part of a rescue mission—"

I started shaking my head as soon as the words were out of Jorge's mouth.

"We want to go on the rescue ship. We want to get out of here," she said, cutting Jorge off.

There was a certain kind of person who, no matter how much life had given them, would always be worried that other people were getting more. I started backpedaling. "It's not a rescue ship, it's a medical emergency ship. We're here making sure that no one in this room is experiencing a medical emergency."

"I'm almost out of wine!" shouted whomever she was related to in the back.

"That's not a medical emergency," I said flatly.

"It's an emergency for me!"

Kate drew herself up to her full five-nothing height. "Look, I just watched my son die horribly downstairs. None of you all look that sick."

Mrs. Avery looked aghast. I smiled and didn't even care that it was fake looking. Another minute of this and I would be happy to throw up all of this lady's shoes. "We're glad you're all present and accounted for. Thanks!" I reached in and slammed the door on us for her.

"That was a little abrupt," Jorge said, finely tweezed eyebrows rising with the hint of an amused smile.

"Sorry." Kate shrugged.

"Don't be. I like your style." I nodded at her. "No one calls it a rescue ship again, okay?" They both nodded.

Marius and his group reappeared in the hall. "Any luck?"

"Can I scratch a dick onto the doorjamb? I feel that symbol would be most descriptive of the occupants inside," Jorge said. Marius made the kind of pained face that said he knew this was a bad idea all along.

"What about you all?" I asked.

"No one was home." Marius held up the master key. "Onward."

CHAPTER TWENTY-THREE

We knocked at the next door as Marius unlocked it for us. I didn't know if I should be relieved or upset that no one answered. I gave Jorge and Kate a look and together we pushed in.

The room was grand. Literally. It had high ceilings—and a piano, bolted in a decorative fashion to the floor. I checked the list. "Mr. and Mrs. Inman?" I called out. No response. Jorge shrugged and started walking in.

We went into a living room bigger than some apartments I'd had. Kate and I went off to the right and Jorge went left. There was a grand bathroom with a grand shower and a grand tub—miles of marble, exquisitely soft towels, and expensive creams and lotions, the spackle of the wealthy-old. Then a bedroom with a huge flat-screen TV, with clothing and shoes tossed out. No one was here. All their belongings, clothing, toiletries. It was a ghost town—a fancy-ass ghost town. Asher was nowhere in sight.

Kate's thoughts were still next door. "Those people are in a room like this, right?"

I grunted. "Probably."

Kate's eyes narrowed. "How come I had to lose my son, and they got all this?"

"One of life's shitty mysteries," Jorge answered her

from the hallway. "Nothing over here. But the door to the balcony over here is unlocked."

The door to the balcony on our side was locked, but I still went outside, just in case. The *Maraschino* seesawed back and forth, and I realized that on this higher floor there was greater motion from the sea, which was doing unkind things to my stomach. I didn't want to lean out too far and see the wino next door—although there was a large partition set up between cabins, so that each fancy room's residents would feel like they had their own private view—but I did look over the edge. Nine floors up, the water looked very far down.

"I think we know what happened to them." Jorge swung the open balcony door back and forth behind me. "Bye-bye birdie."

Kate's expression went cold. "Hopefully."

We returned to the hallway where Marius was drawing another *O* on the outside of the room. "Same here," I said, in response to his curious look. Nathaniel and Tan-man were hanging back behind him. Tan-man still looked unhappy, and Nathaniel appeared smug. What was he getting out of this? The pleasure of watching us dance?

"The Solomons," Marius announced, pointing behind us. I realized he'd already said it twice.

I nodded quickly. "Sure."

The Solomons were also absent after knocking, as were the Foxes, the Doltons, the Catos, the Duffields, and the Schmidts. All of their rooms were empty museum-like testaments to capitalism with eerily open balcony doors, as though the occupants had grown wings and flown away. The sixth room had an occupant—but she was dead. Tied to a chair. Someone had had the sense to strap her down but not the time or inclination to do the same for themselves. She was facing an open balcony window.

The person left strapped behind had managed to tilt her chair over into the couch, and she'd asphyxiated on the firm-yet-giving cushions. I pulled her up and saw the teeth marks she'd left in the couch where she'd tried unsuccessfully to gnaw through its leather to escape.

"Who eats couch cushions?" Kate asked aloud.

I frowned, disgusted. "I don't know."

Marius's group was having the same luck across the hall. And every time I saw Nathaniel in passing I wanted to shake him until he poured out answers. We were only halfway done with this hallway, on this one floor, and the cabins up here were twice as large as the ones below. We wouldn't even finish a tenth of the ship before the rescue boat's arrival put an end to our search. My stomach was churning. What if I never found Asher at all?

It was that thought that got me as we were entering yet another empty room. The *Maraschino* was rocked by a large swell, and I covered my mouth with my hand and pushed Kate aside.

In a large marble bathroom, the sound of me retching echoed particularly well. I didn't make it to the toilet, I just leaned over the nearer of the two sinks, clutching its marble sides.

I hadn't eaten anything in who knew how long. Between my jet lag and the clouds catching up with us outside I couldn't tell what time it was, but it'd been a while. The only thing I had left to heave up was bile, and thanks to my worry about Asher, I had plenty of it, bright neon green.

I leaned over, hurled, and waited, and then hurled again. If my own stomach hadn't been empty I wouldn't have seen it—but there in the pit of the sink, before my own bile pushed them down, were several small frothy things, like the beads of tapioca in those gross bubble drinks that other people liked. I leaned down into the sink, trying to see. I'd been so caught up in the act of puking that I wasn't sure whether they had been there before me or come out of my own mouth.

When I looked up, Kate was in the doorway behind me, looking horrified.

"Are you ill?"

"No, I'm pregnant," I said, scanning the countertops. Maybe the former occupants of this room had left some rich-people version of Listerine.

Her frown grew. "I can't believe you're out here endangering your child!"

I swallowed drily. I knew I was taking risks, but I didn't have a choice. If I didn't find Asher I couldn't make things right, and I doubted Nathaniel's plan had left any safe places on this boat. I couldn't explain that to her, though, not when she was mad at me because her own son had died.

"I'm being as safe as I can."

Jorge's voice saved me from trying to explain more. "Hey, ladies? You should come see this now—" I rushed past Kate toward the sound of his voice.

"What is that?" Jorge stood at the edge of the second fancy bathroom in this suite, a finger pointed at the pedestal tub. I looked where he pointed—and I'd never been so glad I'd just puked.

There was a person in the tub, facedown. The jets were still on, making the water froth and the corpse—now that it had been down for longer than anyone could have possibly been holding his breath—jiggle and dance.

"He's dead, right?" Kate asked.

"He'd better be," Jorge said, picking up a decorative vase with a heavy base.

I reached over, took a lily out of the vase, and walked over to the side of the tub. I had to see who it was. Just in case.

I poked the body twice. It floated farther sideways but did not otherwise respond. I angled the stem in so that it slid beneath the person's face, leveraging it toward me. An overly long tongue dangled out, bloated and purple, but as the face turned it retracted, disappearing inside a water-swollen jaw. Not Asher, I realized with full-body relief.

But.

Dead people's tongues didn't disappear. Fall out, maybe. But not move. Especially not after they'd been cooked.

I'd never seen someone boiled alive before, and some function of the fancy jet control was keeping the water piping hot. The musky scent in the air was stewed human, mixed with churning effluvia. There was a greasy film, which provided just enough tension to create bubbles. Still—something about the way that tongue had moved was wrong. Not that I wanted to reach in there and find out, not even with my worst enemy's hand . . . I grit my teeth. Real nurses don't hide—from anything.

"Hang on." I hooked the stem into the man's mouth and used it to keep his head tilted up at me. I dug around, trying to determine if I could even see a tongue. I couldn't, but—I floated his whole body back inside the tub, and intestines were spooled out underneath. Somehow they were wrapped around one of the jets near the floor of the tub. He'd boiled and split open, like an overripe sausage.

"He's clearly dead. Can we go?" Kate said from the doorway.

"Motion to leave, seconded," Jorge said.

There was no point in searching further. It was wrong, but it wasn't Asher—and there were still hundreds of rooms to go. "Sure."

I dropped the lily, and it bobbed inside the tub with the rest of him.

Marius's group was waiting for us in the hall. "Sorry," I said, apologizing for our delay. "There was a dead man floating in a tub."

Tan-man stood a little behind the other two—which was why they didn't see him shaking.

"Oh, my God—" Kate gasped and pointed at him like he was unclean. Nathaniel glanced at him and watched him slide down the closed door beside them both, making no effort to catch him. Marius turned and, seeing the man fall, whirled into action.

"Are you okay?" He went into medic mode, helping Tan-man lie down without hitting his head. "No fever," he announced to the rest of us, gawking above.

It wasn't a seizure, it was just profound shaking, the kind that in the hospital made the monitors scream that your patient was having ventricular fibrilation, *Come defib me!*—when really he was just cold.

Or—I groaned. "How long's it been since you had a drink, sir?"

"A few hours."

The whites of his eyes were subtly yellowed—I hadn't seen it before, I'd been too wrapped up in my own problems. But I bet the rest of him was yellow too, underneath all that fake tanner.

"You're detoxing?" Marius accused him.

"I told you I didn't want to come along! That doctor made me!" the man shouted, from the floor.

No wonder he'd been trying to steal Valium—benzos were among the only things that helped when detox was inevitable.

Marius looked up at me. We both knew the score. The good news was, Tan-man wasn't dying of whatever mysterious ailment was going around. The bad news was, Tan-man would be useless to us here, or more useless than he already had been. "We've gotta get him downstairs," Marius said, leaning forward to indicate that "we" meant me.

I shook my head. Even if finding Asher was statistically impossible at this point. "I don't want to go."

"I'll take him," Kate volunteered.

Marius grabbed the man by the shoulders. "Can you stand?"

"Yeah. Maybe." He let Marius hoist him aloft, and Marius looked at the woman.

"Go straight back the way we came. No detours."

"Sure." She herded the man slowly, him leaning on every passing door, and cast a glance back at me, eyeing my belly. "You should try to be safe."

Easier said than fucking done, but I smiled and waved anyhow.

CHAPTER TWENTY-FOUR

The four of us looked at one another in the hall.

"I believe Edie and I would like to be paired together now," Nathaniel said, gazing coolly at me.

Jorge's face screwed up into a question, but I shook my head so he wouldn't argue. "You're right. I think we would."

"For whatever good it will do," Marius said. "This is a useless goose chase. Everyone's already gone." Which was, in itself, creepy. Marius gathered himself and held the sheet of paper up with all the names. "Fine. You two—the Kontises; we'll take the Morkins."

Marius naming everyone all the time only made it worse. Marius unlocked the door for us and Nathaniel started rapping on it. "Mr. and Mrs. Kontis?" he said archly as we stepped in. No response. He pressed the door open and gestured with his other arm, looking at me. "After you."

I hesitated long enough that he had to know I was thinking too hard. Should I show him my back so he'd know I wasn't scared of him, or not, so he'd know I was? I went with caution, edging down the narrow entry hall, my back to the wall, until we reached the cabin's main living space. I heard the door shut softly behind us.

My back still against a wall, I watched him enter the room. "What's your game?"

"I have no idea what you mean," he said, with a malevolent smile. "I'm flattered by your attention to me, but I've only just become a widower. I'm afraid a year must pass before we can date."

I didn't know how to respond to that. I wished Asher had told me more while he could.

"I'll take this side," Nathaniel said, and went into a darkened room.

We were *supposed* to be searching. But fuck all these other people, I went into the room after him.

My safe time away from supernatural creatures other than Asher had made me soft. I walked into the room, assuming I'd find him in the bathroom, or at the balcony door, but he was waiting just inside for me. He grabbed one of my arms and twisted it up and behind me, making me rock forward on my toes as he caught me around the chest with his other arm and pulled me close, like we were lovers dancing.

"Let us be clear on two things," he whispered, his voice in my ear. "I could kill you before they heard you scream, and I could fling your body over the edge without thinking twice."

"Let go of my arm," I said, trying not sound scared.

He didn't. He hoisted it higher. I grit my teeth not to yelp in pain, eyes watering.

"What did you do with Asher?" I hissed.

"Is that his real name?" he said. I didn't respond. "I suppose next you'll tell me he's not even a doctor?" Nathaniel went on, voice dripping with irony like venom.

"Where is he?" I couldn't turn around, I couldn't even squirm away from his hot breath in my ear.

"Are you really pregnant by him? I'll know if you're lying."

I didn't want to say anything. His grip on my arm tightened and pulled.

It went. It just went. I could feel a tearing and then heard a pop and it was too late, he'd dislocated my arm. I gasped and cursed in a huge rush. "Yes! Yesyesyes!" He still didn't let go. The pain radiated away from my shoulder in waves, like the ocean outside.

"Good," he said, his voice stretching out the word in my ear like a purr.

I started panting in pain and blinking back tears from my eyes. "What are you doing here? What do you want?"

"Revenge. You've heard the saying an eye for an eye? Well, I want a child for a child."

He let me go and shoved me forward with a laugh. My arm flopped down, disconnected from the rest of me. Unwhole, I staggered forward—anything to get away from him.

"Where's Asher?" I fell to my knees and crawled away before he could think to kick me.

"You won't be seeing him again. I'm feeding him to the fishes, one piece at a time." He peered clinically down. "I love how after everything you've seen in the past two days, you're only interested in one man. One would think your nurse's heart would bleed for the rest of the innocent souls that've been lost, and not that monster you were in love with."

Panic started choking my throat. "What have you done with him?" I begged, my voice raw. I held my loose arm to myself, trying to get my back against a wall, where I could kick out at him if he came for me, someplace where I could protect my belly. "Where is he?" I asked, my voice shrill, as we heard the cabin door open.

"If you want to see what's left of him alive, you'll do what I say. Sort yourself out." He straightened his suit by way of example.

"Edie?" Jorge called from the doorway. "You okay?"

"She's in here," Nathaniel said. When Jorge got to the door, he added, "She fell."

Jorge saw me, eyes wide with panic, clutching my drooping arm. "Oh, honey—" and then he looked at Nathaniel and his fists clenched.

I'd let him get the better of me—and worse yet, I'd have to support him in his lie.

"I fell—I fell!" I said before Jorge could do anything. I could feel myself turning red with pain and shame. I lurched up to standing, ungainly with a quarter of my body knocked out. "I'm clumsy sometimes. I tripped and hit the couch wrong. It's gone out before." I held my arm to me tighter. "Please, can you go get Marius?"

Jorge gave Nathaniel a look, and then leaned out of the room to call for Marius without leaving me alone. I would have hugged him, only I couldn't. Marius came in and looked at me with a cluck.

"Dislocated. How did you—" More slowly than Jorge, he put together two and two.

"I fell," I repeated as Nathaniel nodded, to encourage me. "It happens sometimes. Can you fix me?"

Marius frowned at us both. But at least Marius's medical service had given him enough experience in what to do. He shook a pillow on the bed out of its pillowcase, and cut it with a utility knife to fashion it into a sling. "You know I have to pop it back in now, don't you?"

"Yeah." I nodded and looked away.

Marius took my dangling arm at a ninety-degree angle, twisted it out, and pushed it in, like a kid forcing together unmatched Legos. It didn't take the first time—it took all my strength not to scream in agony. I didn't want to give Nathaniel that too.

The second time it slid home, bone grinding over bone, and it was impossible not to cry out in a combination of pain and relief. Marius wrapped the pillowcase around me, folding my newly reattached arm in across my chest. And over Marius's shoulder, I could see Nathaniel's eyes glittering with amusement at what he'd done. He put his arm across his stomach in mocking imitation of me, the sling forcing me to hold my own stomach.

Jorge kept himself between me and Nathaniel in the hall. "Say the word—" he muttered, and I shook my head.

"It's okay. It's fine."

Jorge looked like he was going to argue with me, but the radio at Marius's waist turned on and piped in Raluca's voice. "How is it going up there?"

Marius unhooked it and brought it to his mouth. "We haven't found anyone sick yet."

"Come down and triage with us then—the rescue ship just radioed, it's near."

Marius looked relieved. He wasn't going to call our "mission" off, but we all knew it hadn't been fruitful. "We'll be there soon." He unclicked the radio and looked at all of us. "Unless anyone here has any objections."

I shook my head and looked away. Jorge shrugged, and I didn't know how Nathaniel responded.

"All right then. Back the way we came." He made a gesture for us all to turn around.

I hung back, and Jorge hung with me. "I mean it," he muttered.

"No. But thank you." My good hand found his and squeezed it, and he squeezed back. We reached the freight elevator we'd first taken up to this floor, and its door slid open—revealing a woman in a room service outfit crouching inside, eating the contents of a tray like a wild animal. Our presence startled her, and she loped past us and down the hall like a startled rabbit. None of us said anything or went after her.

CHAPTER TWENTY-FIVE

Jorge and I lagged behind the other two when we reached the third floor—I was trying to seem meek, and he was being supportive. "You should say something," he whispered to me.

"And what? They'll put him in ship jail?" I would have shrugged, but it would hurt. Plus, Nathaniel still had answers I wanted. Like where Asher was.

Being fed to fishes.

Which isn't the same as already dead—but it's definitely not good. And how did he know that Asher was a "monster"? Maybe Asher had told him about their shared past in an effort to get him to come clean. But then what had happened to him?

After my run-in, it was too easy for me to imagine Asher going the same way. I might not be the only one seven months of safety had made soft.

The only thing I was sure of now was that what Asher had told me was truth. Nathaniel was responsible for whatever was going on here, but I had no way to make him tell me, and I was scared to be alone with him again.

"Are you sure you're okay?" Jorge pressed.

No. Not in the least. But ahead of us, Marius was using the hand sanitizer station, and Nathaniel was determinedly stalking off on his own past the restaurant's entrance entirely. I ran to catch up to Marius and hold him back from going into the Dolphin. "Marius—give me the master key. Please."

He tsked. "It's no use. The ships will be full with the patients we have already. Those who didn't make it downstairs will have to wait for the next round."

"They're not going to make it. Don't you see? This isn't anything normal! This whole ship has been infected somehow—" I looked over my shoulder to make sure that Nathaniel was gone. I couldn't see him in the hall anymore, but I didn't know where he'd run off too, so I lowered my voice as I pleaded. "Someone did this on purpose. They're testing things on us. I've got to find my boyfriend—"

"Testing things?" Marius repeated. It'd been the wrong thing to say. I could see his eyes glaze over in the way I knew mine did every time a patient at work told me the CIA had put a radio transmitter in their head.

"What else explains it?" I tried, realizing as I said it that it only made me sound more mad.

Marius shook his head and sliced both his hands through the air. "I cannot take any more crazy talk!"

"But it's true—"

"No!" he interrupted. We were right in front of the Dolphin's entrance. He straightened his shoulders, and it was clear he was scraping the last of his cruise-ship-employee diplomacy from the bottom of its barrel. "If you'll both excuse me," he said, including Jorge and I, "I have an actual job to do. Raluca needs me." He turned and then disappeared inside, leaving Jorge and me alone in the wide hallway with the Dolphin's wafting smell. It hadn't gotten better in the meantime.

Jorge gave me a side eye. "That . . . is not the direction I thought you were going to go with that."

"Me either."

"Is it true?"

I nodded. "I can't prove it, but it is. And that other man—Nathaniel—he's in on it. And he knows that I know. It's why he tried to pop my arm off like a Barbie-doll head."

"How did you find out?"

I had no idea how to explain. I gave him a wan smile. "Would you believe I'm psychic?"

Jorge snorted. "I'd believe anything for a shot of whiskey right about now."

Raluca's megaphone came on inside the Dolphin. I couldn't hear what she was saying, but she was giving orders. "She'll need our help to get everyone on the rescue ship."

His eyebrows rose. "Call me back when it's called a cure ship."

Jorge was right. What would the rescue ship be able to do for the dying people anyhow? What was the cure for people who wanted to drink so badly that they'd throw themselves overboard or drown in tubs? What a cruel place they'd inadvertently chosen for their sickroom, with water painted on every wall. Dolphins, indeed. I snorted, and for the first time in my life I wished I was a doctor—not that the cruise ship doctor had seemed to be having much luck.

Why was Nathaniel here among us—just to watch? He'd let his own kid and wife die. What kind of man could do such a thing?

A man who'd known all along he wasn't going to get sick.

He'd been here with us, exposed to all the same environmental factors. He must have access to some sort of cure.

Jorge and I walked into the Dolphin's entrance partition. The doctor had abandoned his post, probably to help Raluca, but there were still printouts scattered across his makeshift desk all marked up like homework.

"I'll be there in a second," I told Jorge, and gestured to my slinged arm. I wasn't going to be good for lifting anyone anyhow.

Jorge made a face but let me be. Once he'd left the doorway, I started rifling through piles of paperwork. What was it Asher had said Nathaniel's last name was? Tannin? Some of the sheets were sorted by restaurants eaten and at what times—but one sheaf was alphabetical. I furiously flipped through these until I got to the *T*'s, and as I did so I heard a rustling beyond the curtain. I grabbed the papers five-deep so I'd be sure I got them all, and shoved them into my sling. Dr. Haddad appeared, looking gray.

"Did you figure anything out?" I asked him, so I looked like I had a reason to stay behind.

"I tried. I sorted by restaurant, by dining time, by hometown, by recent travel, by airlines, but I couldn't find any commonalities—other than everyone affected being here." He sat down in his chair and breathed like someone with heart failure, his lungs searching for, but not finding, enough air.

"You don't look well."

"That's no concern of yours."

Outside of the curtain's Raluca's megaphoned voice was getting quieter as it moved farther away. "You should get on the rescue ship—"

"Just as captains go down with the ship, doctors should go down with their sickrooms." He stirred the papers in front of him restlessly, seemingly more out of habit than need.

I prepared to back out of the room to inspect the papers I'd swiped, but then I paused. "Where . . . is the captain?"

"Isolated above. All the officers are quarantined off by floor—the ones upstairs are taking shifts manning the ship."

"You're sure?"

"They're still on the radio with me. Luckily when the quarantine went in place, we had a good crew."

"And all of them are still well? None of them is sick?"

"Not last time I radioed, no. What are you getting at?" He didn't sound angry, just exasperated and tired, and took another wet-sounding breath.

I shook my head. I didn't know, yet. But the utter destruction of an entire ship full of people was a tall order for any single man. Nathaniel must have had help, and it made sense for that help to be on the inside. And if Asher was right, he'd held the right patents to afford it.

Dr. Haddad didn't notice my distraction; he was too busy staring off behind me. I turned to see what he was looking at, and saw where the curtains had parted and a slice of the ocean was visible through the window outside. Shit. Him too. I stepped in front of the window, blocking his view, and knelt down to be in his field of vision. "I'm sorry, I lied to you earlier. I am pregnant, and I cannot have this baby alone. I need to find my husband. Do you have another master key?"

His eyes focused on me slowly. "I gave my last one to Raluca."

"Where's Raluca going now?"

"First floor. Where the tender boats dock."

"Which side of the ship? How can I get there?"

"The freight elevator and down. It'll be aft."

Which the fuck way was aft? "Down by the morgue?" I guessed.

"Yes." He tilted his head so that he could see past me to the window.

I knew what was coming for him, and I knew I didn't know how to help. Should I do what he'd done to the others and tie him to the table bodily, or should I just leash him by his foot?

"Before you go, can you get me a glass of water?" he asked.

"I'm sorry—" I stepped away from him. "I've got to go." If Raluca got on the medical ship, I'd lose my chance to snag her key. I closed the curtain so he couldn't see out anymore. It felt like the only thing I could do. Then I ran into the Dolphin to follow the volunteers down.

CHAPTER TWENTY-SIX

Every jogging step jostled my arm in its socket, and the manifest papers I'd swiped and hidden chafed. The wait on the elevator seemed interminable. I paced in circles trying to figure out how I'd get Raluca—or Marius, as a distant runner-up—to give me a key. I couldn't exactly go and get into a fistfight with anyone in my current state.

The freight elevator doors opened, and I jogged down the hallway to the morgue—I knew I was going the right way from all the flower petals people moving bodies had tracked back to the elevator doorway. If I went past the morgue, hopefully I'd run into them—there was no way transferring so many people over would be a quick process.

The sound of gunfire stopped me in my tracks.

I wanted to pretend I hadn't heard it. I paused, trying to convince myself that it'd been some weird engine noise—but no, another staccato burst and panicked shouting, coming my way—fast.

Without thinking, I ducked into the morgue. Who would look for survivors in here? And maybe I could get some answers. I tapped the nearest body with my shoe.

"Shadows—what's happening?"

The body didn't answer me.

"I know you're in there." The sound of screaming

stopped, but the gunfire didn't. I looked furtively at the doors, and they burst open. I bit back a scream and dropped to the floor, before I saw that it was Rory.

"You!" he said, recognizing me.

"What's going on out there?"

He looked around the room, realizing where he was, and he froze, as still as all the other occupants. "Rory—get away from the window." When he didn't move, I ran for him and pulled him aside. "What's happening?"

He blinked and shook his head and didn't stop shaking it while he talked. "Why did I come here? Did I want to die with them?"

I realized his parents were in here. "No." I grabbed his nearer shoulder with my good hand and looked frantically around the room. "Shadows—" It was too bright in here with the lights on but I knew there were pools of darkness inside each half-opened mouth. The sound of gunfire was getting closer. "I know you can hear me. Can you hide us from this?"

I didn't see which corpse they were speaking from this time, but I heard their voice, gravelly and low. "Turn off the light and cover yourself."

With the nearing gunfire, there wasn't much time. I grabbed up a sheet from the ground, stained with frozen everything, put Rory in the corner of the room where I could find him, and put the sheet around his shoulders like a cape. Then I raced back to swat the light switch down, and ran as carefully as I could in the dark back to his side. I pulled the sheet up over both us, like we were children hiding from monsters beneath our own bed.

There came the sound of scrabbling on the outside of the sheet, and then a weight pressing down around us, like when my cat Minnie joined me on the bed at night—if Minnie had had a hundred more legs and they all ended in claws.

"Not him, not him, just you," the Shadows said.

"Kick him out," a voice suggested.

"Let him die," said another one.

"What?" Rory said. I clapped a hand over his mouth, and wrapped my slinged arm around him.

"Stop scaring him!" I hissed. "Haven't you fed enough?"

"Never," they whispered back.

Rory started to wrestle me, and whapped his head back, catching me in the eye. I let him go involuntarily. "What the—" he began.

"Stop it! They can't hurt you!" It was a total lie, but the guns were getting closer, and it was too easy to imagine each short burst extinguishing a life. "Just calm down!"

The thing atop the sheet curled up on us like an icy snake, and Rory's breathing sounded like a runaway train in my ear. "Hold your breath," I whispered just as the doors to the morgue swung open. I could see a flashlight beam swirl around the room.

I'm not sure what the Shadows showed instead of us, but it worked—either that, or whoever held the flashlight didn't want to spend long in a room where the occupants were clearly dead.

"Clear!" said an unfamiliar male voice. The light from the hallway and the flashlight beam disappeared, and the sound of tromping continued on outside. The weight on top of us scrabbled off, melting away, and Rory and I were alone in the dark.

"What was that?" Rory whispered, his voice breaking in panic.

"I'll explain in a bit, but I need to know what's going on first. What happened with the rescue ship?"

"C—can we turn on the light?"

"That's probably not wise," answered the Shadows from beneath us.

"Shush. Please. Although thank you," I told them, and

then snapped my fingers for attention in front of Rory, even though I couldn't see his face in the dark. "What went on?"

"They—they—" it took him a moment to get himself under control, but then the words poured out like water. "The rescue ship sent a smaller boat over, and we opened the doors up for it to dock—and some of the people started trying to throw themselves overboard. Even the weak ones still wanted to get into the water. We tried to hold them back, but we couldn't. They were too strong. One fell in, and we put a spotlight on him, but we couldn't pull him out—he was too far away. And then this thing, I swear I saw this thing crawl out of his mouth, like a giant worm. The size of my arm." He grabbed hold of me in the dark for strength. "I don't have one of those inside of me, do I?"

"Of course not," I said—although I didn't know for sure. "Where did the people with guns come from?"

"The medical boat. When their transfer boat docked, twenty men got off with guns. They were never here to help us, were they," he said, not actually asking a question. "Is that what happened to my parents? Worms?" His voice broke at the thought.

I couldn't lie to him twice. "I honestly don't know, Rory." There wasn't any time to comfort him, so I just pressed on. "Where's Raluca?"

"She got shot."

"Where?"

"I don't know. I just saw her fall down."

I had to grit my teeth to stop from groaning, and I spoke more slowly. "Focus, Rory. Where'd she fall?"

"Back by the boats. I was a faster runner." I heard him swallow in the dark. "I just left her behind."

"It's okay. Anyone would have done the same in your shoes."

"I got scared," he explained.

"It happens. I know." All the video games I'd imagined he'd played, all those times he'd seen people die on screen, but the real thing was something else. It always was. "Where's Marius?" I asked gently.

"He ran off. I think he got away. I think. I'm not sure."

The darkness hid my frown. "Shadows—is it safe to go out in the hall?"

Their piecemeal voices spoke in eerie synchronicity. "Nowhere on this boat is safe anymore, not even for us. It rises now. He's calling it, and it comes. It will eat all of us, dead or alive—"

"Shadows!" I reprimanded. I was already scared enough; I didn't need to hear any more Vincent Price bullshit from them. "Are you helping us or not?"

They didn't answer me. "Goddammit—if you brought me here the least you could do is help!" I stood and pulled the sheet off us. "Rory, I've got to go back out there. I need a key that Raluca has—"

"Why?" He gathered the sheet up to his chest, as if it would still hide him.

"Because I'm still searching for my friend. And because we can't stay here. We'll wind up like they did." I pointed at the corpse crowd. Now that we were out from underneath the sheet, the windows set into the doors let in some ambient light, enough to see the feet of the first row.

"He can stay here. If he leaves the light off," said the Shadows from somewhere in the dark.

"I'm coming with you." He dropped the sheet and practically ran for the door.

CHAPTER TWENTY-SEVEN

We looked both ways in the hall, and then trotted back the way he'd come. I didn't know what I'd do if we heard or saw anyone—we weren't armed—but luckily no one met us. We opened the last set of doors, out to the tender dock. It was a wide room with garage-like doors that opened out to the sea. Emergency lighting illuminated bodies, and waves from the storm outside grasped like hands, slapping and spraying, reaching in and then sloshing back out. I was about to run across when Rory grabbed my bad shoulder.

"Fuck," I hissed.

"Hang on. If they're military, they might have thermal imaging."

The kid had a point. And way to get his head back in the game. But his hand on me was still like ice from our time in the freezer.

"Where do you think Raluca fell?"

"Over there, I think." He pointed across the berth. If she was still there, if the ocean hadn't pulled her out.

"I'll go. Just—here." I handed him the papers I'd stolen from Dr. Haddad that I still hadn't gotten a chance to look at yet. "Find Nathaniel Tannin's room number for me." I crouched and crept toward where he'd pointed.

I couldn't imagine two boats managing to stay close to

each other with all these waves. I'd probably find out if they had thermal imaging just a second after I got sniped. I snorted, and stayed low, hoping that the spray of water, the fog from outside, and the residual chill from the morgue would hide me—or that no one was even looking in the first place.

The standing water that had gotten trapped inside and the rocking of the waves gave the floating bodies a mockery of life, making them look like they were restless and still breathing. Unlucky helpers, and the sick who'd been queued up for transport outside—the rescue boat must have always been a sham. Nathaniel knew that, as did the officers who were keeping the *Maraschino* hidden by the storm, communications cut—none of the people in here had ever had a chance.

I found Raluca. Machine-gun fire at close range had practically sawed her in two, opening her up like a massive shark-bite. Her radio was still in an outstretched hand. I took it from her and tucked it inside my sling. And then I realized with revulsion that I'd have to stick my good hand into the carnage of her lower half and into her pockets to search for the master key.

That key felt like the only way I'd find Asher. Only my determination to not go through the rest of this alone—the next eighteen years or the next five fucking minutes—made me plunge my hand in, almost blind.

I felt things inside her quivering.

Guts didn't quiver—although whatever I was feeling made mine shake. Bile rose, and only a more profound revulsion about possibly puking into a corpse stopped me from throwing up again.

Raluca was definitely dead. There was no way any part of her had survived. She was practically torn in two. And yet something inside her that wasn't a heart was moving, thrashing around in slowing circles like a lizard's dropped tail. I saw the end of it, dark and leathery.

Rory hadn't been lying. The worms were real.

Had they attacked her after she fell? Or were they inside her all along? I didn't want to know. I found her denim waistband with my fingers and tried not to look as shoved my hand in.

It took me two pockets to find and pull out a keycard drenched in gore. And just in case it was hers and not the master key, I kept going on the other side. It was just as well—there was no way I would ever talk myself into doing this again.

I held the keycard out, damp with blood and worse, and I wanted to run to the open door and wash my hands in the sea. It wasn't safe—and I stopped to wonder if *it*, whatever *it* was, had me. I waited half a second. I wasn't thirsty. My attraction to the water was just me wanting to get clean. Right? I stepped away from her body and found a puddle, one that was seawater and not blood, and tried to rinse my hand and the key off.

I looked back. I couldn't see what I'd felt move inside Raluca anymore. And the thought that maybe it had ditched her and was out here somewhere with me . . . not worrying about snipers, I ran back to meet Rory at the door.

"Did you find it?"

"Yeah."

"Is she dead?" Rory asked, with a mixture of denial and hope.

"Oh, yeah." His expression fell. "Sorry." At least I hadn't told him that I could have worn her colon like a glove. "Did she seem well when you all came down here?"

"Yeah. Why?"

I shook my head. "Nothing."

If the medical ship had never been a rescue ship, why

was it here now? Why were they shooting people? The first and most plausible reason for that was that they didn't want any survivors. The second was that whatever we'd gotten exposed to, they couldn't let back out.

"He's in room eight twenty-two," Rory said, and handed my papers back to me. "Should we go try out your key?"

The emergency lights were just bright enough for me to see the tracks of fresh tears on his cheeks. Everything he'd been through—it wasn't fair. I needed to find Asher, but I also had to live with myself afterward.

"Yeah. But we have to make one more stop first."

We listened—the people canvassing the ship would have no reason to hide themselves, seeing as they were probably covered in body armor. I assumed they would be coming up through the ship slowly—possibly even going down belowdecks to finish the crew off first. I knew from experience that a clearing a cruise ship room-to-room would take a long time.

Rory and I reached the staff elevators, but instead of pressing 8, I hit the 6. Rory gave me a questioning look but didn't say anything.

He followed me as I got my bearings and we jogged down the hall. There was no point in going to my empty room—I knocked on the room next door instead.

The door shifted as someone inside leaned against it to look out, and I relaxed—they hadn't both gone over the balcony at least. I heard the latch go, and Hal opened up the door. "You're back! What happened to you? You look like hell."

"Things aren't good." I pulled Rory inside behind me and quietly closed the door. "There was supposed to be a medical rescue ship for the sickest patients. Instead men with guns got off it and started killing people."

Hal's face turned steely—his hearing aids must have been in.

"Why?" Claire asked. She was turning her wheelchair around to face us.

"We don't know. I wasn't there, and I don't think they took the time to explain themselves to Rory." I nodded at the boy, by way of introduction. "This is Hal, and Claire—" I looked around as an afterthought. "Where's Emily?"

"She wanted to take a bath," Claire said.

Rory and I both blanched. "No. No no no—" I turned away from Claire and started beating at the bathroom door. "Emily? Emily—you need to come out here right now—"

There was no answer. "What's going on?" Claire demanded.

"Emily?" I beat on the door harder. "Emily, get out here!"

The bathroom door's lock unlatched and a bedraggled Emily opened the door. Unbraided, her wet hair was past her waist. She was covered up with a towel, and her glasses were covered in fog. She peered out and spotted me and her face brightened. "Did you find my daddy?"

I exhaled in a rush. "No. Sorry, but no."

"What happened to your face?" she asked next.

My cheekbone hurt where Rory's thrashing had hit it. "I gave you a black eye. Sorry," he explained. I shrugged, and hissed at accidentally moving my bad shoulder.

"Explain what all this is about," Hal said, trying to take charge.

"I can't. There's no time." They deserved answers—and I still needed to explain what had happened in the morgue to Rory—but I had to get to the eighth floor before the gunmen did, just in case Asher was there. "My plan is that I take this master key and go upstairs to try to find my boyfriend. I wanted to warn you all about what was going on, but—" I put a hand to my stomach. "I have to try to find Asher still. He's not dead. He can't be."

"And just where do you suggest we all go?" Claire asked archly.

"The third deck is where the lifeboats are. Maybe if you get into them and hide inside—" I suggested, the taste of my own lies thick in my mouth.

"Is your man higher or lower?" Hal interrupted.

"Eight twenty-two," Rory said.

"Then we'll go there, with you," Claire said, as though that were a reasonable request.

I started shaking my head. "I'm not sure what we'll find there. Maybe nothing—or maybe more people with guns."

Claire snapped her fingers at the young girl. "Emily, grab your clothes, go put them on fast, please,"

"This isn't what—" I protested.

"We're going. You've already left us behind once. We won't let that happen again," Hal said with finality, agreeing with his wife.

"I don't mean to be horrible," I said, while knowing fully that I did, "but I have no idea how we'll manage to take along someone in a wheelchair."

Claire gave me a dangerous smile. "Who said I'd be going in that?"

CHAPTER TWENTY-EIGHT

We were the most motley crew I had ever been a part of. Me, one elderly man carrying his thin elderly wife piggyback, a freaked-out teenager, and a wisely scared kid. Going where? Up to the room I hoped my boyfriend and baby-daddy was being held hostage in. Yee-fucking-haw.

Before we'd left the room, Hal had commandeered the radio and flipped through all the stations like someone familiar with the task. The medical station was silent now, which made sense since Dr. Haddad and Raluca were gone—and most of the other stations were people shouting in languages we couldn't understand.

"We should probably hurry," Hal had said.

"When we get there, I'm going in with you," Rory told me.

I frowned at him. "Why?" His kind of brave was the kind you got from shooting people on a screen, with a respawn point.

He cast a glance full of aspersions at the others and shrugged one shoulder. "I don't want to be left out."

Maybe even video game players had pride. "Fair enough."

We crept up to the eighth floor quietly, using the freight elevator at the end of the hall. At least it wouldn't announce to anyone else what floor we were getting off on. I knew if we met anyone with a gun we'd just get mowed down where we stood, torn in two like Raluca. Hal couldn't run while carrying Claire, and Emily's legs were little. She was trotting along like Whisper the pony, holding the elastics of the mask I'd given her like reins. Like so much else I'd already been through today, it was too awful to really think about. Like what would happen if we did get up to Nathaniel's room and Asher was gone. The dead kind of gone.

We walked down the hall as the numbers rose, and when we neared 822 Hal put his hand out for the key. I shook my head. I wasn't going to let him go in first, especially not with Claire clinging to his back. I waved my hand so that everyone else would press against the wall to one side, and then I crouched down so that I wouldn't get shot if the person inside the room was shooting at chest height.

The sound of the lock would give whoever was in there the upper hand. I reached out, slid the key through the sensor, saw the green light, and waited for the sound of shouting or shooting. When nothing responded, I reached up and pulled the lever of the door down and quietly opened the door.

I was almost disappointed. If there was no one guarding in here, then there was nothing left to guard. These rooms weren't all that different from the ones on the ninth floor—the only difference was the ceiling height. I took off a shoe to keep the door from closing behind me, not so that those in the hall could come in and rescue me, but so that I could quickly run out, and then crept in. I crawled like a monkey holding a piece of fruit to my chest, with my two feet and one good hand. Rory followed me, with slightly more grace.

The first bedroom was full of kid things. Diaper bags, diapers, scattered toys—at least I was in the right place. Rory inhaled to say something and I shook my head before he could speak. Even though it looked abandoned, I still didn't feel safe. I stood, though, and peeked into the attached bathroom. There was a woman's makeup bag on the countertop, presumably Liz's, and oddly unlabeled bottles of pills. I picked one up; it was nearly empty. Whatever was in there hadn't saved her.

I ducked through the living area, empty, Rory silently behind me, and we walked toward the darkened bedroom on the other side.

I caught a whiff of Nathaniel's aftershave, and it stopped me cold. I flung out my good arm to press Rory back. In the silence that followed, I could hear my own heart.

"I think we're alone," he whispered.

I shook my head. I needed to be certain. I was scared. It'd been so long since I'd been scared I'd forgotten that this was how it felt, like something was gnawing a hole in my belly. Like a baby . . . or a horrible worm.

At that thought, I grit my teeth and took a step in, letting my eyes adjust to the dark.

The walls were covered up, papered over, including the balcony's windowed door. After ten more seconds of silence, I turned on the light.

The images on the papers resolved after that. All the bizarre sea monsters that any fevered sailor's imagination had ever thought up were on display, meticulously illustrated. From old "Here There Be Dragons" sketches, complete with tails, to darker and more menacing void-spaced ones, images defined by darkness and absence that hurt to look at until you looked away—and then you were forced to wonder what they were doing without your eyes keeping them pinned.

And so many maps. Scattered on the bed, the desk, the floor, on paper crisped with age, edges drawn by hand with ink that looked frighteningly like blood, and a handful of more recent ones with radiating depths indicated by progressive shades of blue, like pools spread out on the floor.

"Whoa," Rory said, and I didn't shush him. It was good to hear his voice here, to not be in this place alone.

"Yeah," I whispered back, agreeing.

"What the hell is wrong with this guy?"

I shoved a map away with my foot so that I could step on carpeting instead. "I don't know." And with all this crazy on display, I might never figure it out.

Rory looked around the room again, then to me. "I'll check the bathroom."

I realized what he was doing half a second too late—trying to save me from seeing another corpse. I raised my hand to protest, then stopped. If I'd had any doubts about Nathaniel's ability to sacrifice his own child, this room quenched it. If this was what the Shadows were afraid of—well, I understood. A little. And it forced me to confront a darker truth.

A man who was insane enough to create a room like this would have no problems with killing Asher and then lying to me.

"Rory?" I called out, my voice a question.

"It's empty in here." He reappeared in the doorway.

"For real?" I didn't want to go in there; it would smell more like Nathaniel—

"Honest. I'm sorry. I think." He did his one-shoulder-shrug thing again. "I'm not sure if that's worse or better."

"Neither am I." I stepped closer to one of the walls. Not all of this ink was dry. Not all of this ink was even ink. I dabbed a finger though a map on the bed and left a dark red smear behind, taking out the corner of what could have been a continent . . . or, if I squinted right, a horrible leering face. My stomach turned again as I looked at the stain the blood had left on my hand. I would have put it to my mouth to hold my nausea back, but that would make me more likely to throw up. "I'm sorry—" I rushed into the bathroom where he'd just been.

"Take your time!" he called after me.

It did smell like Nathaniel in here. His things, razor, toothbrush, were neatly organized, laid out on a towel. Nothing strange in here, not like the crypt-keeper vault his bedroom was. In here, if I couldn't see the blood on my hands, I could have pretended that housekeeping was on its way soon, with fresh towels. I turned the cold water on and massaged a bar of soap single-handedly, staining it pink. Whose blood was it? Whose?

When I was mostly sure all the blood was gone, I looked up at myself in the mirror, slinged and exhausted. I'd been pushing myself for two days—there wasn't much of me left to go. The *Maraschino* took another sudden turn—away from the "rescue" ship, or toward it?—and my stomach lurched again. That was good, right? It meant that things were okay in there? Or . . . that I was infested, like Raluca had been. One of those two. I looked at myself in the mirror, trying to see the truth.

"Let's go," Rory prompted, his voice farther away. I pushed back from the bathroom counter and looked back into the bedroom, where he stood at the entrance to the doorway at the far side. "I didn't want to wait in there."

"I don't blame you." The bedroom was like a cave, a shrine to one man's insanity, the man who was currently taking the whole ship down. After this, I didn't know if we'd be able to stop him. If I'd been able to find Asher, maybe, there would have been a chance. But not on my own, not now.

All I felt was exhaustion . . . and hate. Hate that I'd had to go through all of this, hate that Asher wasn't here, and above all else hate at my helplessness. Nathaniel had all the power, all the cards, all the guns. I wanted to strike back at him, and I couldn't. I'd burn this place if I could— and I remembered a room that Anna'd wanted to burn, what seemed like ages ago. Maybe this was how she'd felt.

I ran into the room and reached for the highest point I could and clawed my fingers down. My nails caught on staples, yanking vellum and smearing charcoal, tearing strips away.

"Edie—" Rory warned.

"No!" I shouted at him. I needed this. I didn't care that it was a waste of time, it was a small act of rebellion, and I needed it. I raked my fingers through another stack, ripping a horrible face in two, giving it a reason to scream just as it was painted. More ink-blood stuck to my hand and I wiped it on the bedspread, like a murder scene, before starting on the next wall. My nail polished chipped off, bits of red scattering like scabs, and I didn't stop. I would tear this place down, ruin this one thing that was his just as he'd ruined me and mine. I had had a future. For one bright moment, I'd had a husband, a child, a family, perfection. Nathaniel had taken all of that away.

I ran for the balcony window, the last wall, and found the pictures were pasted to the glass. I ripped pieces off in long tears that made it look like I was an animal, clawing to get out of a cage, one strip at a time, as much as the fingers of my one good hand could free. After I'd ruined that I would throw everything Nathaniel owned into the sea, all of it—destroying even some small part of him like he'd destroyed me. I lunged up and grabbed a fistful of his ramblings from where I'd already started a tear and ripped it sideways like I was opening up a door—when I saw a figure, tied to the railing outside.

What had been crazed became frantic. "Rory—help me!"

Arms picked me up and pulled me back. "You can't go to the sea—"

"He's out there!" I fought back, my shoulder burning as I moved. I twisted and found Hal holding me, looking down at me with worried eyes. "I saw him, Asher's out there!"

Hal released me warily. "Stay here." He leaned forward, keeping himself between me and the balcony, in case I might run for it, and peered through a tear. "There is a man out there—"

"It's him!" I rushed forward and leapt up to grab another map away. "He's out there!"

Rory frowned, but joined in when Hal did. We unwrapped the window like a present until we found the door's latch. Pulling together, we managed to slide it open over the remnants of the maps, and their crinkled pieces held it there.

A gust of wet air, trapped between rain and mist, blew in and swept all the papers I'd torn aside like leaves. Asher faced out like an oceanic scarecrow. The suit I'd seen him leave in was in shreds, and he leaned over the railings like he might topple—he would have, were he not tied to the railings at both his hands and feet.

"Asher?" I reached out for him to try to pull him back. His skin was cold and clammy. I instinctively ran my hand up his throat to feel for his pulse. It was present, but slow.

"This could just be a diversion," Rory warned.

"Give her time," said Hal.

I pulled him back as far as I could. His wrists were raw where the ties had chafed, and there was a dressing over his left hand, some wound covered up with a bloody towel. "What did he do to you?" I tried to hold him awkwardly from the side to take the pressure off him. "Get me something that can cut him free. Hurry!"

While they searched Nathaniel's room, I stroked wet hair back from Asher's face. Left alone, he'd changed back into himself. "Please be okay." I kept petting him, trying to hold him up. The *Maraschino* tilted again, caught by a tall wave, and he started to slip through my arms. "Please please please be okay. I can't do all this without you. I love you. Please be okay." I held him so tight my bad shoulder ached and my good one might pop.

Hal's strong arms caught up Asher from me, and Rory began sawing away at the ties with a room service steak knife. Even though I was almost in the way, I wouldn't move, I needed to be there for when he woke up, so he could see me and know that things were going to be fine. Rory made it through one wrist tie, and Asher's arm hung limply free. "Honey, wake up. Be okay."

He shifted. From the Asher that I and others knew to Hector, the doctor I worked with. His skin went from white to tan, and his features changed, cheekbones suddenly malleable, sliding into place.

"What the fuck?" Rory said, and Hal let him drop a few inches in surprise.

"It's okay!" I looked to Rory. "Keep cutting. Please!"

Rory looked from me to Hal, and at an unseen signal kept going, although at a slower pace.

"Asher—it's me. You're safe now."

His eyes fluttered open and he held up his injured hand weakly. *"¿Dónde está?"*

I knew enough Spanish by now to know he was asking where Nathaniel was. "I don't know."

He took in his own condition, legs still lashed, and then looked at me. "Hurry."

CHAPTER TWENTY-NINE

I clung to him to offer him whatever protection from the weather I could. His free hand wrapped around me, bound up with dried blood. "Are you okay?" I whispered, pressed awkwardly against his chest, half hugging him and half hugging Hal.

"I will be. Are you?"

I nodded. Everything was going to be all right now. Somehow we'd all manage to get off this damn boat. He staggered backward, a foot set free, and pulled me close. I felt his lips brush against my hair. "I thought you were gone."

"Me too." It was raining in earnest now, which was good, because it hid my tears.

He shook his head, his chin rubbing against me. "I'll never leave you again." Rory finished sawing and set Asher loose. He wisely waited to change back until then, as Rory still held the knife at the ready. "I know I have a lot to explain," Asher said, taking all of our group in.

Hal jerked a thumb toward the room behind us. "Let's do it indoors."

Asher leaned on me as we went inside. The rest of the room was still there, in all its strange glory, and Claire was sitting on the bed with Emily nearby. I felt Asher groan at the sight of them.

"It's going to be okay," I said, to him, to me, to everyone. I didn't even care if it was a lie. It was all I could do to stop from petting Asher, just to feel him whole beneath my hands, present, there. Maybe the pregnancy hormones were finally running wild, I didn't know, I just couldn't stop crying.

He pulled me into him. "It really is. We're going to be fine."

I nodded into his chest, blind. It was awkward and I didn't care—but after a time I did, and turned around, looking out at the rest of the group, still plastered to Asher's side. If I kept ahold of him, he couldn't ever leave me again.

"Was the room like this when you got here?" Claire asked, after pointing at the destruction I'd left on the floor.

I shook my head. "No. I went a little crazy."

She snorted. "Good for you."

Asher stood straighter, stroking my wet hair, addressing everyone. "We need to get out of here."

"Not before you tell us what you are—" Rory said.

"No, he's right. It's not safe here." Claire gestured for Hal to come and retrieve her. It occurred to me that Hal was a very patient man. "You still have the master key, right?" she asked, looking to me. I nodded. "Then let's discuss this somewhere down the hall. Or on another floor entirely."

Asher grunted. "Hang on." He planted me, and disappeared into Nathaniel's bathroom, then returned. "Okay. Let's go."

By the shaky logic that the gunmen would be rising up going door-to-door, we agreed that getting a floor higher would buy us the most theoretical time. I walked by Asher's side, and I reached for his injured hand as we headed toward the elevator at the end of the hall. The towel-dressing was occupying the space of two digits—he wouldn't be able to wear a wedding ring now even if he'd wanted one. "Why this?"

"He wanted to see if they'd regrow."

That was so awful I stopped walking. "Why more than one?"

"So people would know it was me, not him, if I changed again."

"Oh." I realized if we made it back from this, "Hector" would have to explain two newly missing fingers at work. Despite Asher's being a shapeshifter, Nathaniel had effectively marked him for life. He wasn't a salamander, he couldn't regrow lost limbs.

"He's nothing if not thorough." Asher shook his head and pressed me to him tighter. I bit back a squeak as my shoulder bent a direction it shouldn't. "What's happening to the rest of the ship?" he whispered in my ear.

"The rescue ship brought gunmen over instead of aid. They're tearing through the ship right now, shooting whoever's still alive. I don't suppose you've got an entomologist inside you somewhere?"

"Never had the pleasure of meeting one."

"That's a shame then, because it turns out there's weird worms inside a bunch of people, making them eat everything and then fling themselves overboard."

Asher's nearness slowed our pace. We were already at the back of the group, afforded some privacy for our reunion, although Rory was casting back anxious looks. Claire was hitched up on Hal's back, and Hal had a gentle hand on Emily's shoulder, herding her forward.

"Edie . . . ," Asher said, his voice low in my ear, and then tilted his head at everyone ahead of us.

I didn't need to look into his eyes to know he'd done the math. There was no way we'd manage to get this crazy group of people off this boat. We'd be better off on our own. He knew it, I knew it, we both were right. But.

I shook my head and gave him a bittersweet smile. I loved him more than anyone else I'd ever loved in my entire life. I would walk across glass for him, or run back into a fire. But everyone up ahead had just helped me set him free. I couldn't turn my back on them, not even to save my own hide.

Asher sighed beside me, a sound more felt than heard, and closed his eyes slowly, like a cat resigned to his fate. I would have squeezed his hand, but I didn't want to hurt him.

Our group reached the freight elevators that we'd already used, opened the door, and waited for the elevator hidden behind it to arrive—and when it did it was occupied by a single soldier.

Luckily, our group was more comical than threatening, which gave Claire a chance.

She leaned over Hal's shoulder and whispered, "You didn't see us. Go back the long way." Her voice was the sound of writhing snakes, scales rasping drily over one another. It echoed in the elevator and it felt like it was a personal instruction. I took a step back—and Hal's arm reached out to stop me.

The soldier whom it'd been directed at dropped the barrel of the gun he'd been raising and nodded crisply, order received. He walked around us as though we were not there, and headed down the hallway to the stair.

Asher openly gawked. "I know a lot of languages, lady, but I've never heard one like that before."

Claire smiled down at him. "You're not the only one with secrets."

"Am I the only one without a superpower here?" Rory said.

I gave him a sympathetic look as the elevator door began closing. "Nope."

CHAPTER THIRTY

It didn't take any time at all to rise up a floor, and we deposited ourselves in one of the large rooms facing out to sea and barricaded the door. We'd have warning if anyone entered, but we'd also be trapped inside.

I wasn't surprised to see an unfamiliar dead body in the bathroom. Emily'd found it first, but Rory'd gotten a hand over her mouth to muffle her scream in time.

A man was in his very nice and separate-from-the-bathtub shower. He was slumped in a corner of it, all his clothes on, eyes staring open, jaw dropped wide.

"Shhhhhhhhh," Claire told the girl, but without any weird accent this time.

"It's like this?" Asher asked me.

"All over the ship. That, or people have gone insane and jumped overboard. You don't even know half of what it's like." I stepped back out of the room, and they followed me. "We have to pool resources, and quickly. All our cards on the table. For real." And to encourage full disclosure—"I'm a human. I've got a master key to all the staterooms." I looked over to Rory, standing at my right.

Rory crossed his arms, knife still in hand. "I'm Rory. I'm a human. I'm keeping this." He waggled the knife.

Claire went next. "I'm a siren. I met Hal a long time

ago. I can convince people to do what I want them to do, if they're near enough and willing to listen. My voice travels better underwater."

Rory's eyes narrowed. "I've fought sirens in video games before. You all are never good."

Claire looked affronted. "I hope then that we are at least hard to kill."

"Depends on the difficulty setting."

"Oh, I can be very diffi—" Claire began.

"I'm just a man who loves a siren," Hal interrupted both of them, and Claire looked chagrined.

Emily knew it was her turn after Hal. "I have a radio." She held it up for us to see. Hal must have given it to her. I gave her an encouraging smile, and then looked to Asher, who shrugged.

"I'm a shapeshifter. And I've never met one of you before." He bowed to Claire.

"And I've never met one of you," she said, somewhat regally from her perch.

"You only think you haven't," he said, with a puckish grin.

Now was not the time for my boyfriend to charm people. "What happened to you? Did you find anything out? And what the f—" I started to curse, saw Emily, and bit it back in time. "What was going on in that room?"

I saw the muscles in Asher's jaw clench as he realized that whatever he wanted to tell me, he'd have to share with everyone at once. He inhaled deeply before he began. "I went downstairs to talk to Liz, like I told you— looking like Nathaniel," he explained for the others, who hadn't been there. "She was feverish, babbling things. About sea monsters—which I'd feel silly about sharing, except for present company," he said, with a nod to Claire. "But eventually I figured out she wasn't Nathaniel's wife and Thomas wasn't their child, just hers. He had a rare genetic disorder that Nathaniel promised her a cure for, after they came on this cruise with him."

Maybe that was why she'd been running for pills the other night. "Then what?"

"I was concentrating so much on her that Nathaniel caught me there, looking like him. After that he knew what I was. He said if I went with him, he'd explain everything."

"And just like that, you followed him?" I said, my voice rising. I wasn't the only one whom peaceful months had made soft.

"I needed to know what was going on, Edie. I thought I could stop him," he said, sounding hurt. "And I was right—he is behind all of this."

"So what is he doing here with everyone on the boat?" Claire asked.

Asher inhaled deeply again, to buy himself time to think. "His prior research . . . fell through. And the people he'd been working for killed his daughter to punish him."

I took me a moment, then I filled in between the lines. *Way to not mention vampires or blood substitutes, honey*— and that was what Nathaniel'd meant when he threatened a child for a child. I put a protective hand over my stomach. I'd need to find a way to tell Asher about that, privately.

"So this is his revenge," I said. Asher looked surprised, then nodded.

"I don't know if it's from viruses, bacteria, protozoans, or what—but he infected Thomas first. And then Thomas ran around the whole ship touching things."

Including Asher and me. "No wonder the doctor couldn't figure it out." I wondered what was happening to poor Dr. Haddad right now. "But what does he gain by killing everyone off?"

"He's trying to raise something from the bottom of the

ocean—which apparently requires a vast human sacrifice to awaken."

"And he just told you all of that? Like in a villain monologue?" Rory said.

Asher continued to play coy. "We'd worked together in the past. I've been putting together two plus two."

And so had Nathaniel. Who now knew what Asher was—and what Asher's confession to the Consortium had cost him.

"I don't know what it is that he's raising. He wouldn't say. But he threw my fingers overboard after he cut them off, 'so that it would know my blood.' He wouldn't tell me what 'it' was. And at that point, I wasn't really in a position to ask."

"Whatever it is, the Shadows, those things we met in the morgue"—I looked to Rory to clue him in—"are afraid of it."

There was a moment of silence between Asher and me, as we considered what could worry the Shadows.

"It doesn't get much bigger than the Leviathan," Claire said at last. At seeing our faces, Claire barked a sharp laugh.

Rory made a face. "That's mythology."

"Like me?" Claire said. "Another character in a video game?"

"Actually, yes." He walked across the room and squatted down, putting his head in his hands.

I stirred my hand in the air for her attention. "Leviathan, as in the monster from the book of Job?" My mother would be so proud of me getting to use my Sunday school education now. Asher snorted, and even Hal glanced nervously at his wife.

"Oh, don't look so surprised, the lot of you. Every great religion has a story of a serpent that lives in the sea. It was the most convenient frightening thing in olden times." She looked at Hal in particular and gave him an indulgent smile. "You believe in me, don't you? If you do, then some of the rest has to follow."

He nodded, and she went on. "I don't know what all those insane markings on his maps were about. But I do know what mass human sacrifice looks like. It's not the first time I've seen someone try. I haunted shipwrecks professionally—there's a difference when people jump overboard on their own, versus falling over with slit throats, dead before they can drown. You've only heard of the *Mary Celeste,* or the *Resolven,* but there've been a hundred boats emptied of people and wrecked too, by one loon or another trying to wake the Leviathan, trying to use carnage to lure it up. I'll give this Nathaniel-man that at least—he's got scale."

"But what is it?" I pressed. "A great snake? A dragon?"

"No. The sea holds a lot of life, but eventually everything—from whales to plankton—dies and drifts down. The Leviathan comprises what all of that becomes, death after death, compressed over eons. It gained a slow kind of life, but it's not alive—it's like it's the residue of a memory of what life could be." She bit her lips in thought before speaking again. "You have to remember that most things in the ocean don't live like you or me—the only thing they are is hungry."

"Have you seen it?" asked Hal, rapt at Claire telling a story that was apparently new to him.

"I never went down that far. It's not safe, and the pressure—" She shook her head. "But I know when it's there. You'd feel it too. When you're out in the sea—whenever you're past seeing the ground, where blue stretches beneath you into black, and you're scared of whatever it holds, just like you're scared of the dark. It's that. It's the liquid darkness, somewhere below."

Which sounded like a fair description of the Shadows—

or their older, more frightening cousins—to me. I looked to Asher and could tell he was thinking the same thing.

"Then isn't it always below? Everywhere? All the time?" Rory asked, tone logical and a touch snide.

"Yes. Sleeping. For now. Why someone would try to wake it up to deal with their problems, I don't know."

My lips twisted to one side. If I were trying to get revenge on vampires for killing my daughter, I knew I might try to get something worse than the Shadows on my side, too. It was the only way a human would have a chance.

Asher slashed his hand through the air. "That's that, then. We need to get off this boat."

"What about the worms?" Rory asked.

"Worms?" Claire asked.

"I saw them. With my own eyes." Rory said, daring me to refute him. I couldn't, not after what I'd seen inside Raluca.

"I saw them too." I touched my stomach, just in case.

"It doesn't matter, we still need to go—" Asher went on.

"It matters to me!" Rory protested. "I need to know if they're inside me!"

"That's what he infected Thomas with," I explained, gaining speed as I figured it out. "The worms explain the fevers and seizures, the hunger and thirst—your body tries to fight them off, but if it doesn't, they need energy to grow . . . and they want to reach water before they die. That's why people keep going overboard and drowning."

While I spoke, Asher watched me, weighing what I said—it felt like he was weighing me—and I saw his jaw set as he resolved something. He reached into the pocket of his torn pants, then held out four pills on his palm. "I saw him take one of these. That must be what they're for. To kill the worms."

"And when were you going to share them with us?" Claire asked.

"I forgot I had them," Asher said as she tsked. "I didn't know what they were for until now."

Claire stared him down. At least I wasn't the only one who knew he was a liar. I knew he didn't get sick—but that wouldn't stop him from saving them all for me.

"So we're all infected—" Rory said, finally satisfied now that we'd confirmed his worst fears.

Asher shrugged. "I don't know. Some of you all might have natural immunity, or luck, but Nathaniel doesn't seem like the type to take chances."

"How do you know all this?" Hal asked.

"We'd worked together. Like I said."

"You helped him do this to us? To my parents?" Rory said. He wasn't holding the knife anymore, but I doubted that he'd dropped it.

"Seven years ago," Asher explained, shaking his head. "And I didn't help, so much as steal some research for him. Damning with faint praise, I know." Asher looked around the room to include the rest of the ship, then spoke directly to me. "If I'd known it would lead to this, I sure as hell wouldn't be here."

"I know," I told him. I'd tell him about the Shadows interfering with our travel plans to bring us here as punishment later; it wouldn't make sense to anyone else right now.

Emily's face crinkled. "I don't want there to be worms inside me."

"I know, honey," Claire told her, stroking her hair.

Asher pushed his hand out. "I don't need one of these. And I'm not sure that one dose is enough. But I suggest the rest of you all take one." Asher offered the pills on his palm to me. I picked one up, and then he offered the rest of them around. Rory took one, then Emily, and then it was down to Claire and Hal.

"I suspect sirens are immune," she said. "I should be fine." Hal nodded, her word gospel, and popped the pill into his mouth.

I held the pill up. "What is it?" They were faintly tan, pressed without any markings. My brain was filled with all the things that it could be.

"I don't know. But I know he takes them. So they're safe."

I could tell Asher was overselling it. "For men. Non-pregnant men. I don't feel sick yet," I said, trying to ignore visions of the slowly spinning things dying in Raluca's torso—and how Raluca had seemed fine. I swallowed drily.

"Edie, I can't lose you."

He couldn't lose me—but I couldn't lose this baby. And taking unknown and likely experimental medicine didn't seem safe. Besides, what were the chances of one dose being enough? Or of me not getting reinfected before I got off this boat? I leaned into Asher's shoulder so I wouldn't have to see the look in his eyes. "I never should have left you," he whispered, his head by my ear.

"I know."

"I'm sorry." I nodded into him, accepting his apology. "We can have another child though, Edie. If it can happen once, it can happen again. I need you."

"I need you, too," I said, because it was the truth.

Asher pulled me to him tighter, his roughness revealing his fear. "Please, just take the pill."

"Okay." I'd seen so many patients palm pills before that I knew it wasn't hard. I put my hand to my mouth, faked a swallow, and felt him nod.

"Thank you." His relief was palpable.

"What now?" I asked as he turned around. He didn't see me putting the unmarked pill into the pocket of my jeans.

"Now—we figure out how to get off this boat."

CHAPTER THIRTY-ONE

Asher stood quietly for a moment thinking, and I almost felt safe standing by his side. I'd never be the kind of woman to give over all thought to anyone else, but it was nice, deep-down-in-my-bones nice, to have him here with me again. Despite the odds, with Asher around I almost felt like we had a chance.

Rory was sitting equidistant from Claire and us, trying to keep an eye on everyone who was supernatural at once, and Claire and Hal were whispering to each other just as Asher and I had been. Emily had the radio up to her ear in the semblance of a cell phone. Asher saw this and nodded at her. "Hey Emily—what do you hear?"

She shrugged and handed the radio out to him. He took it, with Rory swinging dramatically backward to be out of his way.

"The medical channel is number five," I said, and Asher grunted, turning up the volume and flipping through the rest of them. Languages I couldn't understand crackled through, sounding just as excited as they had when Hal had done the same earlier. Asher narrowed his eyes and held the TALK button down.

"Hello, is anyone out there? Can you hear me? *Hallo, is daar iemand daar buite? Kan jy my hoor? Alo, este cineva acolo? Poți să mă auzi?*" He started off in English and went through three different languages in quick succession. "What is happening? Are there any survivors?"

"Wie is jy?" came through in a burst of static from the other side.

"Ek is 'n gas hier, wegkruip van die manne met gewere! Wat de hel gaan aan?" Asher said.

"Hoe weet ek dat jy nie een van hulle?" said the man back. I finally recognized the accent.

"It's Marius!" I said and clapped my hands.

Asher broke into a grin. "I believe we met once, outside the medical bay."

There was a staticky pause. "So your girlfriend found you at last?"

"Yes. What's going on out there? Stay in Afrikaans so they won't translate you."

There was another, longer burst of Afrikaans, as Asher nodded.

I didn't know what Marius was saying, but I recognized some names. Jorge—I was so glad he was all right—and Kate.

Asher let go of the button to address us again. "He says they're trying to get to the lifeboat deck, but they're scared of the gunmen. They're getting ready to make a run for it."

I nodded. "Then so should we."

"Hello?" came in another voice, with another accent, shouted over mechanical background noise. I tensed.

"Hello?" Asher answered back, with the same accented English.

"Naririnig mo ba ako! May mga lalake dito na may hawak na baril! Tulungan niyo kami!"

I didn't know what they were saying, but Asher's

expression turned dark, and he asked a series of fast questions.

"Mga trabahador kami sa ibaba ng barko, dito kami sa baba, malapit sa lugar ng makina. Bilis!"

"What language is that?" Rory asked.

Asher let go of the TALK button. "Tagalog. He's one of the fish in the engine room—the workers who live belowdecks."

"Tell them about the guns—"

"They already know," Asher cut in. He pressed the button back down and asked what sounded like questions. His eyes narrowed at their fast response and asked them another question in turn. *"Ano ang itsura ng nilalagay nila? Nakikita mo ba?"*

"Mukhang gam! Isang malaking gam!" came the response, followed by a gun report.

"What's he saying?" Claire demanded.

"He sees gum." Asher rocked back, lowering the radio. "They're putting plastic explosives on the walls."

Hal groaned. "They want to breach the hull."

"But if they do that—" I said in a whisper.

"We'll all die," Rory finished for me.

Asher held the radio up again and asked another question. *"May naiisip ka bang paraan para mapatigil siya?"*

"Bahagi siya ng isang pares. Tinututukan siya ng baril ng isang lalake. Natakasan lang namin yung isa dahil naubusan siya ng bala."

"Lost at sea's no way to die—tell him to escape," Hal suggested as Asher's conversation went on.

"Subukin mo makarating sa ikatlong palapag. Subukin mong makatakas."

There was a bitter laugh on the other end of the line before another response.

"What's he saying?" Emily asked me.

"I don't know, honey," I said, as Asher gave me a look that was both hapless and dismayed, clicking off the line definitively.

"He's injured, a bullet shattered his leg. They took down one gunman, but one remains," he said.

"We have to stop them," I said, and Hal nodded agreement.

Asher took a measured breath and shook his head. "No, we don't. What we need to do is get off this boat. We get to the third deck, and then we get the hell out of here—"

"But there's still people alive on board. Not just the ones we talked to on the radio—we have to try to warn them. If this ship is going down, we have to," I protested.

He paused, and I could tell he was choosing his next words carefully for my sake. "I can't see any possible way this will work." I didn't know whether him being willing to leave everyone else to die was instinct, fear, or love—or maybe all three. Even worse, I knew he was right. But—

"Mercenaries don't sign on for suicide missions." Hal interrupted my thoughts. "Unless somehow those are government guns, those men think they're getting off this boat alive. And if they've got time to get off, we've got time to stop them."

Asher didn't say anything. He just put his hand out toward me, palm up. It said everything he wouldn't. *Please. Just come with me.*

Hal went on, in ignorance, or just plain old ignoring Asher. "I've got a plan. We'll split into two groups. You two and the boy go upstairs, get up to where the intercom is, and see if you can figure out how to warn people to evacuate in all the languages you can think of. Tell them all to get to the lifeboat deck—and see if you can tell anyone on land what's going on out here. Claire, Emily, and I will go downstairs. We'll figure out a way to stop the ones down there from blowing up the boat."

At this, the expression on Asher's face changed to one of complete disbelief—an expression I felt mirrored on my own. An old man, a woman who couldn't walk, and a little girl were going to take on armed men?

"I'll go with you," I blurted out.

"No way in hell," Asher said. He looked from the door to me, his opinion clear. Screw everyone else but the two of us—we could make it if we left right now. I knew he was right, but I wasn't going to go without them—and I was too big for Asher to pick up and carry. "You'll figure out a way?" Asher went on, mocking Hal, his voice incredulous.

As much as I loved him, that was the fundamental difference between him and me. He could displace his guilt, push it away so that it was something reckoned with later or even never, his work with Nathaniel case in point. Whereas with me—I could never manage to feel guilty later for something I could feel guilty about right now. There was a helpless man with a broken leg watching other men put explosives on our boat. There were Marius, and Kate, and Jorge.

I swallowed and looked away from Asher. I loved him with all my heart, but that didn't mean that sometimes he still wasn't wrong. I looked over to Hal. "I'm in."

"Okay. We should get going then." Hal bent over so that Claire could clamber up onto his back.

Asher blocked me. "This is a bad plan and you know it. I didn't just get you back only to lose you again."

"You won't. You'll know where I am the whole time," I said with false bravado.

I watched his jaw clench and his throat swallow. "You're the only thing in the world that matters to me. I won't let you die."

Hal shrugged Claire up into place. "Does that mean you'll help?"

Asher looked to me, giving me one last chance to change my mind. When I shook my head, he shrugged helplessly. "What other choice do I have?"

"I'm sorry. I love you so much."

Watching his face I was afraid for a second that he'd be angry with me. But he looked crestfallen instead, so deeply, deeply sad. He held out his arms and I stepped into them, if not agreed with, then forgiven. He kissed me hard, scared, like he'd never taste my lips again, and then stopped just as fast as he'd begun, his face close to mine, looking deep into my eyes, as if memorizing this new me, the one that I'd changed into since the last time we'd touched. Then he inhaled and exhaled, dropping his frustration, putting on another mood like someone else might put on a mask, becoming the suave charmer who was always in control. "I love you too," he said, then he looked over to Rory. "You ready, boy?"

"My name's Rory."

"That's a yes, then." He walked over and flung open the dead passenger's closet doors, and then looked back to us and started stripping. "I can't do what I do looking like this. I need a minute."

To watch him while he changed would have been too tempting, and maybe that's what he wanted, me to remember what I was missing. So I turned around as the others did, and when he was done, he coughed loudly for our attention and slicked his wet hair back with his good hand. He looked rumpled and under stress, but back in control, and he picked up the radio, pointing it at me.

"Meet you on the lifeboat deck in under an hour, or when we're both underwater, whichever comes first." He didn't risk another kiss, for which I found myself both hurt and grateful. "Live, or else I can't be held responsible for what I'll do."

"I will," I promised.

He jerked his head at Rory, and both of them went for the door.

CHAPTER THIRTY-TWO

After Asher left, it was as if all the air'd gone out of the room. I'd known it would hurt, but—

"Such an interesting fellow!" Claire said, newly re-perched on Hal's back. "Ready?"

"Ready!" Emily said, eager to follow the older woman's lead.

I tried to shake my fears away. Was that the last time I'd see Asher alive? I'd done the right thing but that, as I well knew, was frequently futile. I pressed my fingers to my mouth as though I could hold his last kiss there.

Claire coughed for my attention, and I looked up at her. "Is the siren-thing why your legs don't work?"

"No. I'm just old. Gravity's harder on a girl when you're on land. Water's kinder."

"You used to live in the sea?" Emily asked.

"Yes. I loved it there," Claire said, leaning over to speak to the girl.

"But you loved me more," Hal said, shifting her back.

"Well, you know. You've been sort of fun," Claire said, with an obvious tease. Then she squeezed his thick shoulders tightly. "We'll go first, and if we see anyone, I'll try to talk them down," she said, and Hal opened the door to lead us into the hall.

I felt uncomfortable with Hal and Claire being in the

line of fire ahead of me so I put Emily behind me to at least protect her. If I stopped being brave now, I might be too smart to start again.

"So how does he know so many languages?" Claire asked, looking back at me, using a normal voice.

"Um. Shouldn't we be listening?" I whispered.

"I am," she said, with a toothy smile.

Seeing as she'd heard us the other night, and now I knew she was a siren—"As a shapeshifter he knows the past of everyone he touched before. When he was younger."

"And how did a nice girl like you meet someone like him?"

Little did she know. "I worked in a hospital wing for supernatural creatures once upon a time. We treated shapeshifters, daytimers, and weres."

"Daytimers?"

"Humans who were exposed to vampire blood."

"Ah." She made a thoughtful face. "We don't have vampires under the sea. Our monsters are much bigger, and much worse."

"How did you all meet?" Emily asked. Her parents were seemingly forgotten in all the excitement, or because of something Claire had done.

"That's a very good question," Claire said, smiling down at the child. "Hal was a soldier on a ship a long time ago. When it got torpedoed during the war, some of my sisters and I went to sing for it."

Some remnants of Greek mythology jostled free in my mind, and I squinted at the older woman. "Are you singing for this one?"

"If you're asking if all this is my fault, no. Although I am reaching the time when I need to go back."

There was a hitch in Hal's step when she said this—I wouldn't have noticed if I hadn't been walking right behind him.

"Anyhow," she said, going on with her story, addressing Emily, "I was swimming, watching the sailors drown. There were a lot of sailors drowning in those days. Sometimes we had to fight with the sharks to get the chance to kiss them."

"You kissed boys?" Emily asked, more disturbed about this than the sharks.

"A lot of them." Claire looked back so I would know she was telling this story for my benefit as well. "Not every siren wants to see the world above the sea. But if you do, the only way you can get there is by kissing the air out of a man."

I blinked. Was she saying what I thought she was saying?

"Not just any man," Hal interrupted.

"No, only the right one. I had to kiss hundreds of sailors to find him," she said, squeezing Hal close. "But when I did, I knew."

"For living in the ocean your whole life, you weren't a very good swimmer. We nearly died before we got rescued," he said, and I could almost hear his grin.

Claire squealed. "I'd never had legs before! It was hard!"

I was having a hard time parsing their couple's humor with presented facts. "Do you ever feel bad about all the ones that drowned?" I asked because I didn't want to be the only one who felt bad right now.

"Not originally, no. I was like a child then. Does a child feel pain when she loses a toy, when she knows a shinier one can be gained? I was, as your kind say, shallow. Most sirens are. Not a lot of encouragement for introspection, under the sea."

"Like Ariel!" Emily exclaimed, catching on.

"Much the same. Only with less singing." She smiled at the girl indulgently. "You all are the first humans I've gotten to tell my secret to, since I shared it with Hal all those years ago. It's nice."

I'm glad someone here felt better about things, I thought darkly. But no matter how strangely—horribly?—it'd begun, their relationship had lasted for decades. Would Asher and I get that chance? My heart ached. I couldn't believe I'd let him go again. I hoped I wouldn't be made a fool for leaving his side.

We reached the freight elevator, found it empty, and Hal pushed the button for the lowest floor. Claire pressed a finger to her lips and gave Emily and me a meaningful glance as it lowered.

The doors opened onto a kill zone.

CHAPTER THIRTY-THREE

I realized we were lucky: Whatever ship the soldiers had come in on hadn't held enough of them to man all the doors. And why would they need to anyhow, if they cleared every room as they came through it, and they were the only ones with guns on board? Passengers and crew were the proverbial fish in a barrel.

The slaughter began six feet from the door. I didn't know if those trapped down here had been waiting for good news, or their turn on the "rescue" boat, but they'd gotten bullets instead. Bodies were everywhere, some of them still leaking warm blood. There were spatters on the walls from exit wounds and smears where people had fallen, bleeding. And there were more ropy loops of "intestine" here, worms evacuated from human bodies. I didn't point them out.

It smelled awful—the scent when fear and death make you evacuate your bowels, plus all the warm must of what's normally hidden inside our bodies. Nurse-stomach battled pregnant-stomach and pregnant-stomach won. "I'm going to be sick," I said, and looked for someplace safe to throw up, where I wouldn't be desecrating anyone's body. Emily clung to my leg, her face buried in my thigh, trying not to see.

"Don't remember what you see here," Claire told Emily,

her voice taking on that echoed rasping sound, and the little girl nodded.

"Can you use that on me?" I asked.

"I'd rather not. You might need to react to something suddenly."

I gave her a grim nod and swallowed air, so maybe it could hold everything else down.

Hal picked his way through the small lobby as if it were a minefield. Reaching the other side, he waved to me. "Come on."

It helped that Hal had been a sailor. I supposed that at their core all ships were alike. We followed him down a narrow hall, punctuated with the occasional corpse. All of the fallen crew down here looked surprised, like statues frozen by Medusa in an unending moment of horror. I didn't know what they'd been forced to see down here, but I couldn't imagine the crew had fared any better than we had. Worse, probably, since there'd been no way for them to throw themselves overboard.

We were quiet as Claire tilted her head back and forth, and I wondered darkly if she could use voices like sonar. We didn't stop to go into any of the rooms on either side—from what little I could see through their windows they all appeared to be storage. But I did know it was getting louder ahead of us, and there was a sensation of movement from the decks beneath our feet.

Hal paused and turned back. "We might not be able to hear one another after this next set of doors." He pointed at his own ears. "There's a reason I'm almost deaf."

"That's good, right? They won't hear us coming."

"Yes, but—" Claire shook her head, pointing at her throat. Her vocal skills wouldn't work down here. We'd be on our own. I nodded.

Hal pushed the doors open slowly, crouching, carefully

looking around. Behind him were engines that never stopped thrummed. Pistons as big as sofas pounded up and down, keeping the *Maraschino* still on its space of real estate in the sea. Machinery ran from side to side, reaching the actual edges of the ship. The room had to be three floors tall with catwalks running up and across each side. Where a row of computer terminals lined the bottom-most floor, the remaining crew had been murdered to a man. I wondered where our informant with the broken leg was now, and if we found him, how we'd get him free.

I scanned around, and spotted two parcels of C-4 on each side, in between the giant ribs of the ship, two floors up—and saw a man dressed in body armor wiring up a third one, on the right-hand side. I shook Hal's sleeve and pointed. He nodded when he spotted him.

I made a gesture to Hal, nervous to talk even though the sound of the machinery in here was overwhelming. *What's the plan?* I tried to say with my hands.

Hal held one hand out and made the other into a walking person, two fingers walking quietly along to indicate stealth. And then a sudden rude shoving motion, where we'd push the soldier over the edge, onto the pistons below.

As plans went, it wasn't a great one. But when life gives you lemons—or mercenaries employed by someone psychotic—you do whatever the fuck you can. I nodded.

Then I pried Emily away from my leg. "Stay hidden down here, okay? Like hide and seek," I whispered over the diesel engines. She nodded, and crouched down behind a desk.

I crawled up diamond-deck stairs, this time ahead of Hal. The soldier hadn't looked up from his task. I wasn't sure if C-4 required that much attention, or if he was just that confident that there was no one left who could put up a fight. His gun was slung over his shoulder, across his back, and he was using both of his gloved hands for his task. Feeling like I was pretending to be a ninja, I crept closer, using the ribs of the ship for cover, until he was only ten feet away from me. He looked like he had fifty pounds on me, between muscle and armor. I was going to need every foot of my head start. I was bracing, gritting my shoes onto the deck for traction, when he looked up.

I didn't stop. I ran straight for him, with whatever adrenaline I had left inside. With all my fear of never seeing Asher again, of dying right here, of the worms that might be growing inside me, of the baby that might already be dead—I used all of this to run straight toward him. He lost a moment to surprise and another one to pulling up his gun, and I hit him. He was like a wall.

I didn't hit him with nearly enough energy to send him over the edge of the rails. He took the blow and spun, yanking the gun up. I managed to shove it back down so his hand couldn't get ahold of the trigger. We spun together, wrestling over the gun, whirling around each other until we'd changed spots like dancers, the barrel of the gun still pointing at the floor. I saw Hal near as we whirled and Claire leaned over and caught the soldier's neck from her perch on Hal's back. I half expected her to snap it, while I tried to leverage his rifle out of his hand. I saw her lips move and knew she was trying to say something to him with her voice, but between the engines and his armor, he couldn't hear; he still fought me. So she kissed him instead.

Suddenly I'd won my fight. His hands reached up to clutch his throat, and the gun dropped, forgotten in breathless terror.

I watched him slide to the floor as though he were sinking into water, his lips the only visible part of him with all the armor on, turning from pink to a hypoxic shade of blue. She'd kissed the air out of him, asphyxiating him on dry land.

The soldier forgotten, Hal turned toward the package

of C-4 affixed to the wall. He did something nimble with his fingers and unfastened a timer, still clicking along even though it wasn't attached to anything anymore. He showed it to me.

We had seven minutes and twenty-eight seconds on the clock.

I turned in stunned horror—and I could see another row of C-4 packages affixed between the ribs of the ship on the other side. Eight in a row.

We'd never get to all of them in time, no matter how fast we moved—much less if we did it at Hal's speed. If we tried, we'd die.

I looked back to Hal, who'd already moved on down to the next bundle of explosives. "One side will have to be good enough," he shouted at me.

If only one side of the ship took on water, not both, it would at least buy us some time. The *Maraschino* would sink like a leaf, instead of a rock.

"Go get Emily—run!" Hal shouted over his shoulder. I nodded and raced back down the catwalks, reluctant to leave him behind, but scared shitless at the thought of sharing this much space with so much seawater.

CHAPTER THIRTY-FOUR

"Come on, come on, come on—" I found Emily under her desk and scooped her up, even as she fought to stay behind. Sharp pain radiated out from my shoulder, and I ignored it.

"We can't leave them!"

"We're not! They're meeting us!" I said, even though I was unsure. I shoved her through the doors to the engine room and kept going.

They told you to never take the elevator in an emergency. I looked for the doors marked STAIRS down the hall and ran for them, hoping that Hal would do the same. How far away would be safe? Was anywhere?

The sound of the engine room faded as we raced down the hall, passing sign after sign saying we were almost to the stairs, until my own panicked panting was the only thing I could hear. How much time had passed? Where were Hal and Claire? I closed the most recent set of doors behind us; they were fire doors like we'd had at the hospital, and ought to buy us some time.

Then chimes rang out overhead, and a voice I recognized started speaking in a different language. *"Ang barko ay kailangang lisanin, pakiusap, gumawa ng paraan para makapunta sa isang ligtas na lugar at gawin ito sa maayos at mahinahong pamamaraan."*

Asher was alive. Tears of relief filled my eyes—and I saw Hal and Claire coming at me down the hall. I opened up the door for them, flagged them in, and slammed it shut, for all the good it would do.

"Aceasta nava este evacuat. Vă rugăm să face un fel de punte barca de salvare într-o manieră ordonată."

Hal threw his shoulder against it. "Keep going!" He waved Emily and me on.

"Not without you!" Emily screamed, taking hold of his free arm.

"Hierdie skip ontruim. Maak jou pad na die reddings- boot dek in 'n ordelike wyse."

Claire looked down at something she held in her hand. "We don't have long now. Brace yourselves!"

"This ship is being evacuated." Asher's warning was finally in English. "Please make your way to the lifeboat deck in an orderly fashion. Edie—I'm meeting you there."

My heart leaped up into my throat just as Claire yelled, "Hang on!"

The C-4 they hadn't gotten a chance to disarm went off. The roar of the engine room caught up with us, like a plane landing on our heads. The fire door bucked and threw all of us back, blown open by the pressure of the explosion below, and almost instantly the ship started listing to one side. I imagined the bottom of the *Maraschino* broken open like a piñata, and the dead sailors below dropping like gruesome candy, pouring into the sea.

Hal got up first. I was too dumbfounded with horror.

"Go go go!" he shouted, staggering up, I could read his lips. Claire was still clinging to his back. I swept up Emily again, who was screaming; I could see her mouth open wide. But I couldn't hear her, because my head was buzzing like it was full of bees. Together we raced through the final doors and reached the stairs.

The remaining crew members who were alive were

like us, alerted either by the explosion or Asher's warning, swarmed upward like so many rats. We were at the bottom of things, having started at the lowest floor. I was sure there was shouting, but I couldn't hear it; my head still rang like I was standing too near a church bell. I held Emily close as humanity pressed upward above us, panic blocking all the doors.

"Edie!" Claire called, just a step behind me. Her voice could cut through the sounds in my head.

"We're here!" I shouted back. I picked up Emily on every other step, swinging her forward like a cane. Every time I moved her my shoulder stung.

"Don't stop!"

I wasn't planning on it! But I didn't say that to her, because to say it would be to use air to do anything else but breathe, and breathing was all I could manage right now as we raced from floor to floor. People who hadn't made it, who'd been broken by the escaping mob, gunshot, or mentally bereft by the worms, reached out, trying to grab hold of us so we could help them. It was what I imagined it would be like if I were to run out of hell, with endless hungry hands reaching out for us either side, and the stairs slippery with blood.

I thought could taste salt in the air, but I didn't know if it was from above or below. I didn't want to look back—I was scared I'd see the sea coming up behind me. No matter how much air was trapped on board the *Maraschino*, it wouldn't be enough to keep us buoyant for long.

There was a pause from somewhere up above. It rippled back in line as people stuttered to a stop, hitting one another. I halted before I hit someone, and felt Hal against my back. The staircase started to drift higher on one side. We needed to get off the stairs before they became unusable, before instead of stairs they turned into a slide back down.

"What's going on?" Hal asked—I could only hear him

because his mouth was near my ear and he was shouting half-deaf-loud. And then I heard a sound that cleared out all the others in the hall, the sharp staccato of a gun, cutting through all the fuzz inside my brain.

I froze in fear, reduced to something animal inside by sheer terror and seemingly endless exertion. I couldn't think of what to do next, I could only hear my own heartbeat pumping in time with sound of bullets ricocheting down on us from above. And then screams, loud enough and long enough to get through the cotton in my head. What sounded like endless screaming.

A voice cut through the chaos and terror, the hissing of a hundred hydras. "Hold on to Emily!"

I did as I was told because I had to obey. I would have done it anyway, but Claire gave me no choice. I grabbed Emily, and Hal in turn grabbed me, hauling me down two steps to the landing we'd just passed. We stepped over mob-crushed bodies, and he shoved us inside the door into the hallway behind it. I recognized the carpeting—we were back on the residential floors.

"There's more than one stairway up," he said, slamming the door. "Unless they've sent reinforcements over, they can't be covering every one."

"What floor are we on?" Claire asked. The church-bell sound diminished as she talked.

"Two. One more to go." I saw-heard Hal say.

I was too busy panting to participate in conversation. Emily was as white as a sheet, scared by everything she'd seen. She looked like I felt.

"Can you run?" Hal asked me, soliticiously.

"How can you be this strong?" I asked aloud, but I couldn't hear my own voice.

He laughed. "I keep good company. Come on," he said, and started running down the hall.

The floor tilted beneath us, as if we were in a fun

house at a haunted amusement park. I was having a hard time herding Emily. Like it or not, I was nowhere near as strong as Hal, and I couldn't keep carrying her. I set her down, and she started to cry.

"I know, baby." I wanted to cry too. "How much farther?" I asked Hal, sounding much too loud in my own head.

"We're halfway there."

I realized where we were going. To one of the main public stairwells, the ones that'd been guarded with the quarantine, back in the day. That didn't seem safe to me, but the announcement chimes sounded overhead before I could say so. The shipwide intercom was at the same deafening volume, and a voice that wasn't Asher's echoed overhead.

"If you're still alive, Edie, I have some people you might be interested in saving."

CHAPTER THIRTY-FIVE

Nathaniel. I didn't have to see him to hear the sneer.

There was the sound of a scuffle, and then a nervous voice. "Edie? You can save us?" It was Kate, and she sounded scared.

"Don't come!" said another voice—Jorge. And then he grunted, like he'd just taken a blow.

Nathaniel came back overhead. "I'll be at Le Poisson Affamé for as long as it's above water. Come and try to save your friends."

Claire shook her head, watching my face. "He's taunting you. He knows you'll go, which means you shouldn't."

If Nathaniel had had Asher to lure me with, he would have. Which meant Asher was free, but—"You know who else knows I'll go? Asher."

Her face went grim. She bobbed a little as Hal, her faithful steed, panted. He was tiring, not made of steel after all. "We can't manage without you just yet." She looked pointedly at Emily.

"I won't abandon you three. But the second you're safe you're on your own."

"Fine," Claire said, angry with me for not listening to her advice.

"If that's the way it has to be," Hal said, more kindly.

Going toward the main staircase was still heading

toward the bow and the fancy restaurant up top. I picked up Emily, which set my shoulder rattling around in its socket like a loose doorknob, and started walking.

We had to go more slowly now, not just because we were tired, but because we were fighting the tilt of the boat. Hal staggered and then I staggered—we reached the staircase, and hauled ourselves up using the railing as much as the stairs. Luckily we were only going up one flight, and Emily thought this part was some sort of fun game. I was concentrating on my grip and her. Until Hal started cursing, I didn't look up.

"What?" I asked, then I saw—the entrance to the third floor was barricaded off with chairs from the promenade. They were organized, stacked on top of one another, not just slid over like loose billiard balls on a tilted table. "Oh, fuck." I would have let go to cover Emily's ears, if I could. "They must have been trying to protect themselves from the gunmen."

If we'd all been able-bodied, maybe we could have broken our way through; the chairs weren't nailed into place. But there were so many of them that I couldn't see through to the other side, and we were at a disadvantage in height—there was a chance they'd fall in on us. Then the lights flickered and went out, replaced by dim emergency lights, making wrestling with furniture an even worse idea.

"You still have that key?" Hal asked, sounding as winded as me. I nodded. "Fourth floor then. We can climb down to the boats from there."

We climbed up to the fourth floor, an increasingly laborious process, and fought up to the rooms on the higher side of the ship—the lifeboats on the lower side wouldn't do us any good. It was hard to get out of the stairwell and across the hall to unlock the nearest door, as the *Maraschino* continued its inexorable rise. I pushed Emily inside, then got in myself, holding the door open for Claire and Hal. With him beneath me, I was finally in a position to see how tired he was. I could see the strain on his face.

"Go for the window!" I encouraged Emily, ahead of all of us. She fell to all fours and started crawling, which made a lot of sense. I followed after her, the traction of the carpeting helping, bracing off doorjambs and the edges of the desk and bed.

Emily reached the balcony doors before I did. "Hang on, Emily!"

Her chubby hand reached for the latch, and I put on an extra burst of speed, getting there just as she slid the door open. Sea air and cold rain punched in and took my breath away. Together, she and I made our way out; more slowly, Hal and Claire followed. Hal made sure to put the balcony chair in the way of the door closing behind us, so we wouldn't be trapped outside.

There was no light pollution now. The emergency lights didn't bother illuminating the water outside, it was just us and the waning moon, shining through small breaks in the storm clouds—and the third-floor lifeboats swinging below. If it were dry, if we were all able to walk on our own, if it weren't dark outside, we might have been able to reach them, in theory, clambering down the outside of the ship as it tilted down. But our situation being what it was—I looked down at the swinging lifeboats, my stomach swirling with the ship. Then it began to rain. "This is suicide."

"Can you manage it?" Hal asked aloud of Claire. And I realized what his other problem was. If his wife touched salt water, he'd lose her to the sea.

"Of course," she said, far more confident than I felt.

"We'll get down there and hide inside. They'll detach when the ship goes down."

I looked around. How would they take Emily? If I managed to get her out there with them, how would I reach the bow? Climbing safely out there was one thing, a one-in-a-hundred chance, but then climbing back? Was there a chance I could just throw the girl out to them? Not with my shoulder—

"We'll be fine," Claire said.

"Good." Hal said, and started sinking. I thought he was putting Claire down; it didn't register until a second later that he was falling.

"No!" Claire shouted. "Not yet. No!" Her voice rose up an octave, becoming a harsh animalistic scream as they both dropped to the ground. She clutched him to her chest where they fell. "No!"

"What's going on?" Emily asked, looking scared.

"I don't know—" I looked at Claire accusingly. Had she sucked the air out of him too?

Claire glared back at me and then bent over, sobbing as she ran her hands over Hal's chest. "I can't hear his heartbeat anymore."

"Oh, no—" I pressed Emily to me for a second, trying to give her some wild comfort, and then moved both of them aside.

CPR hardly ever worked by itself on anyone. That's what the TV shows don't show you. You do CPR until someone with a defibrillator comes, and that's what works, if it's going to. Even then it's doubtful. CPR doesn't get your heart back into a working rhythm, all it does is keep your oxygenated blood moving to keep your cells alive, in case the electricity can slap your heart into working order again.

But I didn't know what else to do. I found his sternum with the heel of one hand and started compressions.

Claire clawed at his shoulder with one hand while I pumped. "This wasn't how it was supposed to be," she told him. "We were supposed to make it safely to the lifeboat."

If I talked to her, I'd slow down, and if I slowed down, there was even less of a chance he'd wake up. You were supposed to do CPR until help arrived, or the patient woke up and shoved you away.

"Please, Hal, wake up," she begged him, sobbing against his side. She kissed his lips, and I knew what she was doing, she was trying to give him more life.

I kept going because stopping would mean I'd given up, and it wasn't my place. I was tired and my shoulder was screaming; my compressions weren't effective anymore, but I felt like I had to try. It kept raining, and rumbles of thunder interrupted Claire's sobs. I didn't know how long I'd gone for, or how much longer I had in me. I was just a machine that did this because it was easier than admitting that he wasn't going to come back.

She put her hand out and rested it on mine. "Stop."

I kept going for another three beats.

"I'm sure. You can stop. His heart hasn't started up again." There was another thunderclap, louder now; we were in the middle of the storm. It shook our bodies, and I had a foolish idea to run some piece of metal up on a kite and see if Hal's heart could be restarted by lightning.

Emily was crying behind me, and Claire propped herself up with her arms, her legs together behind her, resting herself across Hal's still chest, and I realized the enormity of the task he'd left me with. Now I'd need to rescue Claire somehow, too.

The lifeboats were nearer, tilting toward the body of

the *Maraschino* as she fell into the ocean on her other side, but I did not have Hal's strength. How would I get both of them out of here, as exhausted as I was, with a shoulder on the verge of going out? There was no way.

Claire was still sobbing. Not knowing what else to do, where to go or what to say, I stroked his wispy hair, and then awkwardly patted her.

Pressing off his chest with both hands, she rose up and howled. Her voice went from low to sonic and high, wild, a keening banshee whale-song that made my teeth ache. It was the sound of the unabashed grief of a creature that wasn't meant to ever have what she loved die.

The sound exposed her for what she was, an alien creature that didn't belong on this side of the waves. Where salt water sprayed up from the splashing ocean, or down from her tears, scales glimmered on her legs, and they were lengthening. Her hair grew to wreath her, damp and dark, like a spreading bed of kelp. She was wild and I had never seen anything so beautiful and frightening at the same time. She put out her hand to me, her transformation half complete.

"Give the girl to me," she commanded, in her otherworldly voice.

Without thinking, my body obeyed. I grabbed Emily and handed her over, even as I questioned the action. "Why?"

"Because she belongs to the sea."

"She's human!" I protested, although Emily didn't fight. She was looking at Claire with complete awe.

"She has no family anymore. I can give her one. She will sing forever with me." Claire petted Emily awkwardly with one hand, leaning up to do so as her change progressed. Things fluttered at the sides of her neck now, with ridges and wicked-looking spines. I took an involuntary step back, and slid a bit, the moisture of the deck overwhelming the traction of my shoes. Her eyes dared me to challenge her—and then she grabbed Emily and rolled backward, like a shark thrashing off a bite. She pulled the little girl toward her unhuman face and kissed her.

"Wait!" I screamed, but it was done.

Emily looked stunned as Claire released her, only to take her up again, beneath one arm. Her awkwardness in her new form only made it more horrible as she clambered toward the railing, balancing between her tail and her free arm, hauling Emily. Then with incredible strength she pulled them up and over the railing. They slid down down down to the sea, leaving me alone with Hal's corpse on the deck.

I couldn't even process what had happened. I ran up to the top of the railing and looked down. I couldn't see where Claire and Emily had fallen in; it was as if the sea had eaten them both whole.

CHAPTER THIRTY-SIX

A wave pushed the *Maraschino* sideways as I watched the ocean nearing. How much longer would we have now? There must be some time left, if Nathaniel was still risking being on board. Another wave hit, timed with a distant flash of lightning, and staring out I could see the "rescue" ship. Two more snaps of electric light and I could make out the outline of a helicopter on its bow, before the thunder hit me. It shook me—and the life rafts, dangling below. There was no way I'd try to reach for them now.

I let go of the railing, and let gravity pull me back to Hal's body. We were both cool and clammy, only he was dead and I was alive. I still had places to be.

Going with the tilt of the ship was more disorienting than fighting against it. I stumbled through the room we'd just come through, and an overstuffed purse slid and tumbled off the bed, sending lipstick tubes and individually wrapped tampons rolling down the floor alongside me.

I made it into the hallway and then back toward the stairs. I was wet from my time outside in the rain, and the smell of the sea was still strong on me—that, plus the tilt, made it feel like the sea was coming for me, like an opening mouth. I ran up not only afraid of what I was running toward, but increasingly horrified by what was gaining behind me.

I reached the ninth-floor landing and only found doors out to the deck.

"Fuck."

Not being Asher, or having had a chance to memorize the entire ship on my own, I'd taken the wrong stairwell up. I was half a ship away from the Le Poisson Affamé. My choices were to get across the deck somehow, or go back down.

The emergency lighting still worked, showing me all the pools that had started to drain, making the decks even more wet. And the plastic railings no longer kept the wind out; instead they acted like miniature sails, keeping the *Maraschino* in a slow spin. Beneath my feet the boat shuddered at irregular intervals, and I imagined room after room burping out air. I stood in the doorway trying to master my fear as a patio umbrella tumbled by outside.

But this was still somehow better than going back inside, and maybe getting trapped there. Taking my cues from Emily, I hit the deck on all fours.

It wasn't long before my hands were numb, my shoulder agonizing, and my feet soaked inside my not-nearly-waterproof-enough shoes. The divots between the fake-wood planks were the only things I could hold on to, and they were peeling back my nails. One by one, deck chairs liberated from gravity slid past, and tables took heavier falls. It was like a horrible video game, only I didn't have any extra lives.

I chose the higher route toward the building that the restaurant occupied—even though climbing down would have been easier, I was too afraid to get any closer to the waves. In a way I couldn't express but felt, I knew the *Maraschino* would reach its tipping point soon, where it would be flatly sideways, before it twisted and flashed its belly to the sky.

I reached the building, barely. It swooped in an organic fashion that had probably seemed sexy to the engineers at the time, but now felt like it would be the death of me. My hands couldn't get traction on its smoothly curved sides, and as the ship leaned my shoes were having less and less luck.

Then doors opened as I reached them. "Edie! Get in!"

I startled and almost lost my grip—and a hand lunged out to catch me. Shivering in the dark, I found myself beside Rory, both of us leaning against a marble counter. As my eyes adjusted to the red-tinted EXIT lights I realized with some irony that we were in the spa, now that the *Maraschino*'s deck had eaten off not only the polish from my nails, but several of my actual nails too.

"You're alive!" Rory gasped.

"You too!" I twisted in his grip and he let me go. "Where's Asher?"

"Hang on. He thought he might have to fish you out of the sea." Rory clicked on his radio. "The irdbay has andedlay." He turned his attention back to me. "You couldn't imagine what we had to go through. He pretended to be someone else that they were expecting and then turned them on each other, stole a gun, and shot someone—he was like James Bond," Rory said with reverent awe, and then looked past me, remembering. "We called out to the mainland, so finally someone knows we're here—we'll get a real rescue boat. Where are the others?"

I shook my head. "They're not coming."

"What happened to them?"

"It's hard to explain." I didn't want to tell him that Hal had died, or that Claire had run back to the sea. His gaze narrowed, but he didn't fight me; maybe he knew he didn't want to know.

"Edie." Asher rose up from behind Rory, rounded him, and reached for me. This time when I went with gravity it felt right. I allowed myself one full breath, one moment of feeling safe with him, before pulling away to talk.

"We weren't able to stop all the bombs. Just one side's worth—"

"I figured as much when we started sinking," he said, and stopped himself. "I thought—I assumed—"

And I realized what he'd thought without him saying it. I'd heard him over the intercom. I'd known he was fine, but he'd thought that I'd died. "I'm alive," I told him, even though he could see me, just so he could hear it again as he crushed me to his side. I ducked into his shoulder and hid there. "I'm alive."

I heard his breath catch as he stroked a strand of wet hair behind my ear. "We were supposed to meet on the lifeboat deck. Waiting there for you, not knowing—it was the most awful thing I've ever done."

"I'm alive," I whispered again.

"I knew it when I heard Nathaniel taunt you over the intercom. But not until then."

How long ago had that been? It hadn't seemed long to me; we were so busy running and then getting shot at. But somehow the lighting in here made him look older and more sad. Happy to see me, but haunted.

"I knew you'd manage to make it up here after that," he went on. "I couldn't dare let myself think otherwise. It would have wrecked me."

"If I'd had a way to tell you, I would have."

He grabbed my shoulders like he was setting me straight. "Can we please go now?"

I hesitated.

"I don't want to die—but he's still got people. You heard them, they're alive."

And the lines on his face drew grim.

"Didn't you hear them?" I pressed.

He made a show of looking behind me. "I noticed you're already missing the three people you left with. What's a few more?"

"Hal and Claire weren't like that—"

"Let's take a vote," he said, and then gave Rory a look. It was clear he and Rory had already discussed things in my absence.

"You think I'm going to be stopped by a plea for democracy?"

Asher's eyes narrowed. "Why does he want you—not me?"

I didn't want to tell him, but he deserved to know. "Because his own daughter died. When we were alone together earlier, before the gunmen, he asked if I was really pregnant, and then said he wanted a child for a child."

Asher's expression became emotionless and flat. "That is the exact opposite of everything you needed to say to get me to go help them. We're going."

"You know what he's capable of! How can you just leave them behind?"

"Look around you. Thousands of people have already died here. Who cares about a few more?" He grabbed my arm. "I'm getting you off this boat."

It truly didn't matter to him. And maybe he was right, but what kind of life with him would I have if I had to live with the knowledge that for me to be happy, we'd just let people die?

Wasn't that kind of thinking what had gotten us here in the first place? I pulled back from him.

"The Shadows made you pick this trip. Because they knew they could use us to figure out what was going on— and to punish us for disobeying them. They say some of this is your fault." Asher looked stunned. I moved closer to him and took his hand back. "We're different. I love you with all my heart, but I'm not like you. I can't just leave them behind without at least trying first."

Rory had been creeping backward, wisely trying to give us space. But then the *Maraschino* swung and he rocked back as the ship did. I saw him reach out for the marble of the spa's registration table, and watched his fingers slip off the cold stone.

He fell to the ground and slid like he was on a slip-and-slide, down the hall, to the other door where Asher'd been waiting for me. It swung open as he hit it and he flew out, just barely catching the doorjamb in time. Behind him was open black.

"Don't leave me!" he howled, holding on to the doorway.

I started up—and so did Asher. I caught his shoulder. "I thought you didn't care about adding a few more deaths to the pile."

For a heart-wrenching second I thought he might actually do it, just to prove his point, even if it broke me. And then he shrugged my hand away and anger crossed his face. "God-fucking-dammit, Edie."

Missing two fingers didn't hurt his agility. He lowered himself through the tumbled wreckage of the spa and reached out for Rory. Rory grabbed hold, and Asher pulled him up, until he could put him down again safely inside.

"Watch out, I won't come for you again," he warned, and Rory nodded wildly.

My stomach reeled watching them climb back up, using the fixtures bolted to the spa's walls for support. I wanted to pretend it was because I was worried about them, or what we still had left to do, or the fact that this entire fucking boat was dropping into the sea, but I couldn't. Asher was too busy concentrating on handholds to see me. I ducked behind the counter and pressed a hand to my stomach, hard. "Stay in," I commanded my stomach contents quietly. I could have sworn I felt an answering thrill to my demand. I knew it was way too early to feel anything from the baby, but I added, "Please be the baby. Don't be a killer worm."

Asher pulled himself even with me. "Other than storm in to our deaths, do we have a plan?"

I smiled at him and tried to be encouraging. "We'll think of something. We always do."

CHAPTER THIRTY-SEVEN

If the spa's display table for all their tonics and brochures hadn't been bolted into the wall, we might not have made it out of the room. But we were able to use it like a ladder, until we reached the door at the top of the store. Rory was shaken by nearly being lost, whatever spell Asher's competence had had on him broken. The second we emerged from the door he started apologizing.

"I don't know what you two are, but I'm not like you." For a second I felt boldly proud—until his next words. "I need to get off this ship."

"Out of the mouths of babes," Asher said, giving me a look.

I wanted to encourage Rory to come with us, but I couldn't in good faith. The deck was getting worse. If he didn't go he might not make it back to where the life rafts were stowed.

"See those canisters?" Asher said, pointing to what looked like oil drums attached to the *Maraschino*'s railings at small intervals. "If all else fails, grab one of those and go overboard. They'll inflate if you pull the string out from the end."

"How do you know?" Rory asked him, like I'd learned how to stop myself from asking long ago.

"I read a lot of books. Hurry up. Good luck."

Rory nodded. "You too." And then he scrambled off as the deck neared forty-five degrees, and another wave hit the *Maraschino*'s side.

"We probably don't have much time," Asher said.

My hand found his injured one. "I know."

Together, we walked over the face of what had been the outer wall of the spa, up to the nice restaurant where we'd eaten a fancy dinner with Liz and Nathaniel just two nights before.

Arriving there like this in this set of circumstances somehow felt more right than the other night when I'd been all nicely dressed. This made more sense—the chaos, the mess, the nearness to death. Of course the last seven months of peace were just a dream; I'd been a fool to ever think they weren't. I didn't know if I didn't deserve happiness, although it sure as hell seemed like someone thought I didn't, or if chaos was in me from the way I was raised. But everything being messed up felt strangely right somehow. Probably because *messed up* could have been my middle name.

"I'm not going to let him kill you, Edie. We'll do what we have to do, and get lucky if we can, but you can't ask that."

"I'm not. I'm asking you to give us a chance to save the others." I nodded at him, and leaned in for a fast kiss. "I promise."

We reached the restaurant door, hung skew by either violence or the current gravity, and carefully crept in.

Nathaniel was there, leaning against a column near the front door. He looked the same as when I'd seen him last, except now he had an orange life jacket on. Two of his gunmen stood to either side.

Jorge, Marius, and Kate were strung up from the exposed beams in the ceiling, trussed like flies caught in a spider's web. They were gagged, but not so much that they couldn't talk around them. Jorge gasped to see us arrive, Marius's soldier's training kept him quiet, and Kate quietly moaned to herself, not in recognition. None of them looked well, but I was no shining example of health right now myself.

Nathaniel leaned forward but didn't take a step. With the unstable deck, he wasn't completely in control. "I knew you weren't dead, even if my men weren't always careful." He gave Asher a nod. "And look, you managed to rescue your man."

"What do you want?" Asher stood in front of me, blocking me with his body.

"Like I already told her. Revenge."

"I didn't kill your daughter. The Consortium did."

Nathaniel's eyes widened and then he laughed, cold and long. "Oh. Of course you would assume that. You couldn't possibly know." He pushed himself forward off the column and took a step nearer us, without blocking his hired guns. "The Consortium didn't come out to punish me themselves. They told my employers to 'clean things up.' Do you know what they did?" he asked us.

I shook my head, mute. Asher didn't move.

"They didn't *kill* her. They took her from me. They've had her, all this time. You ruined a decade of research and made monsters kidnap my only child."

Things fell into place. That was why Nathaniel was willing to sacrifice thousands of people to get the Leviathan on his side. He thought his daughter was still alive.

What wouldn't a parent do to try to rescue their own child?

"When I found out you were on board, with your lovely, stupid, pregnant wife—it was almost too good to be true. I couldn't believe my luck—and that's when I knew my

plan would work. You being here, me getting this chance—
it's fate. The Leviathan is already on its way." He took a
gun from one of his employees. Kate started to moan
louder, and from deep in the restaurant there was the
sound of a rush of water, as though a dam had burst, and
a shallow wave swept in across the back of the floor.

Nathaniel pointed the gun at us, and Asher moved to
stand in front of me. "You know I could have killed you
already, but I didn't. Don't get me wrong, I do want you
dead—but more than that, I want to take something of
yours. Your woman and your child. I'll take them away
from here and make you wonder every waking moment
of your days if they're still alive, or if I've killed them. If
they cursed you when they died. Maybe I'll even raise up
your child as my own. You can spend the rest of your life
imagining him calling me Father."

Despite saying he didn't want to kill us, he pointed the
gun straight at Asher's head—and then twisted it up, to
aim it at Kate. "Your woman will come over here or I'll
shoot them."

Asher flung his arm out to block me. "They're already
going to die."

"Are they? Can you be absolutely sure?"

The water lapped higher behind him, making some of
the fallen tables float. I pressed against Asher's arm.

"I was doing what I had to do to survive. What was
your excuse? You could have been anything! You could
have worked for anyone!"

Nathaniel's lips lifted up in a cruel smile. "So could
you." He shot the ceiling in front of Kate, and both Asher
and I jumped.

The faucet sound got louder, and some distant part of
the structure groaned, as if he'd wounded the *Maraschino*
itself. Kate began to scream around the gag. I thought she
was reacting to Nathaniel pointing the gun at her, but I

realized she was shouting a word. "Water! Water water water!" rising in volume each time.

"You come here, or I'll shoot her," Nathaniel said, addressing me, and then bringing the barrel of the gun down. "Or I'll shoot both of you and be done with it."

I stepped around Asher's arm with finality.

"Edie, don't you dare," he said as Nathaniel returned the gun to point at him.

Kate kept screaming, and water kept rushing in, and it seemed like I didn't have a choice. All I could do was walk slowly toward Nathaniel and block Asher from his gun—when Kate got torn in two.

She shrieked as she came unglued at the seam of her belly, like a doll torn between two dogs. Dark things rolled out of her, dripping down. Worms, cascading out, slithery and black, born one after another.

The previously unflappable gunmen startled at this. They were human, and the sight of a human unraveling and worms shedding out was beyond the pale; even Nathaniel was stunned. Jorge tried swimming away from her in midair, while Marius was impassive; he'd already seen worse in the Dolphin. The still-armed gunmen stepped back into Marius's kicking range, and he gave me a look with his eyes: *Whatever you're going to do, do it now!*

There was only one thing left that I could do. Nathaniel wanted me? Well, he could come and find me then—I intentionally slipped and fell, sliding for the far side of the room.

CHAPTER THIRTY-EIGHT

"No!" Nathaniel and Asher shouted behind me in unison, and I heard the sounds of a fight break out. I had time to register the heat of the friction burn the carpeting gave me as I crossed the entire room on my ass, slid into the water at its bottom, and was blasted with salty cold.

I was lucky not to be impaled on an upturned chair. If the water'd been any shallower, or if my ass had been sliding down tile—I splashed around without thinking about it, sputtering up. My feet found purchase on things that were already sunk in the room and I bobbed.

I was a poor swimmer but an excellent floater, courtesy of my God-given body fat. What I wasn't counting on was the cold. All the heat was leaving my body—I could feel the tables and chairs submerged below me and even stand on them for now, but for how long?

There was a splash beside me as someone slid down in the dark. I bit back a yelp of surprise and ducked, so that only my eyes were above the waterline.

The sound of struggling up above continued. The emergency lighting would have shown me Nathaniel's life jacket, so whoever had followed me down had to have been one of his guards.

Something moved beside me in the water, waving like a snake—one of the worms that had emerged from Kate.

In the seawater it was a patchy sickly green, like a glow stick left in a dirty gutter outside an all-ages club.

Every sphincter in my body clenched, but the awful thing slid on by. It had other places to be, and that was frightening too. It was one thing to be in a room that was filling with water; it would be another to be forced to swim out of here and into the open sea where a monster was rising up.

I heard a gurgle of air escaping from beside me, too near. I'd backed away from the worm without thinking, and gone nearer whoever else had fallen down. But he hadn't come down here on his own—blood was billowing out from his face in a slow wave. Marius must have kicked him and broken his nose, and in falling he hadn't been as lucky as me. The wind had been knocked out of him, or he'd been kicked senseless, and his face was underneath the rising tide.

Living in Port Cavell I'd heard too many stories about sailors climbing onto other sailors' backs to survive to want to be near one waking up. Whoever this man was, he'd watched Kate die, and he'd been willing to sacrifice me—not to mention all the other people who'd already died because of the machine gun that was pulling him below now.

I couldn't stop shivering anymore—I couldn't stay here much longer. I didn't have to bend over to hide; the water was so high I was standing, and soon I'd have to swim.

What kind of monster would you have to be to murder four thousand people? I'd been willing to throw a lot away to find Asher—how much greater destruction would I find myself capable of to save my own child? I wasn't like Nathaniel, but—

The man beside me gurgled again in a final-sounding way. I reached for him and unbuckled his life vest with numb fingers, slinging his limbs out of the armholes one at a time. I pushed him away when I was done. It wasn't the same as holding him under the water with my own hands, but it was close enough. We were swimming in the same blood-colored sea.

"Edie!" Asher called down to me. The fight above me was through.

I took another cautious look around to make sure I didn't see orange anywhere before I shouted out my location.

"Edie!" Asher shouted, voice breaking with desperation.

"I'm here! I'm fine! Come get me!"

Movement above blocked out the lights so I couldn't entirely see what was going on, which frightened me. It was a taste of what it would be like when the ship succumbed to the waves, and everything was dark.

"Hurry, please!" I shouted up.

"Hurrying!" Asher shouted back.

Asher managed to get Jorge and Marius down, and between the ropes that they'd been hung by and their own strength, they were able to lower a rope. I caught hold until they'd pulled me firmly up onto the damp carpeting, and then I clambered as they pulled. On my way I passed by Kate, still twitching and spewing out worm after worm to drop back into the rising sea.

"She's still alive—" I said with sorrow.

"That's not living," Marius said, giving me a final heave up into Asher's arms. He held me for a second, and then shook me once, hard.

"That was reckless and dumb."

"Says the man who said he'd be back in a day!" I shook him off. "Besides—you needed a distraction. Where did he go?" I looked around as if talking about Nathaniel might make him emerge, like saying an evil spirit's name.

"When the fight broke out he dove aside." Jorge clenched

his fists. "I'd like to see him again though—without a gun."

Asher's face said he had more to say to me, but that he'd wait until we were alone.

"Let's get out of here and find a lifeboat—" I said.

"If there are any left," Marius said darkly.

CHAPTER THIRTY-NINE

Asher held my hand like he was never letting go. "That was stupid of you."

"Well, you know. I'm stupid *and* lovely," I said, with a snort. "You couldn't fight him if you were busy protecting me. I took a chance."

"A shitty one."

"But it worked. Now we just need to get off this boat."

Outside, the storm had passed and it was almost dawn. The surface of the sea was eerily calm now in a way that I knew had horrified ancient mariners, courtesy of high school English class, as the *Maraschino* continued her stately descent. There were life rafts scattered around the surrounding sea, bright orange dots, but I couldn't see anyone on board any of them—maybe as the ship sank they'd been knocked loose?

The rest of the life rafts were still attached to the third floor, and we were up on the ninth. It wouldn't be safe for us to go back inside the ship, we all knew that without saying it aloud, although climbing down the outside of the ship still seemed like suicide—what I hadn't wanted to do with Claire and Hal and Emily hadn't gotten any safer since.

"If we follow the vertical railings—" Marius pointed

to the welded pipes that went from floor to floor, providing the structure for the plastic sheets that blocked the wind.

"Sure." Jorge grabbed hold of the first one and shimmied down it until his feet were on the balcony of the next floor. "I hope none of you is afraid of heights," he called back to us.

Marius followed him. Asher and I were bringing up the rear. Asher watched me mount the pipe. "Be careful."

"I will."

By holding on to the edge of the railings above, aligning my body with the pipe, and going slowly, I could just about get my feet down to the railings of the floor below us. It was an easier reach for the taller men, but I was managing, floor after floor. The thought of getting off this boat—even if was onto a smaller one—gave me wings.

Then the first wave hit. Not the *Maraschino*—but me. My stomach cramped, the muscles there turning into a knot. I groaned involuntarily.

"Edie?" Asher asked. Marius and Jorge were already down another floor.

"Sorry. The heights," I lied. My hands went white on the pipe I held as I tried to transfer the pain. My stomach released and I prayed the worst was over while I finished my shimmy—but no. My abdominal muscles had only relented to get a new hold. This time I managed not to groan, but it was harder.

We were almost there. We were so close. And all of my heroism didn't matter. I was losing the baby. Or myself, to a worm.

I threw myself down the pipe, almost spinning on it—if my wet clothing hadn't stuck I might have fallen off and onto the balcony below. But I didn't—I charged, in between seismic bursts of abdominal pain. Asher knew something was wrong. He came down nearly as fast as I did, and we found ourselves together much closer to the water's edge, on the wide promenade of the third floor.

Marius was taking control. "I can operate the davits. You all just push on it so that it starts to slide down the outside of the boat."

Another wave of pain hit. I grit my teeth, trying to bite back a scream.

Oh, God, was this how Kate had felt?

Asher grabbed me. "What's wrong?" he whispered.

"My stomach—I think—" I didn't want to say it aloud. His expression went dark.

Jorge was throwing his back into getting the life raft free from gravity. "A little help here?"

Asher looked at me. "We still have to get off the ship," I said, my voice flat. He stepped away from me reluctantly as I tried to hide another wave of pain. I sank slowly to my knees as he pushed against the lifeboat with his back, eyes on me.

This wasn't fair. I was still alive after all this time. I didn't want to be filling up with worms, or losing this child. It wasn't fair.

Asher and Jorge weren't enough—Marius eyed me warily from the davit controls.

"I'll show you how to do it, so I can help lift."

I nodded, practically crawling over to him, and using the control panel itself to pull myself up. The joysticks were like playing one of those claw-and-grab games. "I can do it. Go."

As the davits pulled from above the three of them managed to get the life raft over the lip of the boat. From there it was a straight drop down the hull into the water. Marius came back to oversee lowering it, letting the ropes down slowly, the metal of the life raft grating against the metal of the *Maraschino*'s side. I sank down, my back against the control panel, curled into a ball.

Jorge was looking over the railing's edge, oblivious to anything other than the life raft's progress. "It's in the sea! You've done it!"

All that was left was to somehow get aboard.

A fresh wave hit, and this time I had to scream. Asher rushed to my side to cradle me.

"Oh, no. No no no," Jorge said, looking back, as he realized what was happening.

Marius started shaking his head and backing away. "She's not getting in my boat."

Asher's grip on me tightened. "We have a greater chance of survival if we're all in the same boat."

"She's infected—"

"You all probably are!"

Marius drew himself up to his full height—the same as Asher, and wider in the shoulders. "She's not getting in my boat," he repeated.

"She risked her life to save you!"

"I'm sorry for your loss, I truly am—but if she's like Kate was, she's already as good as dead."

At this, Asher erupted from my side and went for Marius, swinging.

"Don't!" I said, but neither of them heard me, and maybe I hadn't said it as loud as I'd thought. It felt as if I were getting rabbit-punched in the lower abdomen, over and over again. What the hell was happening inside me?

Marius and Asher couldn't circle each other at the ship's angle, but both of them watched for openings, like people who'd beat the shit out of other people before.

"Stop it—" I pleaded. Jorge knelt by my side, ignoring the other men.

"Are you okay?"

It hurt so bad it was hard to talk. I just nodded while grimacing, holding my stomach, rocking back and forth.

"It's going to be okay," Jorge said, and even though I knew he was lying, it was still nice to hear. I nodded again, and he squeezed my shoulders, until the most recent wave of cramps were done.

"I think it's the baby. I'm losing it," I whispered.

"I'm sure that's what it is," he kindly agreed. Because miscarrying was slightly less awful than being burst apart by worms.

Asher and Marius had gotten a few blows in on each other, but the tilting of the boat was making it hard. It was one of those fights that'd degrade into a wrestling match given the chance, and it wouldn't stop until someone got hurt. "We'll take another boat," I said, but only Jorge could hear me. More cramps hit me, like a physical blow. This was worse than when I'd been stabbed—and Asher'd saved me then, too. I whimpered, and Asher looked toward me, and then Marius—

"Look out!" I hissed.

Marius swung, connected, and followed through, his entire body leaning into his punch. It connected on Asher's jaw with a loud smack and sent him reeling uphill, to fall back on the empty deck. Marius came forward to kick Asher, but Asher recovered, faster than a normal human would. My man was still a little supernatural, after all. He lunged for Marius's outswept leg, grabbed it, and twisted, hauling Marius over himself and down.

Impossibly quick, Asher was up again, on top of Marius like a cat. Marius was facing down on the deck, and Asher was on his back, Marius's head between his hands. He started bashing it against the deck's wood.

"No!" I protested, a fresh wave of cramps turning it into a howl. Jorge turned his face into me so he wouldn't see. I was left gasping as the wave passed, I hurt so badly I was dizzy, it made it hard to see or think—

"Stop! Everyone stop!" A new voice broke over the awful sound of their fighting. "I have a knife!"

There was a lull in the haze of pain. I blinked furiously, and things came into focus.

"Get off him!" someone commanded.

Rory. His voice broke as he shouted, and I could see him brandishing his weapon, the same knife he'd used to help me cut Asher free.

Asher paused, weighing his options. "Why are you still here, boy?" Marius tried to shake Asher off again, and I was relieved: It meant that Marius wasn't dead yet.

Rory laughed harshly, at himself, and then pointed at Asher with his knife. "I was too scared to go alone. I should have been too scared to go with you!" He pointed again with the knife, this time, off to the left. "Take that raft—it's one of those canister rafts you told me about. It's yours. But let him live. He's a good man. I don't know what the fuck you are, but he's a good man."

Asher released his hold on Marius, and the prone man groaned. "Take care, sweetheart," Jorge said, letting go of me and rounding Asher for Marius's side.

Marius's nose was broken, and he was stunned—he'd need help to get into the raft for sure, and who knew what kind of other concussion damage Asher's violence had done—but he was able to stumble to a kneel. Rory gave his knife a warning shake in our direction, and then went to help Marius up.

No way in hell we'd be welcome on their boat.

"Get out of here. All of you," Asher warned, like we were leaving them instead of the other way around. Jorge helped Rory pull Marius up to the side, and then they were over, down the *Maraschino*'s hull to the lifeboat.

CHAPTER FORTY

Asher's face was bloody, his jaw swelling where Marius's fist had hit. "It's just us now. You and me."

I nodded. Talking hurt. Everything hurt.

"I'm so sorry, Edie. I should have listened to you. We should have never gone on this trip."

"S'okay," I gasped out to stop him from blaming himself. We were past that. "S'go."

"After all this you still want to spend time on a boat with me?" Asher said, his damaged face framed by the rising sun. The Shadows may have used us both, but they couldn't change what we had together. I knew I loved him. White hot and pure. Strange, no strange, monster, and man.

I gasped as a new wave of cramps hit, tearing through the muscles of my abdomen like they were on fire. "You're my only," I whispered. I knew it didn't make sense. I knew he'd know what I meant.

He pulled me to him and held me tight as I tried not to scream and wound up sobbing helplessly in pain and fear.

"Stay here, okay?" He set me down carefully. The sound of the ocean was higher now. He went over to the canister Rory'd left and pulled the cord.

There was a hiss, and I was worried the ocean had finally

won its long war against the *Maraschino,* but it was the sound of pressurized air inflating the life raft instead.

"I'll get you into it up here, and then I'll get it over the edge, and then we'll get away," Asher explained, as if saying the words would make doing it easier.

The raft inflated quickly, and Asher hoisted it over the side. It took him longer to get me into it—I tried to help, honestly, but I hurt so badly, all I could do was curl up into a ball while he hefted me up and rolled me in. I landed inside it and it bottomed out, meant to support people in water, not above it, and I worried we'd catch on some puncturing piece of metal that the more solid lifeboat had scratched off the hull on its way down.

I was trying to arch my back enough to prevent this, and Asher was outside, hauling us down to the waterline, when our progress was interrupted by the sound of a wet thump and a voice that couldn't be denied.

"Monster of men, I command you to answer me!"

The dragging sensation outside stopped.

"Monster of men!"

"I have a name," Asher told someone.

"Get down here! Now!"

Even I felt the urge to answer her—and I knew who we were speaking to. I lifted my head weakly out of the raft. Claire was there, beached on the diminishing remnants of the *Maraschino*'s hull like a Renaissance painting come to life. She was as long as a twelve-person dinner table, most of her tail, and looked nothing like the frail elderly woman Hal had loved. Her hair was the color of kelp, from dark brown to translucent yellow, and her tail was covered in variegated scales, ending in an extravagant fin—but the top part of her was human-ish. Her fingers ended in talon-like claws, all the better to spear fish with I assumed, and something about the color and shape of her skin made me feel it would be rubbery to touch.

"Make this work," she said, her monstrous voice an imperious command. She had far too many teeth.

Asher took in whatever she'd shared with him—I couldn't see what it was. "This ship is already lost."

"It's not for this ship. It's for that one," she explained, and then her voice changed again in pitch, becoming one of command. "Make it work. Now."

"Stop that," Asher said, kneeling down. "I'll do it if you can fix her."

I saw Claire's head wave back and forth. "I can't. It's not just your child living inside her now."

Asher stopped whatever he was doing. I saw his shoulders go still. "Heal her," he begged.

"Would that it were that easy," she said snappishly. Then perhaps remembering her years as a human, "It is beyond me. I'm sorry."

I concentrated on pulling myself up so I could see what Asher was working on. Claire had brought him something that looked like putty that I recognized. The packages of C-4 we'd left downstairs, the ones that Hal had stopped from exploding. Claire must have swum below to retrieve them, presumably in through the gaping hole that the ones that had exploded had left.

I hadn't known that Asher had had a demolitions expert inside him, but I shouldn't have been surprised.

"I have no idea how you're going to light all this," Asher said as he worked.

"I overturned lifeboats until one of them gave a flare gun to me."

Asher paused at this, possibly, like me, imagining those lifeboats carrying people she spilled into the water, then shook his head and kept working.

"Emily?" I asked quietly, knowing she would hear.

"She's none of your business now," Claire said. Her

dark eyes were sad, looking at me. "She's safe," she amended, more kindly.

Asher continued to work as the sound of the water came closer. "You only brought me five minutes of fuse. Once you light this—" he warned her.

"I'm built to swim," she cut in.

"And you know where to use it?"

She laughed bitterly, an awful sound. "Hal was a torpedoman."

Asher nodded and gave his finished work to Claire. She took it in one taloned hand and held it to her breast like a child as she used her free arm and tail to propel herself back into the sea. I let myself relax back into the raft as Asher appeared overhead.

"Ready?"

"Yeah." I had my two fists punching in over my stomach, unsuccessfully trying to keep it from knots. Another wave hit, hurt so bad I could puke, and then left me. I could see the fear on Asher's face looking down. Claire had told us both the truth. They were worms. I was going to die.

The pill I'd palmed had already melted in my pocket.

"Where's she going?" I whispered when I could. Anything to stop him from looking down at me like that.

"I think we'll see."

He disappeared again, and I felt us sliding until we hit the water with a slap. Then the edge buckled as Asher jumped in beside me ungracefully, letting cold water in.

It wasn't until I could feel us rocking in the waves like we were in a cradle that I realized we'd escaped the *Maraschino* at last.

CHAPTER FORTY-ONE

The *Maraschino* died as it had lived, slowly and stately. It sank beneath the waves as though it were merely going on another trip, only this time to the bottom of the sea. There was no sucking woosh or danger of us being pulled in after it. Burbles of air escaped, like an ancient volcano burped below, and then it was gone, along with everyone else who hadn't survived, all their deaths red on the hands of a madman.

In between waves of cramps, my curiosity outweighed my pain. I used my elbows to prop my head up on the raft's edge so I could look around outside its canopy. The surrounding waters were full of random debris, clothing, pieces of furniture, and madly swimming worms. Now free of their human hosts they twisted around one another, copulating in the growing dawn, releasing streamers of luminescent eggs into the ocean like scattered stars. Those were what I'd seen frothing in the sink, and out of the weird woman's mouth. Worm eggs.

Like what was growing inside me. I sank back into the raft bleakly.

It wasn't any warmer here than it had been on the *Maraschino*. Jorge, Marius, and Rory had gotten into a lifeboat, but this was only an inflated half-a-foot of air and rubber between us and the sea, and a canvas canopy to protect us from the sun. We didn't even have a paddle. Asher leaned over me and out the raft's door, swirling his hand.

"Edie, look," he said, and I leaned up again to see.

We were pointed at the rescue ship that I felt sure Claire was swimming toward.

I didn't know what we were waiting for—all the explosions I'd ever seen in my life had been televised. But Asher's hand kept us steady, and I was warm where he lay beside me and his skin touched mine.

We were too far away to hear it, but we saw it, half a second before we were sprayed with salt mist.

The bow of Nathaniel's ship hopped up as though it had hit a speed bump beneath the waves. I got the feeling that keeping the explosion underwater made it worse—there was nowhere for all that energy to go but up. It shuddered, and where it had jumped, it broke in two.

"She keel-whipped it," Asher said to himself, sounding like he approved. Maybe Asher had touched a torpedoman in his former life.

"Whoa," I said, trying to bite off the end of the word so it didn't roll into a groan.

The explosion Claire had caused created a chain reaction of combustibles within the ship. Sailors and soldiers flowed overboard like mythical lemmings, jumping into the water to escape the flames. I wondered how many more deaths would feed the Leviathan today because of her.

There was no way for them to reach their lifeboats. Only the helicopter made it off, just in time.

Asher leaned out and paddled bodily toward a field of debris. He pulled out one official orange paddle, a lucky find, and then a piece of a deck chair. It would be useless as a paddle; it wasn't thick on either end, and I didn't think I could help paddle, besides. Asher saw the questioning look on my face.

"In case they make it this far," he said, and jabbed it out the raft's opening demonstratively.

I snorted. "Don't pop the boat."

Soon we'd be alone. Just me, Asher, and whatever else was dying—or coming to life—inside me.

CHAPTER FORTY-TWO

The fleeing helicopter swooped overhead, surveying the destruction below. Lucky bastards, whoever it was inside. Asher pulled me farther inside the raft and I groaned.

"Edie, I'm so sorry—"

I shook my head. I didn't want to hear it. I didn't blame him. Nathaniel, yes, for being crazy and evil, but not Asher, not ever him. I wouldn't take back a moment I'd spent with him, even knowing it would all lead to this. He was the love of my life, even as I felt like it was ending. "I love you," I said, hoping that that would say it all.

He pushed my wet hair away from my face, his hand catching in its tangles. "You don't have to die. You're the strongest person I know—"

Whatever he said next was drowned out by the sound of the helicopter making a second low pass. "Goddammit, they don't have to rub it in," Asher said.

It paused when it arrived over us again. Its attention spun us in a circle, the blades pushing the water below them back in concentric rings, and the top of the life raft shuddered with the force of the sinking air. A door opened on the helicopter's side and a man began to lower himself.

Nathaniel. He hadn't gone down with the *Maraschino* or his mercenaries. Maybe he was right, and this was his fate. The muscles of my stomach roiled again and I screamed in pain and defeat.

No matter what happened, he'd already won.

"If he can save you—" Asher said, pressing forward, waving Nathaniel down.

"No," I gasped out.

"He has a cure—"

"No!" I shouted, letting my anger ride another wave.

The towrope Nathaniel was dangling from lowered, and he held his arms out like he was a descending god—carrying a knife.

"If you save her—" Asher began to shout out, over the whirring sound of the helicopter blades—

And then I felt something beneath us. Like in summertime pools, when your older brother tries to be stealthy and sneak up on you and push you out of your inflatable lounge chair. The bottom layer of the raft rose up and rubbed against the top layer beneath me, making the entire raft subtly rise.

My eyes widened and I looked at Asher, but he was too busy bargaining to feel it.

A tentacle snaked out of the water. Three times as large as any of the worms I'd seen, much much longer, it rose up like a cobra about to strike.

"Asher!" I shouted in warning as the tentacle lunged for Nathaniel's ankle and pulled.

He'd been so busy plotting to hurt us that he didn't see it until it was too late. The harness trapped him upright; he couldn't lean down to get his knife into play. The tentacle tugged down twice, like a fish testing bait on a bob, and then yanked. The helicopter dipped, listing to its open side, and a startled man fell out, while others barely hung on.

The helicopter reeled in line, but only lowered itself

without raising Nathaniel an inch. He was frantically gesturing for them to pull him up—I saw the knife glint in the sun as he dropped it, forgotten—and they were trying to do as he told them, tilting away, but the tentacle yanked again, making the helicopter jump. In the frantic tug-of-war between its panicked pilots and whatever was beneath the waves, Nathaniel lost.

His leg tore off. It dropped into the ocean and blood spattered down like rain. The helicopter, finally free, rose abruptly and started flying sideways at the same time, but not fast enough. A second tentacle rose, and then a third, grabbing Nathaniel's remaining ankle, and then climbing higher up the towrope.

I saw whoever was inside the helicopter run away from the wench. Nathaniel zinged out like a badge on a broken reel, cut loose, dropping into the ocean. The helicopter, now free, bucked up into the sky.

But impossibly long tentacles flew out of the water to catch its running boards. The men inside leaned out to hack them away, and were in turn themselves caught, plucked out of the helicopter as though by Scylla herself, squeezed into halves and thirds, and then those pieces pulled down into the sea.

I knew just enough about physics to know that it wasn't only a matter of strength—that whatever was below had to be more massive than what was above us in the air. It was as if we were watching an old-time woodcut, where an octopus was wrestling a ship, only being reenacted with a helicopter and some kind of demon.

The pilot must have been the only person left, shielded by his seat. He tried valiantly, weaving back and forth against the tentacles, diving down once to buy himself time, but nothing worked. Nothing would work. The Leviathan was hungry.

The helicopter hit the sea like a sack of bricks. The

blades chipped against the water like it was cement and shattered, sending chunks of plastic and metal skipping out. Asher put his arm over me to protect me, and by the time he pulled back, it was done. The helicopter was down. I couldn't even see where it'd landed.

Asher pressed a finger to his lips—as if we could hide from the monster by being very-very-quiet, Elmer Fudd–style—and I would have laughed, if another wave of cramps hadn't hit.

There was a splashing sound from beside us, and then a loud gasp. Both of us turned to look out and saw Nathaniel there, bobbing up courtesy of his life jacket.

"No!" he yelled. Whatever was still below caught hold of him again—and dragged him back down.

CHAPTER FORTY-THREE

I don't know how—if I felt safe, was exhausted, or was dying slightly more slowly than I had been—but I slept as the life raft shaded us from the sun. When I woke up, it was dark, and Asher was asleep too.

Out here, with the moon at quarter strength, I could almost believe we'd done this on purpose, we'd just taken a lovely vacation out to sea. The raft rocked back and forth like a mother's arms as the moonlight filtered in.

My stomach didn't actively hurt anymore—it was just sore, exhausted as the rest of me. I moved slightly away from Asher so that I could see out better. No land in any direction around us. It was as if we were the only people on earth.

And the water looked inviting. I knew it'd be cold, but only for that first second of shock. After that it would welcome me, and draw me in. Who knew how deep it was out here? I could hop off this raft for a moment, dive down, and see.

I could even drink it. Drink it all in.

As though I were in a dream, I pulled my legs into myself and found purchase against the handholds that lined the raft's sides. It was as though a god had drawn this magnificent bathtub just for me; I only had to go and lie down in it.

Without taking in a breath, or any thought of breathing ever again, I went over the side.

The water welcomed me like I thought it would. I didn't know why I'd ever been afraid of it. I heard Asher's panicked scream and then it cut him off for me. Everything was simpler down here, cold, quiet, wet. The water hugged me, pressed in on all sides, and held me close. My hair, ungainly and tangled above, was radiant here, floating out in the moonlight. I dropped down like a stone, and felt my ears pop, but there was still more to the deep.

A luminescence grew beneath me. Down where the sea went black, a hundred-hundred bright eyes opened up, as if seeing for the first time in ages. They blinked up at me in a syncopated rhythm, sending me signals from the dark. I didn't know what the meaning was, but I would learn. I was sure the light would teach me.

Something grabbed my foot. Asher? Ruining this? I kicked, and the thing grabbed up my leg.

There was a ripple in the water in front of me that spun me around, although this far down I didn't know which way was up. Hands grabbed my armpits, shoving me through the water, pulling me where I didn't know. I felt currents of water moving against my flesh, and something strong kept hitting my feet with a thump.

A song kept time with us, so sweet. No wonder I had jumped. If I hadn't, I never would have heard anything like it.

The water got lighter; then we breached and I was divorced from the waves.

A child's smile rose up in front of me, her face low. Emily. I could see the gills on her neck below the waterline, pumping, and envied her them. I knew she was still singing as her new tail beat time.

"Thirsty—" I explained. For water, for answers, for the light-in-the-darkness's touch.

"No," answered a voice behind me, and I felt strong hands on my back hoisting me up and into the life raft again. I felt abandoned as Asher looked back behind himself. "Thank you for this. I'm glad you're well."

I leaned up to fight with him, to get her to take me back, but it was too late, just a ripple and the flick of a tail flapping against the surface of the sea. There was no way to tell where she'd gone. Why wouldn't she take me?

Asher crouched over me in the life raft. I was so mad at him I couldn't even put it into words.

"Thirsty," I spat out, when I could figure out how.

"I love you, but I'm not listening to you say things like that." He took the end of the cord that had inflated the raft and started wrapping it around me.

CHAPTER FORTY-FOUR

Asher tried to stay up, but couldn't—so instead he fell back asleep on top of me, me tied, him perpendicular across to my legs. My mouth ached it was so dry. I would do anything to drink. I wondered if this was how vampires felt.

A piece of the surrounding dark detached itself in the moonlight and crossed the bottom of the life raft, scurrying like a large beetle. I shook my head and tried to free myself, but it came up the side of the raft, so close I couldn't turn my head to see it, but I could feel it crawl into my ear.

"Hello, Edie!"

The Shadows or a piece of them. Of course they'd survived. At my thinking this, they laughed. They were in my head now, and they sounded excited to see me. Great.

"We didn't think you'd manage to last this long!" they said, and sounded cheerful as they said it.

No thanks to you.

"Well, we are the reason that you're here. Maybe you'll thank us later. You never know," they said, and laughed like they'd made a hilarious joke. "Ah, no, really, your son's been doing all the hard work of keeping you alive.

Shapeshifter DNA—if you can call it that—is really quite amazing. Very robust immune systems. We're hoping you live now, so that we can get the chance to meet him. We've never met a human–shapeshifter hybrid before."

I didn't want them to ever meet my son, if that's what he wound up being. I imagined giving birth on the face of the sun, under lights so bright even the Shadows had to hide. They laughed at this—and then all my imagined light reminded me how parched my mouth was, how this night was very dry, and all I wanted to do was drink and never stop—

"That's the worms talking. Don't listen."

But there was nothing else I could think of other than my thirst—my thirst and the thing I'd seen when I'd tried to quench it, the thing beneath the waves, with a thousand all-seeing eyes—and I felt the Shadows inside my ear jump.

"Did you tell it that we were here? Does it know?"

Know what? I rubbed my head against the bottom of the raft, trying to get them out.

"About us!" they whined, painfully loud in my ear.

"I don't know!" I whispered around the gag in my mouth so they'd shut up. *Why are you scared of it?*

"You of all people know what it's like to have relatives you're ashamed of, Edie. Ashamed of, scared of—trust us, our relatives are worse."

Asher stirred, and I willed him to go back to sleep. I thought if he were awake the Shadows would stop talking to me, and for the first time ever they seemed willing to share answers. *Nathaniel's dead, right?*

"Fish food. Literally."

Can you go get help for us?

"We're as stranded as you are. We got here inside your shoe. Decided to hitch a ride on you inside the morgue."

So not only can you not save me, I saved you. Awesome.

"We'd say that we'd owe you one, but we're not entirely sure you'll survive. We're cheering for you though." Then they shouted, "Go Edie!" sarcastically.

I bounced my head off the bottom of the raft, hoping to knock them loose, as they laughed very loudly. I gave up, and they settled down.

I asked the only question I had left to ask. *Are you sure it's going to be a boy?*

The aura of smug mystery finally returned to their voices. "What do you think?"

CHAPTER FORTY-FIVE

I woke up with a start, gasping for air. I have to tell Asher something.

Everything's bright and orange, and I can only see through one eye. The other eye's swollen shut; it burns when I try to open it. Water slaps rubber, over and over, in endless slow applause. I remember the sound from child-hood, floating down a lazy river in an inner tube, drunk from beer my older brother had snuck me when I was sixteen.

"Edie? Are you okay?" Asher's leaning over me. His voice is hoarse.

I have to tell him something.

But I can't. There's rope in my mouth. And I can't pull the rope away because my hands are tied. My feet too. I'm hog-tied, and when I move my shoulder starts to throb.

"Is it still you?" Asher asks me. I don't know why he's asking. I don't know what he means.

I have to tell you something, I try to say around the rope, even though I can't remember what it was.

"I'm so sorry, Edie. I'm so, so sorry. It is you, right?" he asks, and his voice cracks.

I want to comfort him. To tell him that I'm okay, even though it's clear that I am not. He looks so afraid right now. I've never seen him this afraid before.

"We're going to be all right. We're going to get away from here. I'm going to save you," he says, more to himself than me. He scuttles backward and brings up what I realize was a paddle, then leans over the side of the orange thing we're riding on and paddles for all his might.

Inside my mind, things slide into place. My ties, our lifeboat. What I want to say to him.

He's paddling so hard to nowhere that salt water is spraying my face.

And I remember.

Everything.

CHAPTER FORTY-SIX

The sound of helicopters in moonlight. One flits over to us and dips down like a dragonfly.

All this—again?

Men descend from the sky, only this time Asher helps me over to them. Strange hands grab me, fasten me down, and then hoist me up. I'm frantic until Asher's brought up too—they let him sit beside me. They leave me tied.

I lose track of time. I can't hear anything, and Asher's buckled in. I wake up when we land with a bounce.

Men undo the latches that hold the gurney in place and bring it into a room. Somewhere. All I can really see is the ceiling—and I know with unflinching certainty and sadness that they are taking me away from the sea.

"Is there any other way?" Asher's voice breaks through the fog inside my mind. I leave my eyes closed so that I can't see anything, so that I can pretend that we're still on the ocean. If I concentrate hard enough, I can still feel the waves rocking me.

"The fact that it is your child is the only thing that's kept her alive this far. But even now the baby loses strength. When it dies, so will she," says a voice that's strange.

"This is wrong." Asher's again. "I want it to be Anna."

"Anna's the one that sent us." Stranger one again.

"She's on the other side of the country." And stranger two. Both of them sound imperious.

There is a long pause. Long enough that I can almost convince myself I am back at sea, in the water's cold embrace.

"What if she never forgives me?"

"Do, or don't, the choice is yours." Stranger one sounds exhausted. "Anna told us not to force you. But dawn is near."

"And she won't live to see another night if you delay." Stranger two sounds amused by Asher's pain.

What's hurting him? Instinct struggles to mount a response over lassitude, and wins. Whatever's hurting him, I'll kill it. I clench my fists and find my hands still tied. Asher places a calming hand atop my brow.

"Okay. Do it. Now."

"By the order of the Sanguine, and with the permission of Anna Arsov, progenitor of the Arsov Throne, I bind Edith Spence eternally to me, Raven of the Catacombs."

"No—wait—" Asher says.

But whatever he objects to, it's too late. Something flows into my mouth. It tastes like salt, but it's not water.

CHAPTER FORTY-SEVEN

It felt like everything had changed when I woke up. I felt . . . healthy. Like a long fever had broken. And nothing hurt.

"Good morning, sunshine," a voice said. I turned and found Anna standing right beside me. Her blond hair was unkempt, like she'd just woken up.

"Anna?" I leaned over to look past her, and then around at the rest of the strange room, in case I'd been pranked, and then returned my attention to her again. "How come you're here?"

"Because I told them that if I weren't by you when I woke up, I'd slaughter every single one of them. So they put my coffin over there." She pointed behind herself.

I looked past her. It didn't look like a coffin. It looked like a lightproof, bombproof shipping container. Where the hell was I? And what time was it? How long had I been out? I remembered the life raft—and Asher and my child. I put my hand to my stomach as I said Asher's name. "Where is he? Is he all right?"

"He'll be here shortly."

"What's going on? Why are you here?"

Anna took my warm hands gently in her cooler ones. "What he did, he did it for you. You both might regret it

later, but he did what he thought was right at the time.
Don't be mad at him."

"For what?"

She gave me a sad smile. "You know what."

Like a door unlocking, memories slid into place. And
the last one was of a pale stranger looming over me and
the hot taste of blood. "Oh—no."

"It was the only way to save you. He never would have
allowed it otherwise. And I'm just as guilty as him—they
were here because I asked." She swallowed. "I wanted
you to have a choice. I didn't want you to die."

"Am I . . ." *like you* was what I was going to say, but it
was clear that I was not. My skin still had color, and I
could hear my own pulse. Anna had a pulse too, being
living and all, but hers was not like mine.

I knew because I could hear it, beating inside her.

"Oh, no," I said again, more quietly.

She shook her head. "You can tame it, Edie. You're not
one of us, yet. And nothing says you have to be. Daytimers die all the time without knowing another drop of
vampire blood."

"I would have never—" I began.

She stiffened and looked over her shoulder at something I couldn't hear, then leaned in to whisper quickly.
"You'll have a week of almost invulnerability before the
blood goes thin—and don't think ill of me. No matter
what stories you hear."

I nodded because I knew I was supposed to, even if
everything was still too much for me to take in. The door
behind her opened up, and Asher arrived. What would he
make of daytimer-me?

"Edie?" he asked, looking at me in relief. "You're
alive."

I nodded hesitantly. "So far?"

He crossed the room to me in a rush and took me in his arms and I knew everything would be all right.

"Oh Edie—" His arms folded around me and he held me to his chest. "I couldn't just let you die." My beloved, ever strong for me, broke down into sobs. I hopped off the table I was on and fit under his arm just like I always did. He held me close and kissed my face, his hot tears sticking between us.

If our positions were reversed, I would never let him die. It was unfair, even if this . . . was unthinkable. "It's okay, it's okay," I tried to soothe him, running my hands through his hair. "We'll just pretend this never happened. We'll be fine."

He held me like he wanted to press me inside himself, and I would have been fine with that. After all we'd been through I didn't want him to ever let me go again. "I can't believe we made it. We survived." I assumed that if all this had been done for the sake of our child, I in turn still carried it. "Did anyone else make it out?"

Asher nodded, as Anna answered me. "They were turned into daytimers like you were, earlier yesterday. Your smaller raft took longer to find."

I blinked and pulled away from Asher's chest. "Turned?"

"They were all infected, as were you."

At least I knew vampires existed before one turned me. "Wow." I shook my head and dove back into Asher's safe chest. Everything was over. We were finally safe. Changed, but safe. If we were alive—there was hope. I smiled and looked up at Asher, but he didn't look happy yet.

"Hey—I'm scared too. But we'll figure it out somehow," I told him. And I remembered what the Shadows had told me—"It's a boy. We're having a boy."

Happiness lit his face, "Oh, Edie—" There was a knock

at the door behind him, and he bit his lips and bowed his head again.

"Is the family reunion over?" someone asked, and didn't wait for permission to come in.

"Edie, meet Raven," Anna said, introducing the stranger who entered.

Raven smiled at me, as toothy as a shark. "We've already met."

"I apologize, but," Anna went on, her gaze serious and dark, old beyond her years, "my coffin didn't make it here in time. I was two thousand miles away from you when I was notified. I had to call in favors before I could get here myself."

Raven smiled at her in turn. He looked like one of those vampires in the movie Asher and I had watched, with long black hair and clothing that was shiny. "Whoever would think that someday I would be in a position of power over you?"

The private kindness Anna showed toward me left her. "One human life isn't precisely a position of power."

"You're fond of her or you wouldn't be here. It's too late for lies." His lips rose up, and between the paleness of his skin and the oil slick of his clothing, he looked like the reflection of something a whale spit up on the beach. He turned toward me, still snarling. "You're now my servant. And it's time to go."

"Wait—what?"

"Time to go," he commanded again. And just as when Claire had ordered me, I couldn't disobey. I let go of Asher and stepped away. Asher stepped with me, trying to hold me back.

"No—" I protested.

"There's no need to be cruel," Anna said.

"Let me remind you whose territory you are in, Beastly One."

Anna stood taller and got that look in her eye that said she was going to make people pay. "The last Beast alive. I am no stranger to blood."

Raven gave her a withering smile. "Right now if I die, she dies. My blood inside her is very fresh." He snapped his fingers. "Girl, come."

I took another awful step. Asher was still crushing me. "They told me it's only until you have our baby. If you want to keep it. It's up to you."

"Then what?" Hope—any hope—I needed it.

"Then I change you all the way, and take you back as mine," Anna said, loud enough that the entire room could hear.

"Change me now." I looked over at Raven and the follower he'd brought with him. I didn't want to go with them, and I didn't want to be commanded to do things that I couldn't disobey. Being a vampire with Anna was better than that. "Just change me now."

Anna's voice was rich with sorrow when she spoke again. "If I change you now, the child dies. Children don't survive the changing process. Ever."

"Oh." I swallowed. This was Asher's and my only chance. Our child's only chance. Whatever it was, whatever he would become—this was the only way.

"I heard stories from the others that were saved. If she could let anything die, we wouldn't be here," Raven said drolly.

"Just nine months?" I asked Anna. "Eight, if you count time served?"

"Until you have the baby," she said, and then looked to Raven. "I expect you to give her back to me alive."

"Technically, enough of her will be," Raven said.

Asher pressed his forehead to mine. "I'll watch over you somehow. I'll make sure you're all right."

"There's no prohibition about me killing this man, is

there?" Raven asked the air as though it might answer him back.

It was just eight months. Eight months and then I'd be free. I could survive anything for eight months, couldn't I? Couldn't . . . we?

I kissed Asher fiercely, surprising him with my strength. And he knew my kiss for what it was, a promise and a good-bye. We'd had kisses like this before. We'd lost each other—and we'd found each other again. Things had been perfect for a time. If we were both alive, we could get that back.

I twisted my head as if to drink him in, grinding my lips and teeth against his until blood ran between us and found I didn't mind.

"Now," Raven said, and the sound of his voice was like a snapping leash pulling an unseen collar I wore.

"Just eight months," I whispered, stepping back from Asher. He nodded, his intent turning steel. He could wait eight months—but after that, hell wouldn't stop Asher from coming to save me and our boy.

Anna placed herself in my path and stopped me. "I wish I could tell you that it would be easy, or that Raven would be kind. But it would behoove him to do as I say, or risk my wrath. I am the first of my line, and I already have many followers. I can endlessly make more, and would do so, for the sake of you."

I nodded at her. That was all Raven's invisible leash would let me do. Pulled by something I couldn't explain, I was forced to walk to his side.

"At last," he said, and then bowed to the room. "Anna, lovely to be threatened by you, as always. Wolf, get the car."

Raven pulled me outside into the rain. It seemed not to hit him, but I definitely felt myself getting wet. Tears I'd been hiding for Asher's sake leaked from my eyes.

A black car—of course—pulled up, and Raven opened up the back door for me. "Get inside."

I did as I was told, and sat down. I buckled my seat belt, which made Raven laugh. When he was done, Wolf, beside me in the back, pulled out a black velvet hood.

"Can't have you seeing the way to our lair," he said, sliding it over my head. My hands weren't trapped at my sides, but there was no point in fighting him—if I did, they would be.

A blackness darker than the night or the ocean depths came down.

I'd survived, and my child lived, but we weren't going home.

BLOODSHIFTED

By Cassie Alexander

Coming soon from St. Martin's Paperbacks

We were alive.

It didn't matter that I was blindfolded and being kidnapped by vampires, as long as my child and I were still alive.

Right?

We just have to get through the next eight months, baby. The car I was sitting in shifted gears. I felt it speed up, and knew each mile was carrying me farther away from everything I knew and everyone I loved. My past was spooling out behind me like a ribbon and I didn't know if I'd be able to catch the end of it before it ran out.

If Anna was smart, she'd made Asher go back with her on the next flight home. I imagined him looking out a plane window at the same blackness I saw inside my blindfold, wondering if he'd done all he could, if there'd been another way. I wanted to touch him again so badly it burned.

I reached up for the necklace he'd given me instead. The vampire sitting beside me growled in warning and I carefully set my hand back down.

Eight months was longer than Asher and I'd even been dating. But when I'd found out I was pregnant, everything felt right. He loved me and I loved him, and we were going to get married on a beach in Hawaii. I'd have said everything was going according to plan, only there wasn't one at the time. But everything had felt right—up until the cruise ship we'd been on had been taken over by a madman who'd released a parasite designed to ensure the death of everyone on board.

We'd had to fight for our lives and I'd gotten infected. By the time our life raft was found, Anna had called in long-distance favors asking for local vampire thrones to save survivors, vampire blood being the only cure for the supernatural ailment. The blood worked, but it came with a huge side effect—it bound you to the vampire that gave it to you.

So now, not that long after treating daytimers back at floor Y4, I'd been forced to become one.

Anna had offered to change me into a vampire as soon as she'd arrived, and her blood would have trumped Raven's, the vampire who'd healed me. But pregnancies never survived the change, what with the dying and all, and vampires couldn't get pregnant. So this was Asher's and my only chance to have a child. All I had to do was get through the next eight months in one piece and then Anna could still come and rescue us by changing me after I had the baby. I didn't know how I would manage to be a wife or a mother as a vampire afterward, but I'd be free, and it would be enough. When I was back with Asher, we could work everything else out somehow. I had to believe we could—because eight months being enslaved to a strange vampire without thinking I had a semblance of a life to go back to would kill me.

I slid my arms across my stomach to hug myself, and my right hand found the cool metal of the seatbelt buckle.

"You can't escape." A fact, stated by my now-master, Raven. He was driving and his accomplice Wolf was sitting beside me in the backseat. I kept my hand on the buckle in a small act of defiance. But the truth was if he ordered me to let go of it, I'd have to. Or if he told me to open the door and throw myself out onto the open road, I'd have to do that too. I'd survive it—Anna had told me I'd be almost invulnerable for a time, as Raven had given me so much blood to heal me he'd taken me to the edge of turning me himself—but it would still probably hurt.

I'd been hurting for so long that being well now was strange. My last days on the *Maraschino* had been punctuated by pain—morning sickness, a black eye, a dislocated shoulder, the parasitic infection that had taken most of the other cruise passengers' lives, then being stranded on a life raft for days with no water or food. It was ironic to finally feel whole just as everything in my life was becoming irrevocably fucked.

By now my family would know that the *Maraschino* had sunk with everyone on board. There'd never be any safe way to explain what had happened and how I'd survived, much less the vampire blood thing. It would be kinder to just let them think I was dead, and that was an ache that blood couldn't fix.

As I thought about my mom, that she wouldn't ever get to meet her grandson—the velvet bag Wolf had blindfolded me with suddenly felt too tight. My heartbeat sped up before I could control it and I knew the vampires would know—

Cold fingers pressed against mine on the buckle. I knew they would, I felt them coming with some other strange sense, but I still jumped. Wolf chuckled as he pried my fingers off and he ran his hand underneath the sash across my chest, yanking it tight, touching far too much of me along the way. "Safety first," he warned sarcastically.

I stayed absolutely still, like a rabbit when a hawk passes overhead. He noticed that too and I could feel the contour of the seat beside me shift as he leaned even nearer.

"Stay scared," he whispered. "Servants last longer when they're scared."

I twisted my head away from him and toward the window. He laughed as though he'd just made the most amazing joke—and I realized he was laughing at me. The ice of my fear dissipated, thawed by my rising anger, and my heartbeat slowed down, becoming deliberate.

If I died, it would kill Asher. I'd promised him I'd survive—that we both would. *Anything we have to do, baby, we'll do it.*

"Fear makes servants more eager to please, doesn't it, Wolf?" Raven chided, from the front seat. His voice rumbled over both of us with power, giving me a chill.

"Yes, Sire," Wolf agreed, returning to his own side of the seat. I felt the car downshift and take a left-hand turn. I didn't know where were going but I knew for sure we'd be there by dawn.

Raven raced the night. I could feel us swoop around other cars on the road, taking turns at speed. I'd started off trying to memorize things, like I could breadcrumb-trail my way back to my old life, when I realized we were going in circles, probably more to make sure that we weren't being followed than to trick me. But we were slowing down now, making turns more frequently—we'd reached civilization, wherever that was.

Then the car slowed drastically and descended, and I realized a parking garage below ground made sense for vampires. We wheeled sharply to the left, and came to a precise stop as Raven hit the brakes and shifted into park.

"Home sweet home," Raven said, and got out of the car, slamming the door behind himself.

Wolf exited the car as well. I sat still, waiting, until I was startled by a knock at the window to my right. "You can open up your own door."

I felt blindly for the door handle and opened it. I'd been sitting next to an unlocked door this whole time.

Had they'd been hoping I'd run? How foolish had I been to not even try? But there was nowhere I could go that Raven couldn't find me—another one of the perks of being his daytimer. I fought not to grind my teeth.

You'd better grow up to be a really awesome person, baby. I got out of the car and stood beside it, and the blindfold was snatched off me.

Lank pieces of my own hair slapped my face. Being turned into a daytimer hadn't magically fixed my personal hygiene. I stank of sweat, and my clothes were crusted with salt water from my time at sea. I took in the dim room at a glance and saw I was right, we were in a subterranean garage. There were several expensive exotic cars in a row, and Raven was nowhere to be seen.

"He has business to attend to," Wolf informed me. I didn't know if I should grunt or nod—but I did know I didn't want to be alone here with him. I figured Raven wanted me alive to curry favor with Anna, but I didn't know how much safety, if any, that personally guaranteed me.

"Are you sure?" He angled his head toward the hill we'd driven down, where I supposed the entrance to the garage was. "It's not too late for you to run."

And if I did, it wasn't too late for him to chase me down and hurt me. "You're not the first vampire to tell me that."

Years ago, right after I'd started working on Y4, a vampire named Dren had encouraged me to run so he could chase and kill me. I hadn't run then either. My life would have been much different—and probably a lot shorter—if I had. Wolf snorted when it became clear I wouldn't play his game, then turned and walked deeper into the garage. I curled my hands into fists at my side and felt my short nails bruise my palms as I followed him in.

* * *

Wolf led us through a series of unmarked tunnels, but I felt sure I'd be able to remember my way back to the garage. It was easy now as a daytimer to spot the subtle differences between the walls, things I might not have noticed as a human before—a small chunk of cement missing here, a chip in the unrelenting grey paint there. The last leg of the hall opened wide like an entryway, ending in a half-open oak door with ancient-looking iron fastenings, and I could hear a quiet conversation taking place inside the room ahead of us.

"Is she a spy?" a feminine voice asked.

"She's no concern of yours, only mine," I heard Raven say, with a note of warning. The conversation immediately stilled as Wolf led me in.

Raven was in the center of the room, lounging on a backless couch covered in folds of deep purple satin. With his shining black clothing and black hair, the only parts of him that were easy to see were his elegant white hands and his pale face. His lips were pulled into a sneer, but there were dark circles around his closed eyes. Saving me had pained him. Good.

The room itself was huge and carved from stone with no paint. I couldn't see the ceiling above, the light from the naked bulbs strung up on the walls didn't travel that far. Given the cathedral-like nature of the room, and the presumable age of its occupants, I wouldn't have been surprised if there'd been torches illuminating us instead—and I realized that without Raven's vampire blood in me, I probably wouldn't have been able to see.

I took in the rest of the room at a glance. With the exception of one daytimer kneeling beside Raven's couch, the rest of the vampires stood closest to Raven, equidistant to one another as though they didn't trust anyone within arm's length, two men and one woman. Wolf I'd already met—he looked like an old school biker, with mutton chops and a beard, his face as grizzled as his leather vest. The other vampire looked like an action hero, buff with a blonde buzz cut, and the female vampire was dressed in night blue, with smooth waves of long copper hair giving her an old Hollywood look. There were two daytimers in a circle outside of that, ready to attend, a man and a woman, him in a vest and her in a dress, and they appeared to match their owners. I wondered if that was on purpose, or just how things worked out. It was easy to tell the vampires and their daytimers apart, as the vampires only looked at me once, taking all of me in and making up their minds about me in milliseconds, content to ignore me—or to pretend to ignore me—after that. But the daytimers weren't as good at hiding their surprise at having another suddenly join their ranks. Two of them wouldn't stop looking at me in particular—the one whose vest matched Wolf's, and the one kneeling at Raven's side, who looked up at me with complete venom.

Everyone else in the room was wearing dark colors. In the last outfit I'd worn aboard the *Maraschino* before she sank, light t-shirt and jeans, I matched no one and stuck out like a sore thumb. And I realized none of the other people I'd last seen getting into a lifeboat on the *Maraschino* were here either. "Where are the rest of them?"

All of the vampires turned to eye me as one, and I gathered I'd spoken out of turn.

"The rest of the survivors. There were others. I heard you mention them." When I'd been leaving Asher and Anna, only hours ago.

A smile tickled the corners of Raven's mouth as though my concern was droll. "Other Houses. Not ours. Anna wasn't incredibly particular about who saved you, only insistent that you must be saved."

"Oh," I said, because it seemed like he was waiting for a response.

"Oh," he repeated, mocking me. Without taking his eyes off of me, he addressed someone else. "Jackson, teach her manners, will you?"

The daytimer in a leather vest bowed deeply. "Of course, Master."

"Now then," Raven went on, addressing the kneeling man at the bottom of his couch. "With everyone come down here to gawk, who's minding upstairs, Lars?"

The kneeling daytimer's head dropped even lower. Would Raven expect me to grovel like that for him? I couldn't imagine myself doing it now, much less six months from now with a pregnant belly. "We closed early, Master," the kneeling man informed him. Raven's face fell into a profound look of disappointment, as Lars went on. "I–I wanted to make sure your bed was warm."

Raven reached down to pat Lars's head as though he were a particularly obedient dog, and I watched the man's shoulders tense. "Lars, when I need your help hunting, I'll ask for it—or I'll just drain you."

I could see the panic on Raven's daytimer's—his other daytimer, if you counted me—face. Raven's hand wound through Lars's hair as though considering options. The female vampire smirked to see such obvious fear, and then looked at Raven, one impish eyebrow quirked. "I'll eat your dessert if you don't want it, Sire." She had a slight French accent, which made her seem even more exotic.

Raven released Lars and stood. "As it turns out, I'm not in the mood to share tonight." He turned to pierce Lars with one last look of disappointment.

"I apologize, Master," Lars said, nodding eagerly now that he was free.

"Is there anything else of concern?" Raven asked, looking around. One by one, the rest of his vampires shook their head. "Then we'll reconvene tomorrow night." He stood up fluidly, and stalked out of the room via its only other door. The other vampires followed suit, and then it was just me and the other daytimers left inside.

They stared at me, and I stared at them. I swallowed. *Eight months, baby. We can do this.* "Hi. My name is Edie."